Nesting

Renee MacKenzie

Nesting

Renee MacKenzie

Affinity
eBook Press
NZ
2014

Nesting
© 2014 by Renee MacKenzie

Affinity E-Book Press NZ LTD
Canterbury, New Zealand

2nd Edition

ISBN: 978-1-927328-86-6

All rights reserved.

Editor: Nat Burns
Cover Design: Irish Dragon Designs

Acknowledgments

I would like to thank my family at Affinity E-Books Press for having faith in my books and reissuing Nesting. A special thanks to Julie, Mel, and Nancy for making me feel right at home. Thanks to Mel for the formatting and Nancy for the cover.

I would also like to thank my past publisher, Emily Reed, for first bringing out this book; to my Blue Feather Books editor Day Peterson for her attention and care and to Nann Dunne for an exquisite line edit. Blue Feather Books is no longer in business, but I will forever be grateful to them for giving me a chance.

Thanks always to my family and friends, especially my mom, Carol. To early readers, especially Dan Hallman, Parish Howard, and Deb Nichols. Also, thanks to Deb for coming on the adventure to the kaolin mine with me and helping me with priceless insight and in concocting a story— if we got caught. To my coworkers at the lab for putting up with me when my drive in to work on Highway 278 would have me bursting with ideas and bouncing off the walls. To my writing group in Augusta, GA: Karin Gillespie, Steve Fox, Gretchen Hummel, Rhonda Jones, Kyle Steele, Nancy Clements, Donna Jackson, Dawn Johnson, and Rhian Swain, y'all rock. Finally, to Augusta herself, for being such a complex and beautiful place, full of fantastic people, thank you for all the inspiration.

Dedication

For Pam, always

Also by Renee MacKenzie

Confined Spaces

Flight

23 Miles

Table of Contents

Part One

Habitat

Chapter One

Cilantro Soul

Macy Stokes raised the bouquet of cilantro and imagined it as fragrant armor. She marched down Broad Street in downtown Augusta, Georgia, until she reached Emma. She lowered the herb shield as she walked up behind her.

"Eighteen, nineteen, twenty," Macy teased.

Emma leaned back against her and laughed. "I was checking out a painting, not counting." She turned from the gallery window and faced Macy. "I finished counting half an hour ago. What's this?"

Macy offered her best friend the bouquet. "Cilantro. From my garden. Because I know how much you like it." Macy thought about the day she'd introduced Emma to cilantro. She'd made salad with a cilantro and lime vinaigrette and brought it to one of their picnics at the river. Emma had gone wild over it, and Macy couldn't deny how much it pleased her to make Emma that happy.

"How sweet. Thanks."

"Maybe we could put it in your car. People are staring."

"They aren't staring at your cilantro, silly." She gave Macy a pointed look of appraisal and took the herb from her. "Come with me. I want to show you something."

Macy studied Emma's reflection in the window and admired her chin-length auburn hair. Emma wore khaki shorts and a sleeveless denim shirt that made her ever-changing eyes appear to be a light blue. Macy glanced at her own too-tight jeans and black tank top and wished she'd worn something a bit less revealing.

"Come on," Emma said.

Macy clomped along in her new clogs and followed Emma to the next gallery in Artists Row.

Emma grabbed her by the arm and steered her in the door. "You've got to see this."

Macy smiled. She loved seeing through Emma's eyes.

Emma never pretended to know the first thing about art. She would just whisper comments about this detail or that image, and Macy would stand close behind her, close enough that she could feel the heat from Emma's back as she murmured.

Emma stopped short, and Macy bumped into her.

Macy laughed. "I knew you couldn't walk past this painting without stopping."

"I can't help it." Emma smiled. "It reminds me of Chisman Creek in Virginia."

"Where you grew up."

"Yeah." Emma cocked her head. "The dock is just like the one at the Smith place."

Emma had often told Macy about the dark water of Chisman Creek, how it hid the soft muck that sheltered blue crabs and oysters, some with sharp shells that could leave nasty gashes on unwary feet.

Emma pointed at the painting. "I wrote my first poem on a dock just like that one."

"And had your first cigarette. And your first kiss."

Emma bit her lip.

"See, I do pay attention."

"Yeah," Emma whispered. "You do." She moved toward the back of the gallery.

Macy stopped beside Emma and stared at the huge cityscape. "Wow," she said. Acrylic rain pelted faceless people.

"Where are their eyes?" Emma asked.

"Maybe we have to provide them."

"What if we can't?"

Macy's face brushed against Emma's ear. "I'll always remember your eyes," she whispered.

"I don't think so." Emma leaned closer to the painting. "Mine aren't intense like yours."

"Thanks again for the poem that you wrote about my eyes."

"Hematite. Just like the smooth black stones I made with the rock tumbler my dad gave me when I was a kid," Emma said.

Macy's chest pounded as she remembered what else Emma had said about her eyes—that, like hematite, Macy's eyes were impenetrable only to those who lacked imagination. And that Emma found them exciting and inspiring.

Macy took a deep breath and reached around Emma to point at the corner of the painting. "Look how the water swirls down the drain."

"It's so realistic, I can almost smell the rain," Emma said.

"That's my deodorant."

"Brat." She ducked under Macy's arm and moved away from her.

"Let's drink some wine over at the Soul Bar, and we can debate art and eyes and rain." Macy grabbed her hand. "Come on, let's stash that cilantro in your car."

They crossed the street, and Emma unlocked the driver-side door. She tossed the herb into the passenger seat. When she stood back up, Macy was bent over, using the window as a mirror.

"Such a girl," Emma teased. She sat sideways in the car, her feet on the dusty concrete.

In her peripheral vision, Macy watched Emma stick a two-inch sprig of cilantro in her mouth. Emma's lips pursed slightly as she nibbled the end of it.

Macy kneeled beside her and, without thinking, used her mouth to grab the cilantro from between Emma's lips.

Emma looked a bit shocked, started to say something, but couldn't finish because Macy kissed her full on the mouth.

When Macy pulled away, her mind was reeling. *Oh crap*. She panicked. She tried to hide her shock by saying an ultracasual, "Mmm, cilantro."

Then Emma kissed Macy, and Macy shivered when Emma's tongue parted her lips and flicked at the herb in her mouth. They kissed for several moments before Macy backed away.

Emma's eyes were bluer than Macy had ever seen them, and her breathing told her that Emma had attached more meaning to the kiss than she would ever admit. Macy loved Emma, but she wasn't like that.

"Let's go listen to some jazz and find an adventure," Macy said. She stood up, seized Emma's hand, and tried to pull her onto her feet.

"Macy."

"Em, you know you're my best friend." Macy saw the intensity on Emma's face and knew they were in trouble. "Let's go inside. I need an adventure."

"Stay, please. Sit in the car with me."

"I can't." And she really couldn't. As a divorced mother, this was just the kind of thing that could hurt Macy in a potential custody battle. Jack might not be the custody-seeking type, but that wasn't a risk she was willing to take.

Macy knelt in front of Emma. "Please come into the bar with me. Maybe that woman from the coffee shop will be in tonight. She checks you out every time she sees you."

Emma yanked at a thread on the cuff of her shorts and said, "I'm gonna head home."

"Sure you won't come in with me?"

"Yeah. I better go."

Macy tilted Emma's chin up and made Emma look at her. "You'll be okay?"

Emma smiled unconvincingly and whispered, "Of course."

At that moment Macy wanted to get into the car with her. She wanted to tell Emma how her insides were twisting, scaring the hell out of her. Instead, she squeezed Emma's hand and walked away.

With every clop of her clogs, Macy wanted to take back that kiss. She'd crossed a line she'd promised herself she never would. Emma was too serious, too sensitive for that kind of play. Macy knew it, and she'd blown it.

Macy stopped in the doorway of the club and greeted the bouncer. "Hey, Joe, how's everything?"

"Fine, darling."

When Macy pulled her driver's license and some crumpled bills from her back pocket, he waved her in. "No cover for the finest woman in town," he drawled.

"Thanks, Joe." She gave him a smile and meandered into the bar.

"Beer?" the bartender asked as Macy slid onto a barstool.

"No, I think I'll have wine tonight. Red, please." She put a five on the bar and pivoted toward the door. She wanted a good view of any men that came in.

She glanced around and smiled. Within minutes of coming in, Emma would know how many paintings were on the walls. Before long, she'd know how many barstools and how many people there were. Macy loved to tease Emma about her obsessive counting.

Macy picked up her wineglass and took a sip. Its many subtleties danced across her tongue. When she set the glass down, she smelled something familiar. She swore she could smell rain. She spun around, expecting to see Emma.

"Hey." A young guy, probably too young to be legally served, stood in front of her. "You are so beautiful."

She smiled at his youthful directness. "Thank you." Macy turned back to her wine, wondering if guys really expected that line to get them somewhere.

None of the "adventures"—the men Macy ran around with while her mom looked after her son—not one of them ever saw the Macy that Emma captured in conversation or framed with her camera.

It was Emma's quiet resolve that had made Macy agree when she asked her to stand in the fountain on campus, fully clothed, while Emma tested her new camera. The water muted all other sounds and plastered Macy's hair to the sides of her face and her shirt to her breasts.

Macy's fingers trembled against her glass as she imagined hearing Emma's words again, *Stay, please.* She knew that everything would be different now. She couldn't take back that kiss.

Macy stole a few glances at her young admirer as she nursed her wine. He was cute and probably would be a lot of fun. She closed her eyes and envisioned Emma. She knew Em would have dawdled before she finally left, hoping Macy

7

would change her mind. Emma was probably only a block or two down Broad Street but far enough not to know that Macy had left with the young man for an adventure.

But Macy would know. She kept her gaze locked on the door as she made her way across the club. She held her breath until she stepped into the night air.

A sprig of cilantro was tucked under Macy's windshield wiper. She put the herb up to her nose and inhaled deeply. She knew she could never be with Emma like that, but she also knew she had to save their friendship. Macy would give Emma a few days. Then she would call and act as if nothing had happened.

She got into her car, draped the cilantro across her leg, and drove off.

When she got home, the lights were out. Her mother, who'd moved in with Macy and her five-year-old son when she'd left Macy's third stepdad, was asleep in the spare room. Even though she and her mother didn't always agree, Macy had to admit it was nice having a live-in babysitter.

Jeremiah, Macy's little J-man, was asleep under his Batman sheets. She got in bed with him and pulled him close. She could smell sun and sweat in his hair.

Basking in the warmth emanating from her son, Macy let her mind drift off to her favorite spot at the river, the area she and Emma called their grassy knoll. She could picture Emma sitting on the ratty blanket they always lugged along: Emma's camera wedged between her knees, which were pulled halfway up to her chest; her pencil resting in her right hand, its tip barely off the page of her journal. If Jeremiah was with them, Macy would keep one eye on him as he hunted rocks or treasure and one eye on Emma as she snapped pictures or wrote in her journal.

"Hey, J-man," Macy whispered, not intending to wake him, "you think Emma is right, that the river has special energy?"

Jeremiah let out a dream whimper and pressed a little fist against her.

Macy fell asleep coveting both the peace and the rush Emma got from the water's current, the red clay, the surprise chatter of a kingfisher.

The next morning, Macy chopped cilantro and sprinkled it into an omelet. She pretended not to taste Emma's kiss in every bite.

Chapter Two

Undertow

Cam Webber stared at the pale gray of the walls, the slightly darker shade of the carpet. The hues added to her sense of drowning in a sea of overcast. Cam hated the muted colors of the furniture, her relationship with her mother, her life.

"Camille, give it to me."

Cam cringed. She despised it when her mom called her that. She could feel the heat of her mom's glare on her hand, where she clutched the letter from her Aunt Jess. "No." Cam shoved it into her front pocket.

"You've never let me forget how much you'd rather still be with her."

Cam wanted to scream that the six years she lived with her aunt were the best years of her life, but she didn't. "I haven't even mentioned her, Mom," she said.

Mrs. Webber snatched up her purse. "You're nineteen. Do what you want to do. Why should that change now?"

"I don't always do what I want. Don't I clean up around here when you ask me to? And I'm working now, too." She cringed at the thought of seating lunch-goers at the local steakhouse where she'd just gotten a job.

Her mother looked her up and down in that judgmental way Cam couldn't stand. "You are just like her. She made you into a version of herself, and I hate her for that." She clenched and unclenched her fists at her side. "I'm going to work."

Cam wished her mom would just say it. She wanted to yell at her to just get it out into the open about how much of a disappointment Cam was for not dating guys. Hell, her mom probably would have been proud of her if she'd gotten knocked up at fifteen. She glanced down at the androgynous jeans hanging off her narrow hips and the T-shirt that clung to her small breasts. Yes, she was built like Aunt Jess, and she liked that.

"Maybe you *should* go see your aunt, go see that my sister isn't some maternal goddess after all."

"Maybe I will," Cam said.

Cam stopped herself before saying that at least Aunt Jess wouldn't have left her for a week when she was just starting high school. Or saying anything about her sophomore year, when she'd gotten so good at forging her mom's signature, because otherwise she'd have missed out on all the things the other kids' parents were giving them permission to do.

Cam still couldn't believe she'd received the letter from her aunt. It had been seven years since Cam had called her those horrible names because Aunt Jess had given her back to her mother without a fight. After a couple of years during which Cam refused all contact, Aunt Jess had given up, and this letter was her first attempt to reach out to Cam since. Aunt Jess had written that she just wanted Cam to know she loved her.

Forget about that, she told herself. She had a party to go to. She smiled at the thought of spending some time with Courtney and decided that, once she walked out the front door, she wouldn't think about her mom or the letter from her aunt.

†

Cam's head was already fuzzy, and it was still early. She went into the bathroom and stood with her eyes closed for several moments to keep the god-awful striped wallpaper from making her vomit.

After washing her hands and throwing some water onto her face, she picked up her Heineken from the counter and poured half of it down the drain.

The bass from the stereo was vibrating the walls, making the stripes even harder to tolerate.

Someone pounded on the bathroom door. Cam took a long pull of her beer as she exited, putting on a good show.

"Cam, what's up?"

"Hey, Brian."

"Where's your date?" he teased.

Cam's gaze swept the room until she found Courtney sitting beside Aaron on the sofa. Courtney's black hair was slicked back away from her chiseled features; her lips were glossy and inviting. *Maybe too inviting.* Cam worried as Aaron leaned even closer to Courtney.

"You better get over there before it's too late," Brian said.

Cam shrugged. "I need to grab another beer." On her way to the fridge, she kept her eyes locked on Courtney. When the other woman met her gaze, Cam felt her heart catapult into her throat.

Cam set the old beer on the counter and opened a new bottle. She left a huge spit-sip in the bottom of the old bottle. Abandoned, it would be used by someone as an ashtray or absently drained into the sink.

She looked around at the other partiers. Travis was rolling a joint at the kitchen counter. Brian was standing behind him, acting like he was afraid he'd get left out. Billy and Mitch were debating sports. Ashley was giving Laurie a massage, leaning much closer into her friend than she needed to. *Who do they think they're kidding?* Cam wondered.

And then there was Brenda, from Cam's high school softball team. The biggest dyke in their graduating class was holding hands with Derek, the biggest nerd. What a pair. The looks they exchanged made Cam uncomfortable. *Okay, so maybe Brenda isn't a dyke.* Cam *so* needed a tune-up on her gaydar.

She considered Courtney, for instance. When Cam met her at Ashley and Laurie's party, she wouldn't in a million years have guessed that Courtney went both ways. Even if Robyn, Cam's then-girlfriend, swore Courtney was a lesbo and wanted to get into Cam's pants.

Cam had thought it absurd. Until Courtney did get into her pants. They'd been getting high one afternoon, when Courtney straddled Cam on the sofa and pushed her hand down the front of Cam's board shorts.

The heat rising on Cam's face was a flaming reminder of the guilt she'd felt over cheating on Robyn and the thrill of shattering into a million brilliant pieces when Courtney made her come.

As she watched Courtney with Aaron, Cam's guilt dissipated. It wasn't as if she'd set out to cheat on Robyn. She'd just been so carried off on the course Courtney had set for them that she'd barely been able to think. It hadn't been Cam's fault that the chemistry between them had been so wickedly intense. Besides, she'd recently heard that Robyn, now safely graduated from high school, was dating Cam's old softball coach, Ms. Cruise.

Cam chugged down half her beer as she watched Aaron lean closer to Courtney and whisper in her ear. *Prick.* Courtney caught her watching and gave a little wink. Cam angled her head toward the stairs in a "let's go" gesture.

Cam and Courtney met by the bottom of the stairs, and Courtney grabbed her arm to keep her from starting up. "What's the rush?" Courtney asked in a low voice.

Cam looked over to where Aaron stood, watching them. "What's he doing here?"

"Come on, it's a party. Chill out." She ruffled Cam's blonde hair where it was longer on the top and stroked down the sides where it was shorter and darker. "You look hot tonight," she purred.

Cam glanced toward Aaron. "I thought tonight was about you and me." Cam hated the whine in her voice but couldn't help it.

"It is. It will be. Just chill. Okay?"

Cam melted into the smooth sound of Courtney's voice. "Okay." She took a swig of her beer and considered that maybe she should slow down. Then she looked again at Aaron and chugged the rest of the bottle.

Travis wrapped his arm around Cam's shoulder. "Hit?" he asked as he held the joint in front of her face.

Cam was happy to take her turn. As always, she was along for the ride, ready to act the part. She could perform the party animal, softball jock, friend, or smart chick, even if she wasn't any of those things. She was nothing more than a lazy fake. Her mom could tell the whole freaking world that, if her mom was around. She'd certainly told Cam often enough.

"Hell, yeah, I'll take a hit," Cam answered as she reached for it.

When the joint disappeared into the den, Courtney took Cam by the hand and led her up the steps. Courtney's thumb pressed into Cam's sweaty palm, and Cam felt the wetness collecting elsewhere also. She took a deep breath and exhaled just as Courtney pulled her into her arms and kissed her.

"Oh, wow!" Cam's legs turned to jelly. *Oh wow. Oh wow. Ohwowohwowohwow.*

Courtney kissed her again. Movement over Courtney's right shoulder caught Cam's attention, and she jumped when she realized Aaron was standing behind them. "What the fu…"

"Shhh," Courtney whispered.

When Aaron was close enough to touch Courtney, Cam tried to pull away, but Courtney held tight. "Come on, Cam. Go with it."

"Yeah, go with it," Aaron said.

Courtney kissed her hard, and Cam's breath caught in her chest. She let Courtney's tongue explore her mouth. Her heart pounded. Courtney pressed her body against Cam's, and the sensation of being breast to breast rushed blood from her brain to her groin. Cam felt dizzy. Then she felt Aaron press against her from behind. She tried to ignore the hardness of him against her back and focus instead on the softness of Courtney.

"Yeah, baby," Courtney whispered.

"That's right," Aaron added.

He ran his hand between them, and Cam glanced down to see his fingers against Courtney's breast. The image of him groping Courtney jarred her.

"That's right. Get her hot for me."

His words woke her up. Cam slipped sideways, and her sudden absence made Courtney and Aaron fall together. Aaron laughed. Cam held Courtney's gaze through her rising tears.

"Come on, sweetie." Courtney reached for Cam's hand.

"Be adventurous," Aaron said.

"Courtney, don't do this," Cam whispered.

Aaron grabbed Courtney by the hand and pulled her toward the bedroom door. "Come on, Court. You're wasting time with her."

"Please, Cam?"

She thrust out her bottom lip in what Cam was certain Courtney thought was a seductive pout.

Cam stood paralyzed as Courtney followed Aaron into the bedroom, then she ran down the stairs and into the kitchen, where she grabbed a beer and locked herself in the bathroom.

The tacky wallpaper mocked her. The wetness that lingered between her legs mocked her more. *How could Courtney do that to me?* She was humiliated. Did she deserve what she got for how she'd treated Robyn? No, no one deserved this embarrassment. She downed her beer. She thought about smashing the bottle against the countertop but stopped herself. Instead, she picked up the wicker clothes hamper. She held it over her head for a second and brought it down hard on the counter.

Cam awoke to Courtney's parents standing over her, gawking. Rumpled, stinking of beer and sweat, she blinked into the too-bright light, trying not to look at the striped walls.

"You should be ashamed," Courtney's mom muttered as she stared at the shredded wicker strewn about the floor.

"You, too," Cam mumbled. She opened her left eye just enough to look at the mess and was assaulted by the memory of Courtney's betrayal, of her own rage as she beat the wicker hamper against the marble countertop until it was battered to bits. Her hands were in not much better shape. She remembered stripping off the T-shirt and jeans when she'd gotten sick—the result of the beer and the heartache.

She didn't have to look in the mirror to remember that she was only wearing her sports bra and her "I kiss girls" boxers.

As Courtney's parents towered over her, Cam wondered if Courtney and Aaron had been discovered in the bedroom, or if they'd gotten out. Cam considered the coldness of the tile flooring, which was probably imprinted on her face, and the waves of drunkenness breaking against the inside of her head. She braced herself to be dragged down by the undertow, but she wasn't. Instead she was buoyed up, exhilarated by the clarity with which she saw the answer.

Think what you want, the voice in her head told Courtney's parents. It didn't matter, because she knew what to do. She would go to Georgia to see Aunt Jess. As soon as her head quit ricocheting off the tacky striped walls.

Chapter Three

Tyler Mason's Eyes

Kenny Brewer stomped down an aisle in the Piggly Wiggly. He hated grocery shopping, and he hated how his wife knew every damned person in the store and had to stop to gossip with at least half of them.

Kenny listened from a safe distance as Dorianne turned toward her audience of two. "I always knew I had a sister— well, a half-sister, but I only just recently found her."

"Really?" Cindy asked in her whiny, nasal voice.

"And right here in Augusta." Dorianne rubbed the goose bumps on her arms.

Kenny rounded the corner and glared at her. "Dori, are we about done?"

"Yeah, just a minute."

"Tell us about your sister," the second woman said.

Dorianne glanced at Kenny. "Her name is Grace. But I'll have to tell you about her another time. We haven't eaten yet, and you know how men get when they're hungry."

Kenny rolled his eyes when the two women gave Dorianne knowing smiles.

As usual, Dorianne drove them home. She'd been doing the driving since Kenny's most recent DUI. He knew better than to complain about that, seeing how drinking and driving

18

was how her mama and brother had both died. That was one fight he knew not to pick.

Kenny didn't say anything until they got inside, then as she unpacked a case of Diet Coke into the fridge, he said, "Dori, you need to get over that crap."

"Over what?" she asked.

"Your mama set you straight on that crap years ago."

After Dori's daddy died, someone at the Social Security office mentioned she had a sister. Kenny cringed at the memory of how Dorianne's life had changed that day. At first she'd been devastated over having been lied to her entire life, then the need to know had festered in her for years. And now... now she swore... she said she *knew* in her very bones that she'd found her half-sister.

"Your mama explained it was all a big mix-up, and she told you to drop it." Kenny brushed the fine, light hair off his forehead and crossed his arms over his chest.

"Since when do you care if I listen to my mama?"

"She's probably rolling over in her grave at you telling strangers that nonsense about having a sister."

"Why are you getting all riled up, Kenny?"

"I don't know why you can't just keep your mouth shut. Why do you go on and on about this?"

She glared at him. "Because I know for a fact where my half-sister works. I've seen her. And she's got Tyler Mason's eyes and his chin, just like me."

"Give me a break."

"Besides," she said, "her name is Grace. How can you not know the importance of the woman having the same name as my childhood cocker spaniel?"

"You are off your damned rocker, woman!"

Dorianne ran from the kitchen and locked herself in their bedroom. "I hate you, Kenny," she screeched. "I hate you."

†

Kenny stepped out of the cabinet shop into the bright sun. He watched as Dorianne pulled into the parking lot in their old, beat-up, 1977 Ford Maverick. He'd been expecting her. He knew she'd come by to get him, to apologize in that sexy way she had.

Ignoring the smirks of his coworkers, Tank and Gary, he strutted across the parking lot. A smile twitched at the corner of his mouth as he creaked open the door to the Maverick.

The old car was about to fall apart, but it was a classic. He knew it was held together by rust, and it had two more doors than what was cool, but it had been a good car.

"Hi," Dorianne whispered.

"Hi, yourself." He stole a glance at her.

She lit a Salem, and Kenny noticed her eyes were puffy. She'd likely cried most of the night and probably all morning, too.

As she pulled out onto Highway 1, Dorianne handed Kenny a brown paper sack, crease-free except for where the top was folded down. He pulled out a ham sandwich and found a piece of Stir 'n Frost cake, left over from his birthday.

"Looks good," he said.

Dorianne nodded and kept her eyes on the road.

Kenny was just finishing his sandwich and fixing to start on his cake when he saw Dorianne shudder. He followed her gaze. Midway between Thompson's double-wide and Walt's ex-wife's place, two buzzards perched on some road kill. The bloody buffet looked a lot like Bernie Thompson's old bird dog.

Dorianne lit another cigarette and took a few long drags. Kenny watched her concentrate on her driving, and as she pulled the cigarette from her mouth, the smudge of color on the white filter sparked his body to life. *Lord, let's just hurry up and get there.*

When Dorianne slowed the car and flicked on her turn signal, Kenny shifted in his seat, trying to lessen the strain.

Dorianne pulled up alongside the rusting propane tank at Miller's boarded-up service station and killed the engine. She sighed. "Kenny, about last night, I'm so sorry."

He wasn't about to say a thing. No way was he taking any chance of interrupting the apology.

Dorianne crushed out her cigarette. "I know you get mad at me sometimes. And I know I should just leave it alone." She ran her hand along the seam of his Levi's. "Forgive me?"

Her touch made him shiver. He squirmed and pushed his crotch up to meet her hand. He worked his left foot under the seat to wedge up the lever and pressed his right foot into the floorboard to slide the seat back.

A crow called from somewhere out of sight. Kenny took a deep breath and beat back the image of the buzzards feasting.

In their '77 Ford at Miller's place, his hands tangling through her reddish hair to the darker roots and his head thrown back, he accepted Dorianne's apology.

When she'd finished, Dorianne straightened the collar of her blouse and settled back behind the wheel. "Kenny, remember last week when we fought about where I've been going afternoons?"

He remembered the argument *and* the apology. He'd caught Dorianne lying about where she'd been that day. He kept at her, and finally, crying, she told him a real man wouldn't worry, he'd know how sometimes a woman just needed to be alone.

Well, he wasn't stupid. He knew what she really wanted to say was that a *real* man would get her pregnant. A *real* man would give her a baby so she'd have a sense of family, since she lost that when her mama and older brother died.

"I want to take you there."

He turned to Dorianne. "Huh?"

"I want to take you to where I've been going. In town."

"When?"

"Now." Dorianne's hands shook as she lit another cigarette.

He groaned and readjusted his seat. He checked his watch with exaggerated impatience. "I got three minutes to get back to the shop."

"Damn it, Kenny. You wanted to know where I been going. Now I want to show you."

"Can't you just tell me about it while you drive me back?"

"I want to show you. Please?"

"Now ain't the time, Dorianne. I got to get back."

"Martin won't fire you or anything."

Kenny stared at her. Unfortunately for him, his gaze lingered on the pink frost that made her thin lips look full. It made him hot—how her lips looked less perfect after she'd gone down on him. She was a beautiful girl but especially so sitting in the old Ford, smudged from apologizing.

"Damn it, Dori."

"Please," she whispered.

"Girl, you drive me crazy." He sat up straighter in his seat. Then he figured, what the hell? If he did get in trouble at work, Dorianne would be apologizing all week long. "Okay, just drive."

Kenny stared out his window while Dorianne cruised down Highway 1. They passed his aunt and uncle's road, and he caught a glimpse of Macy's black Saturn in their driveway. He looked away real quick. One mistake with that girl years ago, and he had to spend the rest of his life pretending she didn't exist.

When Dorianne took the exit to get on the Bobby Jones Expressway, Kenny nearly shit. She'd always hated that road—the speeding drivers, the construction that didn't end.

She didn't let on, but he was pretty sure she saw him double-check his seatbelt as she merged into traffic. And the easy way she did it showed him just how little he really knew. His wife was driving on Bobby Jones like it was nothing. Her knuckles weren't even going white from vise-gripping the steering wheel.

She drove them through a jumble of red lights, traffic, and turns, and before he knew it, they were parked in front of the Barnes and Noble.

He couldn't help himself. "You been coming to a *bookstore?*"

She responded by nudging him. She was smiling, but her eyes flashed a warning. Then she twisted the rearview mirror toward her and damned if it didn't break off in her hand. He would have yelled at her over it, but he was too busy noticing how it didn't even make her miss a beat. She just held it up and fixed her lipstick.

Dorianne set the mirror on the cracked dash like it belonged there and got out of the car. She stood by his door with her arms crossed over her chest.

He played with her, acting like he wasn't going to budge.

"Kenny Brewer, you better get out here."

He laughed at how unconvincing she could be when she was trying to boss him. When he did get out, the door didn't shut right the first time so he had to try it again. Then it slammed a bit too hard.

Dorianne winced at the noise and clutched his arm with both hands, keeping him close. Not waiting for Kenny to be a gentleman, she rushed to the door and opened it herself.

He stopped two feet inside the bookstore. "Damned place is huge!"

"Shhh." She said it like they were in church or something.

She made Kenny sit in a chair that swallowed him whole. She handed him a *Sports Illustrated* and kept watching the information counter, her finger pads leaving damp ovals on the cover of *True Confessions*.

It seemed like no time before Dorianne gave him a "psst" and nodded toward a tall, brunette employee who was typing into the computer at the information desk. She wrote something down for a customer who'd walked up behind her, and she glanced over at Kenny and Dorianne.

Kenny had a fleeting thought that there was something sexy about her; he just couldn't put his finger on what it was.

The clerk made a phone call and glanced over at them as she talked.

Dorianne leaned closer to Kenny. "I know she's kind of tall for a Mason, but look at those hips."

He wasn't going to look at that woman's hips, or any other part of her. Instead he sat there, swallowed up by an overstuffed chair, and stared at his wife.

"Kenny, you see her eyes? She's got my daddy's eyes. And his chin. There's no doubt, is there?"

He was numb. There was no other way to describe it. His wife had lost her freaking mind, and he just sat there. Dorianne skipped over to the woman, and he wished the chair really would swallow him up. He almost lost his ham sandwich and cake when Dorianne started talking to her.

"Hi, Grace. Remember me? Dorianne *Mason* Brewer."

The woman muttered something and stepped away.

Dorianne grabbed her arm, bony fingers sinking into freckled flesh.

Oh, Lord, Kenny thought, here come the assault charges.

"But, Grace, I told you about my daddy and your mama."

"Please," the woman said, "quit harassing me."

Hearing that, Kenny knew Dori had gone too far. He freed himself from the damned chair and marched over to his wife. He put his best comforting hand on her shoulder, but she wheeled around.

"Look at her eyes, Kenny. You can't tell me those eyes aren't Tyler Mason's."

"Dorianne, please," he whispered, his face getting hotter just knowing people were staring at them. "Let's go."

"No, we aren't going!" she said. "Why can't you just accept that I got family other than you?" Her hands clenched into fists. "You may be able to keep me from having a baby, but you can't deny me my sister."

The Grace woman squared her shoulders and breathed deep. "I am not your sister. I don't know you or Tyler Mason, and I don't care to know either one of you." She turned to Kenny, teeth clenched. "The police are on their way. I suggest you get your crazy wife the hell out of here."

Kenny grabbed hold of Dorianne and wouldn't let her shake him off. "Come on, Dori."

"But she's my sister."

"No, baby, she's not." He held her wrist in his right hand, put his left arm around her waist, and propelled her out of the store.

As they left, Kenny looked back at the woman. He saw that same stare Dorianne could give, like when she was mad about him tracking red clay in on his boots or making fun of her Shake 'n Bake. It must have been his turn for crazy, because for a minute, he would have sworn that Grace woman was staring at them with Tyler Mason's eyes. They were the same eyes that peered over the top of a Bud can in the old photo stuck to their fridge with a Pizza Hut magnet.

He looked from the door to the police car pulling up and back to Dorianne. Her wet eyes were her daddy's eyes, and Grace's eyes, but Kenny would never tell Dori that he'd seen it.

So there they stood in the parking lot, police car in the background, Dorianne shaking and crying, and Kenny holding her.

"It's okay, baby," he said.

"I'm sorry. I'm so sorry." She sobbed. "I'll make it up to you. I will."

His heart hurt so bad for her. "No, Dori. No more apologizing."

She shook in his arms.

"Swear you won't be sorry for every little thing. You don't got to apologize for everything."

"Okay," she muttered.

As far as the *not* apologizing went, he could only hope that, like usual, the girl wouldn't listen.

Chapter Four

Do Over

Macy listened to the message from Emma again, as she had a hundred times in the last few days. Her heart pounded. She should call Emma back. Or not. *Crap.*

She hit the button to listen again. "Hey, Macy, it's me, Emma. Listen, I really need to talk to you. Please call me back."

Macy hit the button for the next message. "Macy, hi, it's Emma. I'm leaving town tomorrow. I'd really like to talk to you before I go. Please call me back."

According to the message, Emma would have left two days earlier. Macy felt dizzy. She needed to talk to Emma. Maybe Emma hadn't left after all. Macy told herself that if she did call, and Emma was still in Augusta, Macy would ask her out to dinner. Then what? Tell her she was sorry, but there could never be *that* between them?

She wished she could turn back time. She wanted a do-over, as her son Jeremiah often requested when they played games. If she could go back and fix things, she could undo that kiss. She would leave the cilantro at home that night and not be so flirtatious.

Or, her do-over could have been very different. She could have gotten in the car with Emma instead of going into the bar. She could have gone home with Emma and explored the feelings she had whenever they stood close, or touched, or even just looked at each other from across the table at The Metro coffee shop or the blanket at their canal picnics.

Before she could chicken out, Macy picked up the phone and dialed. "Be home, be home," she chanted as the phone rang. She was startled to hear the message that the number she was calling was no longer in service. She knew she should have expected it; she'd waited too long to call Emma back, but it didn't make it any easier to actually hear it.

She dialed Emma's cell number and received a similar message.

There would be no do-over. Part of Macy wanted to cry; another part was relieved.

†

The man peered around the ivy-draped trellis, expectation obvious on his face. He gave Macy a shy smile. "Are you Brenda?"

"No. Sorry."

He shrugged, smiled again. "Me, too."

Macy watched from her perch on the veranda as a handful of cars motored down Walton Way. The view was her favorite part of the Partridge Inn's restaurant.

She tried to count the calls from Emma that she hadn't returned. She wasn't as good with counting as Emma was, but she knew there were too many. She couldn't blame her friend for leaving Augusta without saying goodbye. Emma had tried.

Turning to look inside the bar, Macy sipped her beer and watched the guy waiting for his blind date. He was a little bumbling but in a cute way. He fiddled with his drink, checked his watch, and looked at Macy.

The beer was bitter and cold, and it tickled Macy's tongue.

The man came over to her table and gave her a big, crooked smile. She smiled back, a practiced gesture.

"I guess I've been stood up. Pretty sad when a blind date goes bad before it even starts."

"Brenda?" she asked.

"Yeah. When I walked up, I was really hoping you were her." He laughed ruefully. "And you truly aren't?"

"Truly." Macy drew a line through the condensation on her glass.

He stuck out his hand. "I'm Michael."

She hesitated before accepting his overture and responding, "Brenda. No, just kidding." She laughed. "I'm Macy."

He released her hand. "Do you mind if I join you?"

She did mind but didn't say so. "I guess that's okay."

"I'm sorry. You're meeting someone?"

"No. I'm not."

He set his drink down on the white tablecloth and sat opposite her. "It's a beautiful night."

She nodded. The ceiling fan stirred the air, slightly shifting the fronds of a hanging fern.

"So, what do you do?" he asked.

"Accounting." The irony was that she was pretty bad with numbers. "How about you?"

"I'm a doctor."

"Oh," she said.

He fiddled with his drink, clear and on the rocks, and looked up at Macy. "No wedding ring?"

She studied her hands. "I'm divorced." *And very, very, not interested.*

"Kids?"

"One. A son. Jeremiah." Her face felt warm. She credited the beer for that. "He's only five, but he's quite the little man."

"Wow."

"What?"

"Do you know you lit up when you said his name? I mean, really lit up."

Macy smiled.

"There's nothing sexier than a woman who gushes over her child."

She dismissed his comment. She dismissed him. Macy needed something, and for once she was sure it wasn't approval from a stranger or validation from sex.

"What are you doing out here tonight?" he asked.

She hesitated. *Why am I still sitting here with this man?* "I'm hiding from my empty house."

"Empty?"

"My son's spending the night with his father, over at his grandparents' house. It's the first full night I've ever spent without Jeremiah."

"Ah, tough one," he said.

Tough in more ways than one. Macy was afraid that if she sat home, she'd end up driving over to check on J-man at Russ and Eileen's, peeking in the windows at her former in-laws until the cops snagged her as a peeper. Or else she'd find herself online, one Google search after another, trying to track down Emma.

"I should probably get going," Macy said.

"Maybe we could get together sometime."

"Yeah, I guess." She just wanted to get in her car and drive.

"Can I get your phone number?"

"How about you give me yours, and I'll call you," she said.

"That means 'get lost.'"

"No, that means give me your number and I'll call you." Part of her was irritated at him, but a bigger part was irritated with herself. She knew she'd have to call him, just to prove him wrong.

Michael jotted his number on a napkin, then he walked Macy out and they said a polite goodbye.

Macy pulled onto Walton Way, knowing where she was headed. Even though she hadn't planned on going to Aiken, she knew as she left the Partridge Inn that she would end up there.

The traffic on River Watch Parkway was light and fast. Macy rolled down her window and relished the feel of the air against her skin. The more the current ran over her arms, the faster she drove, until the sensation became almost too intense. Only minutes passed before she merged onto I-20, then crossed the bridge over the Augusta Canal and the Savannah River into South Carolina.

The air rushed in, flirted, urged her on. She laughed out loud at the idea that she was thinking like one of Emma's poems. She could hear the breathlessly long lines of a poem born at the river's edge, scratched into Emma's journal, and read aloud only after much editing on Emma's part and much begging on Macy's.

Macy took what she hoped was the correct exit off the interstate and pulled out her cell phone. She speed-dialed Russ and Eileen's. Eileen picked it up on the first ring.

"Hello."

"Hey there."

"Oh, Macy. Hello."

"What's wrong?"

"What do you mean what's wrong? Nothing's wrong."

"You've got that tone in your voice."

"Well, Jack didn't show. He said he got tied up at work."

"How's Jeremiah taking it?" Macy steered into a gas station to turn around.

"He's building a birdfeeder with his grandpa. I don't think it matters too much to him."

Macy could tell it broke Eileen's heart to say that her grandson wasn't dying to see her son. She pulled in under an Exxon sign. "Do you want me to come get him?"

"Oh, heavens no. Let him stay. Russ loves having the boy around. Have you thought about what I said?"

"Yeah." Macy quickly pulled back onto the highway before she could change her mind and return to Augusta.

"Now that your mother's moved back to Burke County, don't you agree that Jeremiah should come here after school?"

Macy hesitated. She knew it was silly to worry about Russ and Eileen's neighborhood. Timmy Jones had disappeared from his yard three houses away from their house, but that was nearly a decade earlier. And the speculation had been that his daddy had snatched him during a nasty custody battle.

Macy took a deep breath. "Yeah, I think you're right. We'll start doing that instead of the afterschool program."

"Great, then it's settled."

"Thanks, Eileen."

Macy turned into the parking lot at the bar and switched off her car. She watched as mostly men drove in and out.

She'd been online to check out gay clubs outside of Augusta. The club had to be out of town, so she wouldn't risk running into anyone she knew.

The longer she sat, the more panicked she became about going in. When a Subaru parked beside her, she turned to see who was in the car. Two women—one with short hair and very red lipstick, the other wearing a T-shirt with block lettering: DYKE. These women were not Emma. Even if

Emma were there, then what? Macy hadn't realized she was staring until the short-haired woman whirled around. "What are you looking at?"

Macy started the car and pulled to the other side of the building. A good-looking man emerged from a Jeep Cherokee and strode across the parking lot. It was one of the executives from Odom Construction, one of Macy's employer's biggest clients. *What was I thinking?* Aiken was still way too close to home. A queasiness roiled her stomach as the man disappeared inside.

She yanked a Wet Wipe from the console between the seats and ran it over her face. The wipes were Emma's thing. Emma was a bit of a germ freak, and it had rubbed off on Macy.

"What am I doing?" She slammed her hand against the steering wheel. "This isn't me," she told her reflection in her rearview mirror.

As she sped away, she thought about her mother. If she could see Macy now, she'd say she always knew there was something unnatural about her, more than just the darkness of her eyes.

At a red light, Macy pulled out the napkin with Michael's phone number on it. She was straight, and she'd prove it. She dialed the number and waited for the ring, for Michael's deep voice, to feel something familiar stir inside her. Nothing. There was no signal, no service.

"Damn it!" She hurled the phone onto the passenger-side floor. When the light turned green, she stomped on the accelerator.

Macy hopped onto the interstate and tried to reach down to the phone. All she came up with were a few discarded Wet Wipes. She'd told J-man a hundred times not to throw them on the floor. He didn't listen, but that was okay. When he looked at her with those sweet, searching eyes, she couldn't speak harshly to him.

That made her think about J-man getting in trouble at school. The teacher told the kids to put their fingers over their mouths to keep quiet. Jeremiah wouldn't do as he was told. He tried to explain to the teacher that he'd have to wash his hands first. That night he was so proud when he told his mama he'd remembered what she and Emma had said about germs. The sound of their names juxtaposed had sent alternating waves of longing and regret through her.

Macy didn't remember the rest of the drive. The next thing she knew, she was turning onto her ex-in-laws' street. She was looking so hard at the dark, sleeping house, that she didn't see the white Mustang until it pulled up beside her.

"What are you doing?" Macy said.

Her ex-husband shrugged. "I guess it's too late to go on up, huh?"

"I would think so, Jack."

"I really was working."

"It doesn't matter if *I* believe you or not." She considered the importance of consistency in raising kids. If that was a big deal, at least Jack was consistently absent from his son's life.

Macy checked out Jack's new car. He was always trading for a newer model, just like he did with employment. He'd start a job, make it work pretty well financially, and then decide it wasn't enough. Instead of sticking it out, he'd move on to the next "perfect opportunity."

"I'm moving into a new apartment the first of the month. When I get settled in, I want to take Jeremiah for a weekend," he said.

"Another new apartment?"

He rolled his eyes, and she noticed his face looked fuller. "Does that mean another new girlfriend, too?" she asked.

The low rumble of his Mustang sounded like he was growling at her. More consistency.

"And what are you doing? Taking the night off from screwing around?" he asked.

Macy sighed. "Goodnight, Jack."

He gunned the engine, creating a brief squeal of tires and leaving her behind to mutter, "Jerk."

She looked again at the dark house, its hedges cut into perfect rectangles. Their symmetry was comforting. She imagined J-man asleep, undoubtedly curled under a blanket, and realized she was more than a little relieved that Jack hadn't spent time with his son.

Chapter Five

Rezoned

Kenny looked around at all the people who had the same idea as he had to hit the flea market early. Dorianne made a beeline to a small pen of black puppies. Kenny sighed as she squatted beside them and reached in to stroke their soft heads.

"I've been wanting a puppy," she said.

"Yeah, but you want one in the house."

"That's where they belong. I don't want a yard dog."

"I wasn't brought up with no dogs in the house. You weren't either." Kenny had always had bird dogs penned up out back. And no way Dori's daddy would have any dogs in his house. Even her cocker spaniel had stayed in the garage at night.

One of the puppies licked Dorianne's hand, and she smiled. Kenny realized it was the first time he'd seen her smile since the bad scene at the Barnes and Noble.

Kenny knew a cuddly puppy wouldn't fix everything, but that was all he could think of to do for Dori. So he bought one of the puppies for her, on account of her being so upset over that Grace woman calling her a liar about them being kin. Besides, twenty bucks for a Lab was a great deal.

†

Later that night, Kenny went out with Tank and Tank's cousin Eddie. They walked into a bar that changed names every two years or so, all depending on whether they were playing loose with the alcohol laws or the taxes. Kenny didn't care that the place was small and dark, or that the stale beer and smoke smells mingled with what could have been urine. It was where he'd had his first legal drink, and that counted for something with him.

"Hey, Kenny," Tank said.

"Huh?"

Tank pointed to the right. "Check out up at the bar. It's your dad."

"Son of a bitch," Kenny muttered. "I'll catch up with you guys later, okay?"

Tank nodded. Kenny had already told Tank a little about how him and his dad almost never got to see each other on account of Kenny's mama being mad at Kenny for taking sides with Dorianne against her.

His mama constantly talked Dorianne down, always dogged her about something or other. Kenny had finally had enough when his mama ticked Dori off with some meanness over a chicken potpie. Ever since then, they exchanged Christmas cards from three streets away.

As Kenny crossed the few feet between them, he studied his dad. The lines on his face seemed a little deeper, his hair grayer, but he looked good.

"Hey, Dad," Kenny said.

Ken, Sr., extended his hand. Kenny shook it and looked closely at his dad for any sign of discomfort at seeing him.

"How you been, son?"

Kenny smiled. "I been good. You?"

"Fine. How's Dori?"

"She's still putting up with me." Kenny thought his dad was a bit too thin, maybe a little haggard. "You okay, really?"

Ken, Sr., nodded. "Yeah, really. Your mama's about honey-doing me half to death, but I'm okay."

"How is Mama?"

"She's still making me put up with her." He chuckled as he held up his mug to get the bartender's attention. "One more for me, and get one for my son."

When Kenny got home four or five hours later, Dori was pissed. He wasn't whipped or anything. He did get to go out with his buddies every now and again, but the rules were that he had to give Dori an estimated time of when he'd be home. So she wouldn't worry. He'd missed his expected time by at least two hours.

"Where the hell you been so late?"

"Out at the bar with Tank and Eddie."

"Just Tank and Eddie?"

"Who the hell else would I be with?"

"You damned well better not have been hanging out up there with any women. And I know Macy goes there sometimes."

"Macy wasn't there." He wanted to remind Dori that he hadn't technically cheated on her back then, that they'd been broken up, but he didn't.

"Then why are you so late?"

"We were just hanging out." Kenny didn't want to say anything about seeing his dad. He wanted to wait and tell Dori in the morning, when he wasn't feeling so raw.

"You're sure Macy wasn't there?"

Kenny clenched his jaw. "I was at the bar talking to my dad. Okay?"

He could see shock on her face. Hell, he was shocked, too.

"So, me and the guys walked in, and there's Dad having a beer. Right away I went up and we started talking, and it was like no time at all had gone on since the last time I saw him."

He took a deep breath and started talking fast. "I figured, screw it, I'm going to talk to my own father. We talked and talked, and it was real nice, and I didn't want to mess it up by leaving to call you. I was afraid if I walked away, even just long enough to make a call or take a piss, Dad might decide talking to me wasn't worth Mama's wrath, and he'd leave, and that would be that."

"Oh, Kenny." Dorianne hugged him and pressed her body against his.

†

When Dorianne didn't show up at the shop to get Kenny, he couldn't figure out what was going on, since they hadn't fought or anything.

Tank drove him home. They pulled up to Kenny's house in Tank's spit-shined F-250. There sat the old Maverick. Kenny shrugged, figuring time must have slipped by Dorianne. He got a brief flash in his head of Dori on her knees, apologizing in that sexy way of hers.

Kenny went inside and saw Dori with her back to him, on tiptoe to reach the mantle over the spotless fireplace. She wouldn't let him burn any wood in it because she didn't want the neat rows of brick to get charred and dirty. The dust rag in her hand reminded Kenny a lot of his old Johnny Cash T-shirt that up and disappeared awhile back.

Dorianne held the ceramic owl, the same owl Kenny wasn't allowed to touch because she always said his big hands were just itching to break any pretty thing she had.

Then she was dusting the glass sea turtle. Her precious, hands-off-or-die, glass sea turtle she said was a symbol of fertility from Hawaii, but he'd seen the little oval stuck on the bottom that said it was made in China.

Kenny looked at her whitish face and her feathery-perfect hair, and thought, *Damn, my wife is beautiful.* Then he noticed the smudged eye makeup.

She heaved loudly a few times and went to him. He held her, because he'd learned a long time ago that was what females wanted you to do.

"What's wrong, babe?"

He knew she'd get that mascara stuff all over the shoulder of his T-shirt, but that was okay, since she was the one who did the laundry.

It took a lot of crying and standing there before she tried to talk. And then it was just words—some he recognized, some he didn't.

Just when he was about to give up on figuring out what she was saying, she said it so he understood. The doctor found something during her yearly "girl exam."

"They might need to operate, and I'll probably never have kids now, and God, why's it all so unfair?"

"It'll be all right." He held her tighter. "You'll see. It'll be fine."

Knowing she had a way of being overly dramatic, he figured it probably wasn't as bad as she was making out.

†

"You got to go to work when we get done?" Dorianne asked.

"No. Martin gave me the whole day off," Kenny said.

"Good. I hope I can remember how to get to the Medical College."

Dori drove, sitting all stiff behind the wheel of the Maverick. They'd talked about getting another car, something newer and more reliable, but decided to wait until they'd started their family.

She stuck to the speed limit, and Kenny just sat there, thinking about how he'd always figured if he could get her to relax—get her mind off it—they could actually pull off getting pregnant. He thought if he could just quit influencing her apologies, if they'd quit wasting so much of it doing *that*, they'd have a baby eventually. And there he sat—dog that he was—getting aroused at the idea of her going down on him. He thought how maybe he didn't deserve a baby, or a beautiful wife like Dori, for that matter.

The parking garage at the Medical College of Georgia got a bit confusing, but Dori did real good. They took the stairs and followed the directions she'd written down on the back of a grocery receipt.

They waited a long time in the clinic, both of them holding magazines they weren't reading.

"Did you give the puppy fresh water?" Dori asked.

"Yeah," Kenny answered, but then they fell silent.

Eventually a nurse called Dorianne to the back.

Still gripping his magazine, Kenny sat there thinking. He was doing more and more of that lately—thinking about Dori and kids and family in general.

He sighed. At least he did still see his Aunt Eileen and Uncle Russ. They were his cousin Jack's parents. Jack and Kenny didn't get along, especially not since Kenny had a thing with Macy their senior year. *Hell, Jack shouldn't still be mad after all that time—he done married and divorced Macy since then.*

Kenny quit faking it with the magazine and tossed it onto the table. He walked across the room to see what other magazines were around but didn't pick one up.

Yes, he remembered putting water down for the puppy, but he couldn't be sure there was clean newspaper on the bathroom floor. Oh well, a puppy mess wasn't the worst thing going on those days. Kenny would even surprise Dori and clean it up himself.

"Kenny Brewer."

He stopped pacing and looked at the nurse in the doorway. He followed her into a room where Dori sat in the corner with her eyes all red and puffy. Dori nodded toward a chair a few feet from her, but she wouldn't actually look at him. After a few minutes, when she still wouldn't look him in the eye, he started glancing around.

A red trash container was stuck in the corner. It had a black, tribal-art-looking symbol on it. Kenny wasn't so much of a hick that he didn't know what bio-hazard meant, and he couldn't help but wonder what in the world about his wife could be that dangerous.

"You okay?" he asked.

Dorianne stared straight ahead.

He shrugged, and his attention went to a paper liner on the padded table. He could still see where Dori's body had crinkled it. Kenny couldn't stop looking at the paper, and he figured it had to be killing Dori, the way she hated wrinkles. At home she'd iron everything—clothes, sheets, curtains. Once she'd even chased Kenny around the room trying to iron the shirt he was wearing.

"Them wrinkles driving you crazy?" Kenny teased.

"What?"

The strained look on her face shut him up.

Then he saw the stirrups he'd heard women talking about when they wanted to embarrass their husbands or boyfriends. Women knew they could clear men from a room with just a word about their periods or girl-exams.

42

The doctor came in, introduced himself to Kenny, and took a seat across from them. "Dorianne has told you…"

"Nothing," Kenny said, stealing a look at his wife.

"Okay, then. We found two large tumors, both in or on the uterus. So far, there's nothing to indicate the ovaries are involved, so we hope to save them."

Kenny studied Dori's imprint on the paper liner.

"We should schedule the surgery sooner rather than later. Any questions?" the doctor asked.

Kenny looked at Dorianne.

"No, no questions," she whispered.

The doctor looked at Kenny.

"No, me neither," Kenny said, thinking if there was a pop quiz, he'd flunk for sure.

They left the exam room and made their way back to the Maverick.

In the car, Dori started shaking something terrible. "All I ever wanted was to have a baby."

"I know," Kenny whispered.

"It's all I ever wanted." She shook harder and harder.

The next thing Kenny knew, he was shaking too, and he leaned into her, but she shrugged him off. She pivoted so she was just out of his reach, and he knew her body was telling him, "Not even *you* can fix this one."

He didn't know how to tell her he needed fixing, too, that he needed her to hold him and tell him it'd be okay. He couldn't ask her for that, so instead he said, "You'll have your baby, one way or another."

He knew his voice came out way too loud and clumsy. But, Lord help him, no matter how stupid it sounded, he'd never meant anything more.

Part Two

Migration

Chapter Six

Flying South

Orange dust clouded Cam's view as she ran toward the braking Chevy truck. She stepped onto the road to avoid the blood- and dirt-matted roadkill in front of Jim Bob's Used Cars on Highway 278. The door of the blue and white pickup creaked when Cam pulled it open. She hesitated before climbing in, and a calloused hand swept a Coca Cola can, snuff tins, and other debris from the passenger seat onto the floor.

With her duffle bag balanced on her lap, Cam gingerly fumbled around for the seatbelt, running her injured hand between the frayed seat and the door.

"Ain't none."

"Excuse me?" She was caught off guard by the gruff tone of her new ride.

"If you're looking for the seatbelt, ain't none."

The driver, probably old enough to be her grandfather, pushed black-framed glasses up the thin bridge of his nose. Cam marveled that the old man could even see through the heavily scratched lenses.

"Isn't it the law?"

"*That's* the point." The old man gripped the steering wheel with fingers swollen close to splitting. The late March sun filtered through the nicotine-yellowed windshield. "What's your name, kid?"

"Cam Webber."

"Hmm. Where you headed all alone?"

"Augusta." She struggled to ignore the stench of sour mint and rotten meat that caught her attention.

"I ain't got it in my mind to go into Georgia today, but I'll take you as far as the bridge."

"Thanks, every little bit helps." Cam pushed some of the trash to one side with the toe of her Reebok. She studied the writing on a cracked cassette case until finally identifying it as Anne Murray. "How far will I be from Augusta at the bridge?"

The man's soiled shirt hung limply over his bony shoulders. "You ain't from around here."

Trying not to stare at hands too big for an otherwise thin man, Cam glanced at two shepherd-dog mixes rooting around in the overgrown weeds on the side of the road. "No, sir. Baltimore. Maryland."

"Maryland? You should have stayed on the interstate. It would've been quicker." He tapped the brakes on the way down the hill, keeping below the speed limit. "What's in Augusta?"

To the left, a hand-painted sign for a gift-and-bait shop advertised worms and crickets. "My aunt. She's been living in Augusta for a while now. I'm surprising her."

The old man laughed. "Boy, never surprise a woman, family or not." He coughed and cleared his throat. "I'll drop you at the bridge. That's the Savannah River, the state line. Augusta."

"Thanks." Then it sank in. The old man thought she was a guy. Heat rose on her neck as she remembered the first time someone had tried to stop her from going into the ladies' room, thinking she was male. At the time she was mortified.

These days it didn't really bother her as much, and in this case it might even be a plus.

The old man's tongue slid behind his bristly cheek and lingered at his lower lip. "You see, seatbelts are just one more way for the government to chip away at our rights."

Another downhill stretch brought more brake tapping. At the bottom of the hill, they stopped for a red light. Four men sat on chairs or overturned milk crates under a large shade tree. The light turned green, and the old man half-crooked his finger in greeting as they passed the loiterers.

At the next light, Cam eyed a pair of rusted gas pumps beneath a faded Schlitz sign hanging in front of a shack. On the other side of the road was a dilapidated building lettered in time-streaked black print: Petticoat Junction. For the first time since she'd gotten into the truck, she wished the old man was going slower so she could get a better look. Everything was so different from what Cam was used to in Baltimore.

Noticing scenery was nothing new to Cam. It was a familiar thing to do, since she was always along for the ride. Starting up another hill, the truck fought the slope and Cam sat up straighter in the seat.

The old man flipped off the air conditioner, and the truck lurched forward with the extra power. "So, why ain't you stayed on the interstate?"

"One of my rides said this way was quicker." A couple Cam rode with in North Carolina had fought for miles. It got so bad, she'd asked to be dropped at a country store when they left the interstate for gas. From there she'd been zigzagged all over North and South Carolina. It seemed everyone knew a different best way to get to Augusta.

Just past a store called Stop 'n Shop, the old man slowed down. "Ten dollars says it's that one," he said as he pointed a fat finger.

"Huh?"

He pointed toward three dogs by the road, ahead and to their left. The scrawniest, a yellow one, was sandwiched between two black dogs. "There been five dogs so far. Odds are one's roadkill before the day is over." Again he jabbed his finger toward the dogs. "Ten dollars says it's the yellow one."

"Yeah, sure," Cam answered, nudging the Anne Murray cassette case with her running shoe. She wondered if her aunt had any dogs. Aunt Jess had been about to get her one from the pound when Cam's mother came and took her away.

The old man leaned forward. "Yeah?"

Cam sighed. "Sure." After six years of living with her aunt, it was over just like that—no fighting to keep her, no nothing, just "I'm sorry, it's for the best." She wondered if her trek to see Jess in Augusta was the right thing to do.

The old man gunned the engine and turned left, cutting off a logging truck. Cam held on and planted her feet against the floorboard. She cracked the Anne Murray case in at least two more places.

The old man turned the truck around at the mouth of a red clay driveway and faced it back the way they had come. The dogs scattered when he accelerated. He maneuvered the truck past one black dog and swerved wide to the right. He almost broadsided the yellow dog and barely missed the second black one.

"What the hell?" Cam's duffle bag slid off her lap as the old man jerked the truck back onto the road. "You almost hit… What did you do that for?"

Without looking at her, the old man held out his hand, palm up. "I missed on purpose. But you still owe me ten dollars."

"Are you nuts?" Cam leaned away from him and stared at the almost lineless palm of his hand.

"A bet's a bet. Gimme my ten dollars." He laughed. "Or you want me to go back and finish it up?"

Cam just stared at him, and the old man pulled off the road again.

"Please don't. Don't go back." Cam turned around and watched the dogs shuffle around the shoulder of the road.

The old man threw the truck into reverse and backed closer to the dogs. Another logging truck raced by.

"Paying up?" the old man asked as he stopped the truck about fifteen feet from the dogs. "Whatcha say?" He extended a fat hand to her.

She fought the taste of bile as she shifted her hips to pull her wallet from her back pocket. Her hands shook as she fingered the ragged edge of the address she'd torn from the envelope that had contained her aunt's letter. When she handed over the ten dollar bill, only seven dollars remained.

The old man grinned and stuffed the bill into his shirt pocket. He pulled his glasses from his face, studied them a moment, and rubbed the lenses against the rough, stained truck upholstery. After putting his glasses back on, he jerked the truck into gear and turned back toward Augusta.

That did not just almost happen, Cam told herself. She automatically reached for the absent seatbelt. She worried that she should have seen it coming, that she was a grownup now and should have known better.

How could she possibly describe to Aunt Jess what had just happened? Even after her mom stopped chasing men and dreams all over the country, even after her mom returned home and ripped Cam away from her aunt, even after Cam had grown so angry at Aunt Jess for not insisting Cam stay with her, even after all that, Cam imagined telling Jess about the things in her life that mattered. She'd daydreamed of telling her aunt about the state track meet her junior year, getting her driver's license, graduating.

The old man chuckled. "So, he's gonna surprise a woman, huh?"

It took Cam a minute to remember that her ride thought she was a dude, and that he was referring to her surprising her aunt.

"Women are funny things." He glanced at Cam. "Yes, they are."

They passed a small, brick church. This Baptist Church, that Missionary Church. She must have passed a hundred of them so far, all with cutesy slogans on signs, like bumper stickers for churches. Cam wondered if the old man went to church. She sneaked a peek at him as he fiddled with the snuff in his mouth. Did his fat hands grip a leather-bound Bible every Sunday? Did the minty stink linger about him as he sang hymns?

Cam could imagine Aunt Jess going to one of the small, white churches, or even to one of the huge, brick, neatly landscaped churches. She could picture her going to an Episcopal church, like the one where Cam had been confirmed back when she was twelve and still living with Jess. Cam would have known more about her aunt if she hadn't thrown a temper tantrum and cut off all contact. She'd just been so hurt when Jess handed her back to her mother.

Another church, another sign. "Fear God and you will have nothing else to fear." At least it wasn't another "If God is your copilot, swap seats."

The old man's head jerked toward a small church. His fat fingers thumped against the steering wheel and punctuated his distracted words, "God and country."

Cam gave the old man a questioning look and glanced in the side mirror as a BMW came up fast behind them. A sign welcomed them to Beech Island. She didn't feel welcomed. Aunt Jess saying she loved her was one thing, but welcoming Cam into her home was another.

Just past a fire station, there were two more dogs on the side of the road. Cam braced her feet against the floor. She was going to be ready for whatever stunt the old man might pull with those dogs. She consciously slowed her breathing, hoping to hide her nervousness. When the dogs were flea-sized specks in the side mirror, she relaxed.

"God, and country, and history," the old man said.

Cam's stomach was doing flips and flops that got worse the closer they got to Augusta. She took several long breaths and tried to calm herself. "History is important," she said.

"See there, you know." Over and over, the old man nodded his small, gray-haired head. "You know what else is important?"

"Family," Cam whispered.

"Yes, family. Exactly."

Ahead, smokestacks ascended into the blue-gray sky and exhaled a mustard-colored breath that dissipated into the clouds. A burnt smell permeated the truck, mixing with the ever-present odor of stale mint.

The old man drove over the bridge in the left lane, going much slower than the speed limit. The smokestacks continued their belching.

"Is that the river?" Cam asked.

"Yep."

Cam coughed as she looked down into the brown water.

"Yep, I figured I'd drive you over, seeing how dangerous it is these days." He poked at his glasses. "You're a pretty good kid."

The river was mottled with irregular patches of rippled texture and mirrored smoothness. The smell worsened. Cam's eyes watered. She held her breath and looked over at the old man, silently asking for an explanation for the burnt feces smell filling the truck.

The old man smiled, and said, "Cricket crap." He kept his gaze on the road. "You know, it's the best fertilizer. Cricket crap's even better than chicken shit. More nitrogen. Next time someone says to you that you don't know shit, tell them, 'Oh yes I do.'"

Suddenly the old man put on the brakes and cut hard to the left. The car behind them laid on the horn as the truck pulled to a stop in the median. The old man announced, "Augusta."

Cam stepped out of the truck, and the old man called out to her, "Hey, kid." He held out the ten dollar bill.

"Yes?"

"Thanks." The old man laughed as he stuffed it back into his shirt pocket and put the truck into gear. "Don't let anyone get you on that one again."

Cam hoisted her bag onto her shoulder. She closed the door, and seconds later, the old man drove off.

Standing across the street from a sign with a cartoon cricket, Cam breathed in the smell of mound after mound of dark, acrid fertilizer and the foul, yellow breath of industry. Amazed that something smelling that awful could help something else grow, she turned away from it, toward Augusta.

Chapter Seven

Stoney-Faced Sea Urchin

Macy wasn't exactly sure why she had gone to the hospital. It wasn't like she and Kenny were close. However, she had once been good friends with Dorianne. Her heartbeat quickened as she thought of those early days.

"Macy, look here!" Dorianne had had a French fry stuffed up each nostril, then crossed her eyes when Macy looked at her. Macy had laughed until soda came out of her nose.

Macy studied Kenny, his legs stretched out in front of him, the heel of his right foot balancing on the toe of his left. She couldn't help but notice how well he'd matured.

As she walked toward him, Macy worried that he'd tell her to leave. Palms sweating, she wondered who she thought she was, showing up at the hospital. But it was too late to retreat—he'd looked up, recognized her. She tried to feel secure in her back-up story of being there to see Michael.

Kenny stood, glanced around. "Where's Jeremiah? He's okay, isn't he?"

"Oh, yeah." Macy thought his concern was sweet. "I'm not here about J-man. He's with my mom for the day. I'm here to see Michael, a man I'm dating."

"Oh." His eyebrows knitted closer together.

"Michael works here. Actually, he's not *working-*working today. He's with friends. His friend Jess has been in the hospital, and she's going home today. Cancer." *God, why am I rambling on about that?*

"It's good she's getting out."

"Not really. They're letting her go because there's nothing else they can do for her." Macy's voice faltered, but she fought against giving in to grief for her new friend. "Enough about that. You've got your own things going on."

"Yeah. Dori's having surgery today." He gave her a puzzled look.

"Your Aunt Eileen mentioned it."

Kenny nodded, and Macy motioned toward the seats. "Mind if I sit with you for a while?"

"No, of course not." He returned to his same seat.

Macy sat one over, facing him. He looked better than she ever remembered seeing him, although understandably a little tired. "So, tell me about Dori's surgery."

"Hysterectomy. Big word to be coming out of my mouth, huh?" He leaned forward. "Dori ain't never gonna have kids, Macy."

"That's got to be tough."

"It's hell. That's all she ever wanted. You know that."

"Yeah, I know."

When they were real young, Dorianne had a thing about not forsaking old dolls or stuffed animals for new ones. The guilt of abandoning one was too much for her, so she'd have them all lined up on her bed, the ragged with the brand new, careful to give them equal attention.

It amazed Macy to think of how little she'd thought about Dori the last couple of years. She had kept Dori tucked away, safe in an insulated compartment of her brain.

Kenny took a deep breath. "And the doctor's making a fuss about trying to save an ovary. Without the other equipment, what's the difference?"

"If they save an ovary, Dori won't need hormone replacement therapy. Trust me, she'll be glad for that much."

"You women know all about this stuff, huh?"

"We learn it along the way—if we're lucky and pay attention."

"Dori's been on the computer looking all this up. She's smart like that."

"Yes, she is. Did the doctor say anything about using a surrogate with Dori's eggs?"

"Dori don't want nothing like that. She said she don't want no baby that isn't really ours."

"But it would be."

He shrugged. "Dori says no."

"What do *you* say?"

"Guess it don't matter to me anymore." He shrugged again, then the color drained from his face as he looked toward the door. "What's taking so long? God, I couldn't handle nothing happening to her." His breathing grew ragged.

Macy took his hand. "I know, Kenny." She didn't know, yet she did, too. She may not have known the mature, intimate love between two adults, but she did know about loving someone so much it made breathing hard, loving someone so much it made you swear the world was spinning in a whirl of worry and wonder, heartburn, and gratitude. She wouldn't tell Kenny how she loved her son that way, not now that he and Dori wouldn't have kids.

She let go of his hand.

Kenny sighed. "It's good to talk to someone about this. And it's good that you understand, being a girl and all."

She smiled. Ever since she and Emma had taken a feminist theory class, she hadn't been able to tolerate being called a girl. But coming from Kenny, it didn't bother her.

"Dori would kill me if she knew I was talking to you, of all people."

"Still that bad, huh?"

He nodded. "She'd get all riled up. You know you ain't her favorite person."

"Yeah, but I'm sure she'd understand that you need someone to talk to," Macy said.

"That girl understands a lot, but not nothing to do with you."

Macy felt the heat rising on her face, and she was pretty sure Kenny could see the blush.

He gave her a weak smile. "Hey, how's your mom?"

"Good. She had been staying with me, but she and Harold got back together, so she's moved back to Burke County with him."

"Harold. Which one's that?"

"Husband number three." Macy kept it to herself that he was probably her least favorite of her mother's husbands. And she didn't admit how much she liked her household being back to just her and Jeremiah.

"Ah," he said. "Tell me about your new boyfriend."

"Michael's a doctor. He's sweet."

"Where did you meet him?"

"The Partridge Inn." She'd only called Michael to prove that she would. The next thing she knew, she was going out with him, trying to take it slow and make it work. She thought about the veranda, the warm breeze, the mess she'd made of her friendship with Emma.

"You like him a lot?"

She hesitated, trying not to let the thoughts of Emma take hold. "Yeah. We haven't been dating long, but so far so good."

An image from the night before flashed through her mind. She and Michael had sat on her sofa talking, while Jeremiah watched TV in his bedroom. Michael kissed her, and she kissed him back, thinking, *"This is nice."* It wasn't lost on her that *nice* and *I can't get enough of you* were two very different things.

Then J-man had barreled into the room. "Mama, mama, do we need a new slicer-dicer?" Macy had laughed, knowing what was coming next. "For only nineteen ninety-nine we could get a heavy duty slicer-dicer. With its own case."

"No, J-man, I don't think we need one." She moved a few inches away from Michael.

"But if we act now, there's also a knife set—for free!"

Macy's amusement had faded as she considered how, a year earlier, J-man would have told her his daddy would buy him one if she didn't. Now Jeremiah barely mentioned Jack.

"That's great." Kenny shifted in the narrow hospital seat. "You deserve to find someone special."

It took her a moment to realize Kenny wasn't referring to a new slicer-dicer. Even though she didn't believe that bit about her deserving anything, she smiled anyway. "Speaking of someone special, have you talked to Jack lately?"

"Special, my ass. No, ain't talked to him lately. I see him every now and again when I go by Uncle Russ and Aunt Eileen's."

As they grew up, there had always been comparisons made between Jack and Kenny. Jack was considered the better looking of the cousins, always better at sports, always smarter. Kenny's eyes were a little closer together, his nose just slightly bigger. But they had the same fine, light brown hair, the same quick, easy smile.

"I see Jeremiah over there some, too. Sure is a handsome devil," Kenny said.

"J-man is that. He always tells me when he sees his Uncle Kenny. He really likes you."

Kenny stood and walked several feet away. Fumbling through some magazines, he mumbled, "He's a good kid."

Kenny picked up a *Family Circle* and sat back down. He drummed his fingers against it in an uneasy beat while they sat without talking for several long moments.

He tossed the magazine back onto the table. "Hell, Macy, you and me screwed up something fierce. Dori ain't got no close girlfriends. Hasn't, not since you, not since high school."

She just stared at the magazine Kenny had thrown down. Brightly colored magazine covers bombarded her. Growing up, she and Dorianne had stashed a collection of cheesy romance comics under Macy's mattress. They'd commandeered the 1960s comics from a box of Macy's mom's stuff in the attic.

"You and Dori were always together," Kenny said.

Locked in Macy's bedroom, they read *Romance!* and *First Love* out loud. Their overly dramatic voices were laced with an undercurrent of giggles trying to burst up to the surface.

"Back then, it was like you and Dori lived in your own little world," Kenny said.

Macy blushed. One hero—"stony faced" according to the literary account—carried the beauty to the safety of the beach after she was felled by a sea urchin. Dori usually got to be the beauty because she had breasts first, but Macy didn't mind because she got to hover over Dori, attempting resuscitation. Macy would place a hand over her mouth, and through that barrier, she, being the brave hero, kissed the

beautiful woman. Later, they jokingly called that story their
Stony-faced Sea Urchin.

Macy was amazed that she'd kept the memories of
playing "hero" at bay for so long.

"Yeah, you and Dori were such good friends before we
messed it all up."

"She and I had been drifting apart before you and I had
our thing."

"But nothing too serious," Kenny said. "I mean, I know
y'all didn't hang out as much after you and Jack hooked up,
but it always happens that way with girls, don't it?"

"I guess."

But things like the comic books don't always happen, she
mused. She and Dori started acting them out when they were
nine. They did a lot at first, then not so much, but always
seemed to go back to it. Then Dori had confided she always
envisioned Jack as her hero, and Macy had bristled with
jealousy.

Even after role-playing dwindled to an end, they still
shared private jokes about the magazines. But when Macy
started dating Jack, all references to them ended.

Not long after that, Dorianne started spending a lot of
time with Kenny. The closer Dori got to him, the further
Macy let things go with Jack. She only had sex with Jack
after she heard whispers that Dori and Kenny were doing it.

"You do know that me and Dori were broke up when—
well, when you and me fooled around? I didn't cheat on her.
I ain't never cheated on her."

"I know."

"I never did find out what you and Jack had fought about
that night."

"It was something so stupid that I don't even remember
it now," Macy said.

But she did remember Jack's anger when he saw her with Kenny. After Macy and Kenny had slept together, they went out for a bite to eat. They sat in Macy's car in the parking lot of the Dairy Queen, sorting through their burgers and shakes. Jack and two of his jock friends walked up. He tapped on her window, and she reluctantly rolled it down a few inches.

"One little fight," Jack hollered, "and this is what I get? Look at you. You got that fresh-fucked look. What a slut."

The memory made Macy cringe.

Kenny laughed. "Jack was madder than hell when he saw us out that night."

Macy remembered the muscles around Jack's jaws tightening under his smooth skin.

"And the look on your face when he started walking to my side of your car," Kenny said.

Jack had gotten halfway to Kenny when Kenny opened the car door. Macy wasn't about to let them fight, so she put her old Ford into reverse and stepped on the gas. The force of it made Kenny's door swing open wide, and he lurched forward and smacked his head on the dash. Just as he tried to straighten up, Macy gunned the car forward. The motion threw him back against the seat and slammed the door shut, almost catching him and Jack in it. They both yelled "shit" at the same time, and Macy remembered thinking about it being in stereo.

Macy looked at Kenny as he shifted in the hospital chair. Her cheeks grew warm, and she tried for a sheepish grin. "You got so mad at me that night."

"It looked like I was running from Jack, and damn it, I'd been waiting for a real reason to stand up to him ever since that time in the seventh grade when he nailed me in the face with the ball during smear-the-queer."

In Kenny's breathless sentence, Macy could feel years of one cousin living in the long shadow of another. She knew there was more to what had happened than one night of sex between him and his cousin's girlfriend.

"The ball hit me so hard, it made my eyes water, but not no crying tears like Jack swore they were. He teased me about that for years."

Macy saw now that for Kenny, that night in the Dairy Queen parking lot was about taking a stand, about challenging a lifetime of always being second to Jack.

Understanding that made Macy question her own motivation for what had happened that night. For years she refused to consider why she slept with Kenny, why she always felt betrayed by Dorianne when she was the one who'd messed up. And now, after kissing Emma and liking it way too much, she started putting things into perspective. She was finally seeing things about herself that she hadn't ever allowed herself to think about. And it scared the hell out of her.

"Even if Dori won't never appreciate you being here today, I sure do," Kenny said.

"I'm glad I could be here. You and Dorianne are terrific people. I'm sorry I made it impossible to have you both in my life."

At first the lack of closure had overwhelmed Macy, creating a restlessness she couldn't quite contain. But, paralyzed by guilt, she hadn't been able to do anything about it.

"Kenny, are we okay?"

"I can say you and me are cool, but I gotta tell you, Dori ain't never gonna be your friend."

"I just want her not to hate me, to forgive me."

Kenny started to say something, but a nurse came in and told him he could see Dorianne. He was following her through a door, being reassured that the surgery had gone well, when he turned toward Macy and mouthed "thank you" before disappearing to be with his wife.

Macy sighed. She'd have to be content with fifty-percent closure on that front. She left the waiting room and headed toward Michael, toward a relationship she hadn't screwed up yet.

Chapter Eight

Tilt-A-Whirl

The woman pulling over in the dusty Cavalier looked safer than any of her other rides, but something felt wrong when Cam peered through the smudged passenger window. Still, she opened the door and folded herself into the car.

"Get in, darling. You'll have to excuse the mess. Just push that to the side. That's my daughter's, Olivia Dawn's. I try to get her to keep her stuff in the backseat, but hell, you try telling a seven-year-old to do anything."

Cam smiled, grateful for the empty juice boxes instead of snuff tins.

"Hi, I'm Grace." She reached over to shake Cam's hand.

"I'm Cam."

She looked Cam over thoroughly. Cam waited for the recognition that she was a girl, but Grace just smiled.

Cam reached for the seatbelt, thankful to have access to one again, and secured it.

"Where you headed? You planning to camp out on Washington Road for Masters tickets?"

"What's a Masters ticket?" Cam asked.

"The Masters is only *the* golf tournament of all golf tournaments. I'm not a huge fan of the game myself, but the

Augusta National is absolutely gorgeous." Grace sighed. "Ah, when the azaleas bloom."

Cam looked behind them as Grace stopped talking and whipped her Cavalier out onto the road.

"Where'd you say you're headed?"

Cam smoothed the scrap of paper against her leg and read the address aloud.

"Oh, yeah, I know that neighborhood. That's where my doc lives. Doc and I dated, but it didn't work out, and that's a shame, because he would have made a great daddy for Olivia Dawn."

Cam stared at the address. She wanted nothing more than to hurry up and get there.

"Whose address did you say that was?"

"My aunt's."

"Well then, let's get you to your aunt's."

Grace turned left, zigzagged past several auto shops, and made another left. "You would not believe how bad the traffic gets during the tournament. It quadruples at the very least. But there is an upside. I can bartend and make more that week than the whole rest of the year at the bookstore."

Half a block later, she turned right onto Greene Street, and the sight floored Cam. Bright pink flowers smothered bush after bush. The splotchy sun, finding its way through the canopies of huge trees, made the color glow. She knew immediately that this was the Augusta that Aunt Jess had fallen in love with.

Grace kept talking about the tournament and money, and Cam's mind drifted. She looked up at the trees. They lined both sides of the road and met in the middle, where their branches barely brushed overhead. Cam thought of the painting on the ceiling of a cathedral in Rome. She couldn't remember what it was called, but she remembered the image from her art history book where God and Adam were reaching out toward each other but not quite touching.

By the end of the next block, the trees had begun clasping hands.

"It's about time."

"Excuse me?" Cam was jolted back into the discussion.

"Finally the weather's cooperating, and the azaleas are blooming right on time. The last couple of years, it's been downright cold for the Masters."

The traffic light turned red, and a gate came down. Cam heard a train whistle.

"No telling how long this will take." Grace sighed and shoved the gearshift into park.

As the train came into view, the back of Cam's head started throbbing.

"Oh, no," Grace said.

Cam looked up and saw that the train stretched out in front of them wasn't moving.

"Oh well, such is life." Grace reached over Cam's legs and started rooting through the glove box. Pulling out a photo in one hand, she let the other rest on Cam's leg. "This is my child, Olivia Dawn."

"She's precious." Cam knew all kids were, especially to their parents. Well, maybe not Cam in her mom's eyes, but she wasn't going there.

"Too bad her daddy's a deadbeat, but he does come around to see his daughter. I have to give him credit for that."

Grace looked at Cam but didn't wait for her to respond before she started in again. "I didn't know my daddy when I was growing up. Matter of fact, I just found out he's a drunk roofer from right here in town, not a banker from Atlanta like I thought." She paused. "Wow, that's the first time I've said that out loud." Her voice caught briefly, and she looked away.

"That's got to be tough."

"Was I devastated? Yes. Surprised? Not really. As a kid I often overheard the speculation. That can really hurt a child, you know."

Cam nodded, the only contribution she was comfortable making.

"Anyway, this roofer died years ago, so it's not like I'll ever have to meet him or anything."

Cam considered the lack of a male presence in her own life as she grew up. The only decent men active in her life were Coach Barnes, the track coach, and Mr. Moore, her English teacher.

"Hey, since they're neighbors, I wonder if your aunt knows my doc. What's her name?"

"Jess Almond."

Grace's mouth opened a little wider. "Jess. As in Jess and Sharon?"

"Sharon?"

"Your aunt's girlfriend, or lover, or whatever the hell is PC these days. I'll tell you what—I like your aunt just fine, but not that other one. She is so uptight. One night my doc and I went on a double date with them. I hadn't met them up to that point. Matter of fact, I assumed we were going out with a man named Jess and his wife. Was I ever surprised. Anyway, I ask one little question, and that Sharon gets all pissed off."

Sharon? The same friend Aunt Jess had all those years ago?

Grace went on. "I asked them who was the husband and who was the wife. Jess told me neither, that they were partners. So I said if there's no husband, who changes the light bulbs and mows the grass?" Grace shrugged. "Later, I felt like things were going well enough to get a little personal, so I asked Jess if she'd at least ever tried it. She was like, 'Tried what?' 'Tried *it*,' I said. That's when Sharon butted in with something like, 'Give me a break.' And then she changed the subject, and I was like, 'Well, screw you, too.'"

The pounding moved up the back of Cam's head and wrapped around her forehead. She couldn't stop thinking about calling Aunt Jess a dyke when lashing out at her years earlier. Back then, she didn't really know what it meant and surely didn't know how it applied to herself, but she knew enough to use the word as a weapon.

Cam stared ahead, and as the last car of the train passed, she could again see the road in front of them, the trees, the new green of the grass. It was all much too bright.

Grace gave her a pouty smile. "It's so difficult being a single mother. Mothers have to work so hard, and when we don't get any help, well, we have to do what we have to do."

Cam nodded, pretending to understand more than she did.

"With Olivia Dawn's curls and sweet blue eyes, I just can't be too careful, you know?"

Grace put her car in gear and moved forward through the intersection. She pulled over and parked at the curb in front of a plain, brick building.

"I have no choice but to put Olivia Dawn in the most affordable daycare I can find. I don't like it, but I have no choice. It would be so much easier if I had some peace of mind, if I only knew for sure she is safe there."

Cam looked at the neat rows of brick that made up the Georgia Department of Labor beside them. "Why did we stop here?"

"To discuss what I need you to do for me."

"I really need to go see Aunt Jess."

"This won't take but a few minutes. Besides, I know a shortcut that will more than make up for the time."

"Grace, I—"

"Look, Cam, this time of day, Jess probably won't be home anyway." She took Cam's hand in hers, ran a painted fingernail across Cam's sweaty palm. "You have all day, and this will only take a few minutes. I'll make it up to you."

Not liking the vibe she was picking up, Cam yanked her hand away. "I'm not like that."

"You're not gay like your aunt?"

"I am gay, but this is not my style." Cam tried to make an expansive gesture with her hands, unable to tell this stranger how screwed up the last couple of days had been, how panicked she was becoming, how much she just needed to get to Aunt Jess.

"I'm talking about ten minutes of your time. That could sure help me sleep better at night. I worry so much. One day you'll have kids—okay, or not—but try to understand. I really need to know that she's safe there. I need to know that someone couldn't just walk out of that daycare with my little girl."

Before Cam knew it, she'd agreed to Grace's crazy plan. Anything to get things headed back toward Aunt Jess.

Grace pulled around the corner from the converted house with the white vinyl siding. The muffled sounds of children at play drifted from behind the stockade fence enclosing the yard. Cam took a deep breath and glanced back once as she walked away from Grace's car.

Cam went in and tentatively approached the young, bleached-blonde woman at the front desk. "Excuse me. I'm Olivia's aunt. My sister asked me to pick her up and take her home."

"I see. Let me just check Olivia's file."

Cam tried to stay calm by concentrating on the teddy bear wallpaper.

"I'm sorry, our records don't list an aunt for Olivia. Do you have ID on you?"

"Oh, that. I left it at home. Sorry." *Crap.* "Listen, my sister is a hard-working single mother, and she's overwhelmed right now and just asked for this one tiny favor, for me to help her out by picking up Olivia Dawn. Would you begrudge a poor woman that little bit of help?"

Cam didn't have a clue where that had come from, and it left her feeling more than a little uncomfortable, but she was impressed by her own fast thinking.

The young woman must not have been as impressed, because she was on the phone talking to the director and Cam was pretty sure she heard something about the police.

Cam bolted.

She ran around the corner and found that Grace's car was no longer there. She thought about her duffle, left behind in a stranger's vehicle. *Damn it.* She needed to keep running, until she passed out or the cops caught up to her. Two blocks and a major case of shin splints later, she almost got hit when Grace pulled from behind a big 4x4.

Cam jumped in, panting, "She's calling the police."

"Thank God." Grace accelerated.

"I'll be arrested for attempted kidnapping. They'll register me as a sex offender, and all you can say is 'Thank God'?"

"Now I know my child is safe there. That's what counts. Don't worry, they'll never see you again. It won't matter."

"Aunt Jess will shoot me if she ever finds out about this."

"Oh, don't worry. Your aunt won't care. She's got other stuff on her mind."

"What other stuff?" Cam rubbed her right shin.

"Well, like the chemo. I imagine when you're going through that, you couldn't care less what favors your niece does, or has done for her." Grace winked.

"Chemo?"

"Oh, yeah. I hadn't gotten around to the part about the cancer."

"Cancer?"

"I'm sure she's fine now. It's been awhile, but the last time I talked to my doc, he said she was doing much better."

"You couldn't wait to tell me she's a lesbian, but *this* you forgot to tell me?"

Grace made an *oops* face.

"Christ, Grace." Cam pulled her duffle bag into her lap. "Just take me there, please."

"Okay, okay, we'll be there in no time."

Cam sat back and tried to visualize her aunt. She hoped Jess hadn't lost too much weight from the chemo; she'd always been on the thin side as it was.

Grace tapped on her steering wheel as they sat through a red light. "Hey, sorry for not telling you about the cancer. But I'm not sorry about asking you to go into the daycare. I had to know what would happen."

Cam closed her eyes. Her headache eased as she thought about Aunt Jess being pleased with her for reading between the lines, for knowing she wanted Cam to come see her without Jess having to actually say it.

She figured at first Jess would pretend to scold her for hitching all that way, but then she'd see how Cam had become a woman, capable and strong. They would share laughs as Cam told her witty stories about her journey—both to adulthood and to Georgia.

Grace drove into a McDonald's parking lot. Cam wanted to punch the dash. She wanted to tell Grace to go screw herself, but she didn't. She would not let herself lose it, not after all those miles. When Grace pulled up to the drive-thru window, Cam undid her seatbelt, grabbed her duffle, and got out of the car.

As Cam walked away, she could hear Grace calling after her. "Come on, Cam. This will only take a second."

Cam crossed the parking lot and walked up to the first person she saw. When she read the address to the white-haired man in the khakis and pink golf shirt, he pointed across the street.

"Just go about a half mile in that direction, and you'll run right into the road."

With every step, the pounding in Cam's head dissolved, replaced by a drumming in her chest. She was so close.

Cam unclenched her fist and double-checked the number. The ink was smudged, but she could still make it out, if not from the paper, then from memory.

†

Jess and Sharon's kitchen was very bright, with white floor tile, cabinets, and countertops. They provided a nice contrast with black appliances, right down to the refrigerator. But Macy's favorite details were the splashes of red: the toaster, the coffeemaker, the ceramic fondue pot. The dish towels and pot holders were imprinted with a chili pepper motif.

Another pepper, a magnet, held a grocery list on the fridge—milk, bread, Pop-Tarts. Jess had a thing for chocolate Pop-Tarts, but Macy didn't know which of the women had written the list that ended in, "I love you!" Their handwriting was so similar, something she figured had happened over time.

Macy stood at the sink and stared into the pale froth of the soapy water. It was hard to believe that just a few days ago, Jess and Sharon had eaten off the plates she was soaking, and now Jess was gone.

"Hey." Michael leaned against the doorway. "That can wait." He gestured toward the dishes.

"I'd rather just get it done."

"Okay," Michael said. "Jeremiah's still in the spare room playing."

She smiled, and Michael disappeared back into the living room. She could hear the low sounds of a ballgame murmuring from the TV.

Macy sighed. Jess and Sharon had been so passionate with one another, right up to the very end. Once she'd overheard Sharon telling Jess, "Baby, after all these years, you still give me goose bumps."

She imagined them before the cancer started taking Jess away bit by bit. Surely they gave one another that heart-pounding, butterfly-stomach feeling of near panic.

Long ago, that kind of passion would sneak up on Macy whenever Dorianne brought up the hero characters in *First Love*. Like the time Dori went to the roller rink with Kathy and Debbie, without inviting Macy. Dori felt so bad about it afterward. She said she was sorry, squeezed Macy's hand, and whispered with hot bubblegum breath in her ear, "Macy, come play hero." Her words were toe-numbing, belly-tingling.

Macy had felt something like that with Jack, briefly. But she was never quite sure how much of her fervor was about him, and how much was panic over losing Dorianne's friendship. The tornado of confusing feelings was nauseating, much like at the county fair when Macy rode the Tilt-A-Whirl for the first time. She threw up cotton candy all over Jack and turned his white T-shirt into a sour tie-dye of blue and pink. When he took her home, he didn't even try to kiss her goodnight or put his hands up her shirt, and she remembered thinking that maybe girls should puke on their dates more often.

Standing over Jess and Sharon's white sink, Macy felt a little dizzy. She hadn't known them long. She'd met them through Michael. By then, Jess's cancer had taken a heavy toll on them both. But Macy liked them immediately and quickly grew attached.

She went out front for fresh air. It felt nice to be outside, even in the early, sweltering heat. Sitting on the porch steps, she thought she tasted cilantro. She knew it was absurd, a product of the unopened manila envelope in her car, the one with Macy's name in Emma's handwriting. She wasn't afraid of what might be in the envelope, just of her possible reaction to it. She really missed Emma.

But being with Michael was safe, calming. There were times Macy missed the rush of an adventure with a stranger, and of course there were times when she thought of Emma, but she was okay with Michael. He was kind and unassuming and didn't pressure her for too much too soon. She'd wanted to take it slow, do it right, so they had only just started sleeping together.

Best of all, though, Michael was good with Jeremiah. And her J-man seemed to like him a lot.

Macy looked up as a young man crossed the yard. His blonde-streaked hair was disheveled, his jeans rumpled. His smile was self-conscious, a combination of nervous and giddy. She was just thinking how cute the guy was when she realized it was a young woman.

Macy smiled. "Can I help you?"

The young woman shifted her duffle bag from her right arm to her left. "I'm Cam, Jess's niece."

Macy's eyes widened. "I'm Macy Stokes." She extended her hand, and the girl shook it. "Let me go inside and get Michael."

She mumbled something about wanting Jess, not someone named Michael, but Macy hurried inside.

When Macy came out with Michael, the young woman was massaging her temples. Michael introduced himself as a friend of Jess and Sharon's and asked if Sharon was expecting her.

"Where's Jess?"

The words were a knowing whisper, and Macy's heart broke for her.

Cam crumpled onto the sun-scorched lawn.

They walked Cam inside and settled her onto the sofa. Macy went into the kitchen to get Cam a glass of water. When Macy came back, Michael was talking about Jess. Cam was on the sofa, on her back. Macy handed her a damp rag to place across her forehead.

Michael used his soft doctor voice, telling Cam how Jess had gone in her sleep, relaxed in Sharon's arms.

After a brief conference in the kitchen, Macy and Michael decided Cam would stay with Michael for a few days, until she could sort things out. They tried unsuccessfully to reach Sharon on her cell phone but still planned to honor her wishes and lock up the house after they'd cleaned the kitchen for her.

Macy wiped down the counters and put away the dishes, tiptoed past Michael and Cam, and touched Michael's shoulder softly as she passed his chair. She was quiet as she approached the spare bedroom. She didn't want to wake J-man if he'd fallen asleep.

She stood in the doorway and watched him fly one of his action figures through the air. Lingering there, Macy noticed for the first time the red accents in that room—a red table lamp, a crimson-faced clock on the wall. She looked back to J-man, but when he caught her watching, he stopped mid-flight. He turned his action figure to face her. "Mama, can you help me cream him so we can spread his ashes?"

She didn't know what to say. When had he started knowing stuff like that?

✝

At home that night, with J-man bathed and off to bed, Macy retrieved the envelope from her car. The postmark was the same as the one on the card Emma had sent J-man for his sixth birthday. Macy carefully pulled two 8x10s and a note from the envelope. Placing the photos on the table to her left, she put the note down in front of her. Her hands shook too much to hold it still enough to read.

Macy, I hope this finds you well. I wanted to share these images with you, as they are my favorites. I'm in Virginia, finally feeling like I'm home. I've found what I was looking for. Hope you're finding yours, too. Hugs and kisses to Jeremiah. Much love, Emma.

The first photo had been taken in downtown Augusta. Macy focused on the background, not wanting to see her own restless image staring back at her. The rough brick of the buildings on Reynolds Street served as a stoic backdrop to her half-smirk expression. The look was probably in response to one of the off-the-wall, pseudo-philosophical comments Emma loved to throw out.

It struck her then how unselfconscious she'd become over Emma's photography. At first it made her feel a little uncomfortable, but Emma was good at what she did, and Macy savored the excuse to relinquish control, however momentarily.

The second photo was of Macy and J-man. She didn't remember Emma taking the picture of her squatting with him near the riverbank, looking closely at something he held in his hand. There was a sweetness in the curve of J-man's hand, the concentration on his face. But there was also something very unsettling, something Macy couldn't quite place. The longer she looked at the picture, the harder it became for her to breathe.

She stuffed it all back into the envelope and stashed it on top of the refrigerator.

✝

Damp earth under their feet, Macy and Cam hiked along the path between the canal and the river, through an occasional cloud of gnats. On the far side of the canal, sunbathing turtles lined a dark, slanted log, like precariously placed dominoes.

"This place is really cool," Cam said. "You come out here a lot?"

"Not as much as I used to."

If Macy could manage it being just her and J-man, that was fine, but she didn't like going to the canal with Michael. They'd all gone there together once, and J-man kept asking her if she remembered the time he beat Emma when they raced to the river, or when they'd all ridden their bikes down the canal path. Michael had smiled and reached for Macy's hand. Right at that moment, his touch burned her. She'd pulled away. The look of bewilderment on his face made her feel ashamed. From then on, it was just easier not to share her and Emma's special place with him.

Macy was okay being in that space with Cam, because she wasn't trying to replace Emma; Cam wasn't trying to do anything but come to terms with what was on her own plate.

Macy watched her out of the corner of her eye. Cam had a cute, androgynous look to her, one that she pulled off well with her smooth skin, stylish hair, and lean body. *Obviously gay*, Macy thought, then she wondered whether Cam and Emma would hit it off if Emma was still there, and if that would have made Macy jealous. *Yes*, Macy thought. *Very jealous.*

Macy turned toward a rustling near the riverbank, and she thought about seeing otters and beavers and squirrels near there with Emma and J-man.

Thinking of squirrels, her mind drifted to a time at her in-laws' when Jeremiah was little and she and Jack were still married. She and J-man lazed around under one of Russ and Eileen's shade trees, while inside, Jack raided his dad's tool chest. J-man rambled over to her and climbed into her lap. She directed his gaze to two squirrels playing tag along a tree trunk. Several moments later, Macy watched as one of the squirrels hurled the other from the tree, right into a tabby cat's ready claws. She thanked God J-man's attention had already drifted to something else. He glanced up only briefly from the He-Man figure he was playing with.

Macy thought about the squirrels a lot after seeing that. She'd even told Emma about the incident one afternoon out at the river. Emma said she'd read somewhere that squirrels of different troops would do things like that if one strayed into the other's territory.

"Troops?" Macy had asked. Emma said she didn't know if she had read that term somewhere or made it up, but it didn't matter to Macy. She loved it.

When Macy had commented that people had similar tendencies, Emma agreed then swore she'd never throw Macy from a tree.

As Macy and Cam walked, Cam told her about a time she and Jess tried to feed a stray dog. They were luring it toward them, when a man came out of nowhere, waved a badminton racket at them, and chased them away.

"Aunt Jess was devastated. She was worried the incident would make me afraid to do good things. So, we drove around all day until we finally found a real stray to feed."

"That sounds so much like her." It reminded Macy of something Emma would do, too.

Cam walked over to the weathered, crumbling wall and looked out over the river. "She was terrific, wasn't she?"

"Yes, she was," Macy said, referring to both Jess and Emma.

Cam leaned against the wall and ran her fingers along the rough surface. "The last time I saw Aunt Jess, I said some pretty hurtful things to her."

Macy had guessed that something had transpired between them.

"I was only twelve. I didn't mean any of it. I was just hurt that she'd let my mom come waltzing back into town and take me away from her."

"I'm sure she understood," Macy said.

Cam dug her fingernails into the wall. "Was there a funeral?"

"Sharon said maybe we'd have a memorial service when she gets back. Something small."

"She hasn't been buried someplace already?"

"She was cremated."

Cam shuddered.

"Does that surprise you?"

"No, not really. It's just not something I've ever imagined." She sighed, fought back tears. "I feel like such a dork. After I found out she had cancer, I walked that last little bit to her house and had the goofiest fantasy."

When Cam looked at her, Macy didn't say anything. She wasn't sure she wanted to hear the rest.

Cam went on. "I imagined her sitting on the sofa, with her legs crossed under her. I'd tell her she looked beautiful,

78

and I'd mean it. She'd shyly rub the stubble on her head, and I'd offer to shave my own, you know, as a symbol of solidarity." She heaved a loud sigh. "So much for that, huh?"

Macy paused for a few moments before speaking. She hoped the kid wouldn't get her crying, too. "Look, Cam, I hope you aren't beating yourself up over not getting here in time to see Jess. She wouldn't want that."

"I just feel so lost. I always imagined having all the time in the world to show her she'd done a good job with me. Now she'll never know."

"You don't really believe that, do you?"

Cam didn't answer right away, just stared out across the brown water. "If she's watching right now, what would you guess she's thinking?"

"That you're a fine young woman, and that she can't wait to see what you'll make of yourself."

"That I still need quite a bit of work."

"Don't we all, though," Macy said.

"Not you. You're pretty and smart and a great mother to Jeremiah. And a good girlfriend for Michael."

Macy felt uncomfortable. Not only did she not feel like she was those things, she didn't want anyone else to feel them about her.

"You think you and Michael will get married one day?"

She started to say no, thought of J-man, and said, "Maybe."

"What about kids?"

Macy had enjoyed being pregnant but didn't know if she'd ever *choose* to be pregnant. With J-man, she just was.

"I'm getting too personal. Sorry."

Macy waved off the apology. "You have other family, right?"

"My mom's in Maryland. She's kind of in and out of my life. Pretty much always has been."

"So, it's just you two?"

"Yeah. Now." Cam shoved her hands into her jeans pockets. "What's Sharon like?"

"Super nice. She and Jess were great together." Macy sighed. "You know, Sharon's not sure when she's coming back."

"She knows I'm here, right?"

Macy nodded. That morning Michael had told her that Sharon wasn't interested in coming back to Augusta yet, especially not to see a snotty-nosed niece who'd hurt Jess the way Cam had. Sharon was taking time for herself in the mountains, where she and Jess had loved to vacation, and would come back in a week or two, as planned. The bottom line: Cam was not her responsibility.

"What did Sharon say about me being here?"

Macy shrugged.

"Really, I want to know."

"She's got a lot to deal with now, so don't take it personally. She's just not interested in connecting with you."

"She's hoping I'll be gone by the time she gets back."

"I don't know." Macy wiped at the sweat collecting at her hairline. "Do you know what you'll do now?"

"You think I could find a job around here? I don't really want to go back to Maryland right now. I have nowhere I need to be. Pretty pathetic, huh?"

"I imagine there's something you could do here." Macy studied Cam's lanky frame and watched the young woman push at a twig with her shoe. If Macy's life often felt like a Tilt-A-Whirl, she imagined that Cam felt like she was stranded on a stalled Ferris wheel.

Chapter Nine

Whirligigs

Kenny was the first one at the shop. He piddled around a bit, rinsing the coffee mugs everyone always left in the break room. If Dori had gotten anything through his thick head, it was to not leave coffee mugs sitting around getting stained. He ran water into the mug and knew it was too late—the coffee goo at the bottom wasn't coming out. While he watched the water and the stain melt into the color of a puddle, he thought that he could be one of those metaphor things. *My life's a puddle.*

He stepped away from the sink and the coffee mugs when he heard someone fiddling with the shop door. He knew it wasn't Tank, because he'd gone fishing in Florida for a week. It sure wasn't Gary. He never came in that early. And since their sometime receptionist, Miss Anna, wasn't scheduled for that day, Kenny figured it had to be his new trainee. Macy had talked to her neighbor Alan, who knew Kenny's boss, Martin, and Kenny got stuck training this new kid, Cam. What girl wanted to work in a cabinet shop, for Christ's sake?

To make matters worse, the chick hadn't done any more work than sacking groceries or hostessing a restaurant, but here was Kenny, having to teach her stuff. At least it was

Macy or her boyfriend stuck driving the girl to the shop mornings, and not one of the other workers.

Hell, the kid couldn't even get in the door. Kenny went over to give her a hand and realized he must have locked the door behind him.

The girl wore baggy jeans and a light blue T-shirt. Hell, she looked like a dude.

When Kenny started showing her around, Cam had her hands shoved down in her pockets. Kenny wanted to tell her cabinets wouldn't get made like that, but he didn't. He figured she didn't know any better, yet.

He kicked a two-inch scrap of oak out of his way. "Safety comes first—blah, blah, blah. When working the machines, no long sleeves and no rings or watches or anything. Obvious stuff."

He showed Cam the goggles, the first-aid kit, the eyewash station. He led her to a small closet. "And here's where the broom's kept. It ain't real technical, but somebody's got to sweep. Every couple of hours, you need to straighten up." He smiled. "And it'll be your job to gather the coffee mugs at the end of the day and make sure they at least get a rinsing." He looked around. "You get on the broom, while I check some wood that's just come in."

The shop used mostly poplar and maple, some alder, and oak on the pricier jobs. They didn't use so much pine anymore. Cherry wasn't bad, but maple was Kenny's favorite. Maple always looked good, and damn it did smell nice.

Cam was about done sweeping in the shop area when Kenny asked her if she had a boyfriend back in Maryland.

"No," she said.

"Do you even like boys?" Kenny asked.

"What?"

Kenny was fixing to ask Cam if she was gay, like her aunt, but figured maybe he shouldn't bring her up. Kenny hadn't ever lost any family, but Dorianne had lost plenty, and he knew how hard that had been for her.

"Miss Anna's our receptionist. She comes in two or three days a week to do the books. She's older than God now, so she ain't expected to vacuum and clean up in the front office anymore." Kenny pointed back at the closet. "The vacuum and cleaning stuff's in there, too. Just do enough to make it look good if customers come in. All us employees come in and out the back door mostly, so keeping the front office looking okay ain't so hard."

Kenny kept thinking that, at any second, Cam would say she wasn't a maid at the Holiday Inn, but she didn't. He was beginning to think training was pretty cool, seeing how much he hated cleaning.

"Should I vacuum now?" Cam asked.

"Yeah, why not."

When Kenny looked over a few minutes later to see how Cam was doing, he saw that the girl flitted around like a bird, especially the way she fiddled with the cord and pushed the vacuum around in jerky movements.

Kenny drove home for lunch. He'd been doing his own driving. When they found out Dorianne needed surgery, he went and got his driver's license. Even though he could have gotten it back awhile ago, he hadn't bothered because Dori driving him around had gotten to be their normal way. And since neither of them minded, they figured if it ain't broke, don't fix it.

But then it broke.

Dorianne had been home from the hospital for a while, but she still wasn't supposed to do a lot. Kenny put her under orders not to do anything until he got home for lunch, because he knew that girl would overdo it and end up hurting herself.

Kenny got home and could tell she'd been crying. She went back and forth between sad and mad, before he finally got that it was about the laundry. He'd done some washing the day before, trying to help, and he guessed those clothes got all shrunk up.

She'd sure been moody. He didn't know if it was the surgery, a hormone thing, or the fact that she hadn't had a cigarette since her hysterectomy. Probably all of the above. At least she wasn't still mad at him for not realizing on his own that she'd quit smoking.

Kenny slapped some ham and cheese between slices of white bread for himself. Dorianne wanted a Slim-Fast, so he shook one real good, the way she liked it, and poured it in a glass. She had this thing where she wouldn't drink it right out of the can. He bitched a little that she needed to eat something more than that, but as usual, she didn't listen.

Dorianne sipped her lunch. "Have you talked to your Aunt Eileen lately?"

"Yeah, yesterday."

"How's my puppy doing?" she asked.

Aunt Eileen and Uncle Russ had agreed to look after the new pup when Dori had the surgery. They still had her, since Dori wasn't up to par yet.

"The puppy's fine," Kenny said. "Jeremiah's been staying with Aunt Eileen afternoons while his mama's at work." Kenny was careful not to say Macy's name. He fidgeted with the crust of his sandwich. "Is it okay that Jeremiah named the puppy?"

Dorianne looked up from her glass. "What's he calling her?"

"Bella."

"What kind of name is that? They want to keep her, don't they?"

He'd been wondering how to bring that up. "Yeah. They really like her, and she's used to being over there now. And Jeremiah sure is attached to her."

What Kenny didn't tell Dorianne was that Uncle Russ informed him, in his law-like way, that Bella would be staying there. Russ said Kenny and Dori could see the dog anytime they wanted, but that she needed to just stay put with them.

"Okay, tell them they can keep her. At least I know they'll take good care of her."

Smiling, Kenny gave Dorianne's hand a little squeeze.

"You know, it would make sense to have a blood relative carry our child," Dori said.

Kenny almost choked on his sandwich. When he'd brought up the surrogate thing, Dori had said she didn't want to hear it. And that was without her knowing he'd gotten the idea from Macy.

"We should ask Grace to be our surrogate," Dorianne said.

Kenny stared at her. "Dori, stop. Please."

"What? She's my half-sister. Why wouldn't I think of her?"

He hated to do it, but he had no choice. "Because she don't consider you kin."

"I found the truth online, Kenny. You saw it." She pushed the half-finished Slim-Fast away from her.

"I know."

"And soon I'll be able to show her in writing."

Kenny walked over to stand behind her and kissed the top of her reddish head. Then he spoke into her darker roots, letting his words soften through her hair, "Baby, you can't make people act like family."

When Kenny got back to work, he was more tired than he was before his break, but he wasn't too tired to tease Cam while he showed her about putting up some tools.

"People ever think you're a dude?"

Cam just stared at him.

"Seriously, I'm curious. With your hair and the way you dress, I bet some people get mixed up. Does that bother you?"

"Not really."

"Do people think you're gay?"

Cam looked away.

"Are you? Gay, I mean?" Kenny noticed how red Cam was turning. "I mean, I don't care if you are."

"Yes, I'm gay. Now can we just get back to work?"

"No, not yet." Kenny laughed. "Now you can teach me some things. You know, like how do you—"

"Oh, hell no! We aren't going there."

Kenny laughed harder. "What? I was just gonna ask you how you know if other chicks are like you."

Cam rolled her eyes.

"Hell, you probably get more action than most of the guys you know."

Cam turned a darker shade of red.

"That's what I figured. Okay, back to training, stud." Kenny realized then that before long, he'd probably just think of Cam as one of the guys. "Commercial shops like ours use pneumatic tools. They'll outlast the electric ones as long as the oilers are full and the condensation's drained."

Cam cocked her head to the side, and Kenny could tell she wasn't getting any of it.

Next Kenny showed her the table saw. Cam looked at it a bit nervous-like, but she'd get over that. She'd have to, because, hell, if she couldn't get on the saw, then she couldn't do anything.

Kenny wouldn't have her working on the saw for a couple of days, but it was time to get her down to business. He showed her how to true-up material with the planer and noted Cam did okay with it, for a beginner and a girl.

As Cam clumsily put the wood cup-side down on the planer, she reminded Kenny of a band geek in the pre-game show at a football game—the one dressed up in a big hat and blue polyester uniform, looking like a giant blue jay with a drum.

Kenny went to the finishing room where he matched up some wood, making sure the grains came together just right. He was wanting to put the hardware on that job.

Gary came in, took one look at the tool room where Cam had straightened up, and started cussing. "Now I won't be able to find a goddamned thing. Do you even know what tools you stuck where? Hell, do you have any idea what any tool is?" His voice grew louder with each complaint.

Kenny sighed. It was no secret Gary didn't like change, unless the idea for it was his. Maybe Kenny shouldn't have asked Cam to clean up in there.

Gary was an installer and mostly worked on the road. In order to do that, he had to be able to do practically anything from scratch, which Gary pretty much could. He wasn't as good as Kenny, but without a driver's license all those years, working the road wasn't an option for Kenny. But that was okay, too. Kenny was much more of a shop kind of guy anyway.

Since Kenny had gotten his license, Martin had him doing deliveries and stuff when things got behind. In return, Martin let Kenny take a company truck home most nights. That was pretty cool.

Gary marched up to Cam, a hammer in each hand. He held up one. "This is a claw hammer." He held up the other.

"And this is a straight claw hammer. They each have their right place. Got it?"

The little hairs on Kenny's neck got prickly, back where Dorianne tickled him with the clippers when she trimmed his hair. Cam didn't remind him of a blue jay after all. No, the kid reminded him of a dove he'd seen once. Kenny had been cutting grass at the Johnson's and scared three doves up onto the roof of the house next door. The whole way up, they made that whistling-whimper noise. They were just hanging out up there when—BOOM—a falcon swooped down and grabbed one in an explosion of feathers and perched right there on the roof and ate it. Cam reminded Kenny of a dove that didn't know any better than to hang out on a roof.

Gary had always been downright goofy, but Kenny didn't remember him being such a prick. Not until after Kenny and Jack quit going fishing with him out near the clay mines when they were kids. Kenny couldn't say exactly when Gary had changed, but it was sometime after that.

Finally Grumpy Gary left for the day. Kenny could tell Cam relaxed once he'd gone. At least Gary was the only jerk working there. Tank, Eddie, and even Martin, were all decent.

Putting away his tools, Kenny asked Cam, "So, how's it going, staying with the doc?"

"He's pretty cool. He said I can stay with him as long as I need to. I'm gonna pay him some rent and save up for a car. I might even go to college. Eventually."

"That's cool, if you're into that."

"Macy took me out to the campus at Augusta State. She's been showing me around town."

"Sounds cozy," Kenny said, teasing.

Cam blushed. "She's got the prettiest eyes," she muttered. "The darkest, most intense eyes I've ever seen."

As Kenny was fixing to lock down the electrical panels so they could call it a day, he saw Cam grab coffee mugs from the counter in the break room. He was impressed that the kid remembered to do that. She even washed them up with soap.

Kenny had to admit Cam had done well. First, she caught on right away to the planer. Second, she made it until almost quitting time before bringing up how pretty Macy's eyes were.

†

Macy hadn't planned on going out, it just happened. J-man wanted to spend the night with his grandparents. Macy knew he liked staying over there, especially since Eileen started letting *his* dog, Bella, sleep in bed with him. She forced the thought of germs out of her head and let the boy be a boy.

Next thing Macy knew, she found herself downtown at Whirligig's. It was a new club, and she'd heard on the radio that they played good music. She leaned against the slick, wood bar with her beer and started contemplating possible adventures.

Several young guys in Army fatigues stood by the door. They usually traveled in groups, but it was easy enough to cut one from the herd.

Closest to the stage were two couples. Nothing there. To their left was someone more Macy's type. His dark, rebellious hair reminded her of a South American soccer player, or Cat Stevens before his Muhammad days. She'd definitely keep that guy in mind.

Macy's scanning brought her gaze to the opposite end of the bar. She wasn't going to allow herself to check out the trio of women, but before she could pan past them, Macy saw her: the short, light bob pushed behind her ears; the fine features; one very responsive eyebrow that seemed to rise up to ask questions on its own. It was Sharon, sitting at the bar with two women. Sharon saw her about the same time the soccer-playing Cat Stevens started walking her way.

Macy glanced again at the man and knew that was not what she wanted. She almost tripped over her barstool hustling over to Sharon and her friends.

Macy took a deep breath and smiled. "Hey, stranger, when did you get back?"

Sharon looked at her watch. "About two hours ago." She glanced over Macy's shoulder. "Where's Michael?"

Heat rose on Macy's cheeks. "He has an early appointment tomorrow, so he wanted to stay in tonight." She punctuated the statement with a shrug. Macy had wanted—no, needed—to go out, so she told Michael she was going out with some girlfriends. He hadn't noticed that she didn't really have any.

Sharon introduced Macy to her friends. Allie and Pat said hello and made the usual pleasantries. Pat mumbled something about kidnapping Sharon for the evening.

When Pat and Allie excused themselves to go to the ladies' room, Macy swiveled her barstool around to face Sharon. "You look good," she said.

"Liar. I look like hell."

Macy nodded and gave a little smile. "You're allowed."

Sharon shrugged. "I shouldn't be here. I don't want to be here, but I don't want to be at home, either."

Macy couldn't imagine how hard it would be to go home and be that alone. It would be unbearable to lose the most important person in her life. The thought threatened to send Macy into a panic. She knew she'd never survive losing J-man. Wanting to wash away the very idea of it, she quaffed her beer.

"Planning to get drunk tonight?"

Macy looked at Sharon from behind her beer glass. She hadn't realized she'd gulped so much. "No, I'm driving."

"Just remember, I don't represent DUIs."

She tried to picture Sharon in the courtroom. It dawned on her that she didn't know what kind of lawyer Sharon was. She was about to ask, when a familiar-looking man approached from the back of the room. He paused, almost like he was going to ask the time, but instead he lifted Macys hand, kissed the back of it, and walked away.

"A friend of yours?" Sharon asked.

Macy pretended to look over at him. "No, I don't believe I've ever seen him before." She didn't look at Sharon as she lied.

She thought about past decisions, about choosing adventures over friendship. It felt strange, looking back, that she was so afraid of the consequences of kissing one woman yet barely thought twice about doing a lot more with any man.

Allie and Pat rejoined them. Macy placed her beer on a coaster and studied the neon orange lettering. Whirligig's. She caught Sharon watching her, so she asked, "What is a whirligig anyway?"

"Beats me," Sharon answered.

Pat picked up another coaster and looked at it. "Is a whirligig a something, or is it something you do?"

"It's possessive, a noun, so it's a something," Allie said.

Pat laughed. "I think it's a sexual position."

"Don't go there," Allie teased.

"It can be a noun or a verb." Sharon traced her finger over the letters.

"A very active verb," Allie said.

Sharon smiled at Macy and nodded toward her friend. "Allie's an English teacher. Can you tell?"

The bartender brought Macy another beer, telling her it was from the gentleman at the end of the bar. Macy's past adventure, the hand kisser, winked at her when she looked over at him.

"I can't accept this," Macy said.

"Yes, you can," Allie said. "If you don't drink it, Pat will."

Macy looked at Sharon. Sharon raised her glass and mouthed, "Cheers."

She prayed the guy wouldn't expect conversation in return.

"So," Pat asked Sharon, "how do you two know each other?"

"Macy dates my neighbor, Michael."

"The doctor?"

Macy nodded. But she didn't want to talk about Michael. Contemplating whirligigs and active verbs was more in line with her mood. That, and she wanted to know if Pat and Allie were lesbians, and if they could tell she had her own thoughts about women.

Halfway through her beer, the idea of a past adventure clashing with the pleasure of spending time with these women became unacceptable to Macy. When the guy who'd bought her the beer left the end of the bar, she decided to make her getaway, preferring to leave rather than have him come back and maybe embarrass her in front of Sharon. She told Sharon and the others she was leaving.

"Let one of us walk you out," Sharon said.

Macy shook her head. "That's not necessary," she said when Pat started to stand. "I'm parked right outside. I can manage on my own. Macy glanced one last time at the whirligig coaster, then squeezed Sharon's hand. "It was good seeing you."

As she left, the door barely thumped shut, and something about the muffle of it told Macy to look behind her. The same discomfort kept her from turning around. She stared straight ahead, counting her steps. That made her think about Emma, and she wished she would find a sprig of cilantro on her windshield. Macy was almost to her car when her past adventure caught up to her.

"Hey, gorgeous, where you headed?" When Macy didn't answer, he said, "I know you remember me. And I couldn't forget you if I tried."

"I have to go." She tried to get around him, but he stepped between her and her car.

"Not so fast. How about we hook up again? I'll bet an encore is just what you need." He moved closer.

"Really, I have to go." Macy looked behind her, toward the door to Whirligig's. She took a step back and considered bolting to the bar.

He grabbed her arm. "Darling, why so cold? That's not how I remember you." He tightened his grip.

Macy tried to pull free. He maneuvered her around and pushed her against her car door. He smelled good—a hint of beer mingling with strong soap. She grew angry with herself for noticing.

He pressed his body into her, and she could feel his hardness against her stomach. It flashed through her mind that Sharon might see, might think she'd asked for it, or wanted it. *No,* she told herself, *Sharon's not like that.* Besides, she wouldn't see anything, because there wouldn't be anything to see.

"Get off me." Macy pushed him.

"I don't remember you liking it rough, but I can get into that." He shoved her hard against the car. His mouth found her neck, and his hand moved between her legs.

Fear and anger amalgamated into a rock that settled into Macy's throat and threatened to suffocate her if this man didn't kill her first. No, he would not. He would not kill her, or hurt her, or have her.

Rage rose from somewhere deep inside. It freed her voice and allowed her to roar her dissent. "No!" She pushed him away, and her fingernails grazed his face.

"Bitch."

When he reached up to feel his cheek, Macy shoved her key into the car door. She managed to get inside and lock the door behind her.

Her hands shook so hard, she could barely pull the seatbelt across her. As she pulled out of her space, she saw him crossing the street. Gripping the steering wheel, she stomped on the accelerator. He sprinted to get out of her way. She tried not to think about the possibility that she might not have swerved to miss him.

She glanced into the rearview mirror. She sped, and her hands shook even harder. Sharon wouldn't represent her for DUI but how about for vehicular homicide?

Macy looked again in the rearview mirror, worried about being followed. Maybe he wouldn't try anything that night, but what about later, sometime when J-man was home? There was no way she'd risk that. She headed to Washington Road, toward the other side of town.

Sharon's Miata was in her driveway, probably where she'd left it when Allie and Pat had kidnapped her. Michael's car, of course, was in his driveway. Macy was mad at herself for running to Michael. How could she be independent if she was afraid to go home alone? And what kind of aura did she have that a man thought he could approach her in that way?

She used the key Michael had given her weeks earlier, the key she hadn't yet initiated.

Cam was stretched out on the sofa, watching the Comedy Channel. She lowered the volume when Macy walked into the living room. "You okay?" She jumped up and moved toward Macy.

"Yeah, I'm fine." Macy stopped short, realizing Cam had caught her crying. She hated that her frustration often brought tears with it. "I'm fine," she repeated.

"Did something happen? Did someone—"

"I'm fine." Macy was a little overwhelmed by Cam's concern. "It's nothing, really." She walked around the sofa, thinking, *Great, now my aura says, 'Comfort me.'* "I'm gonna jump in the shower."

Macy scrubbed until her skin screamed for her to stop, then she stood under the hot water until it began to cool. She didn't bother blow-drying her hair. She found a pair of Michael's pajamas at the bottom of the linen closet and slipped into them.

Cam was watching Macy closely when she came out of the bathroom, the area between her eyebrows squinched up. Macy glanced at the coffee table. Just as she focused on a bowl coated in remnants of fudge swirl ice cream, Cam grabbed the dirty dish and took it into the kitchen.

When she came back in, Macy asked, "What's on?"

Cam snatched up the remote and handed it to her. "Put on whatever you'd like. I wasn't really watching."

Cam was a sweet girl, but her age was reflected in her choice of humor. Apparently, bodily function jokes still made her laugh. Macy chuckled. "This is fine." She took a seat on the far end of the sofa to see if she could find something funny in toilet humor.

During the next commercial, Macy caught Cam staring at her. She slipped in a little reminder of Cam's living arrangements. "When did Michael go to bed?"

"About an hour ago." Cam shifted around to face Macy and hit the mute button. "Is that Sharon's car next door?"

"Yeah, she's back."

"When do you think you'll talk to her? Do you think she'll be over to see you and Michael tomorrow?"

"Relax, Cam."

"Sorry. I'm just anxious to meet her."

"You'll meet her soon enough." Macy smiled at Cam, hoping her words hadn't sounded too harsh.

Macy moved over to the loveseat and snuggled into its arm. She didn't want to go to Michael's bed, but she didn't want to talk either. She shut her eyes and could hear Cam settling on the sofa. The scent of herbal shampoo lingered in her wet hair. The light of the muted TV played against the inside of her eyelids in a swirl of images from her evening out. *What was I thinking?*

Part Three

Molting

Chapter Ten

Dreams and Games

Dream currents wrap around her, holding, warming from the inside out. A light fog tickles the drowsy Savannah River and traps heat beneath its surface. She and Emma lie on the grassy knoll, on their sides, facing one another. When Emma opens her mouth to speak, Macy steals her words and her breath and holds them hostage, clearing the way for their mouths. Emma's cilantro scent binds them and transforms Macy. She is supple, hungry, on fire.

But it was Michael who was waking Macy with his shower dampness, his deep, male voice. If he had just kept quiet, she could have moved with him; she could have been making love to Emma. But his voice wasn't Emma's voice, and Macy couldn't make it be, and it became impossible to finish the make believe.

Macy rolled away from him and faced his beige bedroom wall.

"Come on, honey," he said.

"Shhh." She desperately wanted to go back to sleep, back to the grassy knoll.

"Jeremiah's two rooms away and out like a light." Michael nuzzled her neck.

"Yeah, but Cam's still up," she mumbled. "She might hear."

Michael pulled away. "Oh, for God's sake."

"What?" She didn't really want an answer.

"Why are you so worried about your precious little baby dyke hearing, huh? Afraid it'll assault her sensitivities to find out straight people actually fuck, too?"

"What?" Now she did want an answer. Now she was wide awake and angry about more than being robbed of her dream. "Where in the hell did that come from? And don't think I haven't noticed the way you treat her has changed."

"You think I don't see how she looks at you? I'm letting her stay with me. What the hell else do you want from me?" Michael leaned back against his pillow.

"Does this have anything to do with Sharon?" Macy asked. "I heard what she said about letting Cam stay with you."

"No. Sharon will be fine." He rested a hand over his eyes, as if shielding them, even though there was only the faintest light sneaking in through the blinds.

When Sharon had come back and found Cam living with Michael, she was unhappy with him. She apparently felt betrayed, like he had sided with Cam. Macy hadn't ever mentioned overhearing Michael's response—that he had only asked Cam to stay with him because he feared if he didn't, Macy would invite her to stay with her. She wondered if doing something nice still counted if your motivation was whacked.

Michael gave the sheets a playful tug. "I'm sorry."

"Me, too."

He lowered the sheet and exposed her breasts. When he moved in to kiss her neck, she held him off with both arms.

"What now?" he asked.

She was exasperated and feeling a little hurtful. "What do you mean, what now? I don't want that any more now than I did five minutes ago. What do you imagine has changed?"

"Jesus Christ."

Macy whipped off the sheet and flung open her arms in a crucifixion position. "Okay, okay, whatever you want." She didn't try to hide the sarcasm.

Michael sprang from the bed. "This is not right."

As he yanked on his pants, Macy pulled the sheet back over herself. She rolled to face the wall and heard his keys jangling when he left the room.

She heard no response from him as Cam muttered, "Hey, what's up?" Michael was polite enough not to slam the front door on his way out.

Cam. Macy knew Cam had a bit of a crush on her, but it was harmless. She was a sweet kid who would soon meet a girl her own age, and then she'd forget all about whatever feelings she imagined she had for Macy.

Macy knew the routine with young men and women. She'd seen it before.

Macy had to ask herself, was she living *her* same old routine? Was she, on some level, repeating her past of game playing, maybe even provoking Michael's jealousy over Cam?

She thought about Emma's note and asked herself, *Have I found mine?* Or was being with Michael just one more game in a long line of games? Maybe she *was* just playing house with him. That could explain her lack of desire to go to the next level. He'd asked her to move in with him several times, and she always answered that it was too soon.

Then there was the intimacy issue. Macy's desire for Michael was sporadic, at best. She knew on one level that this was directly related to her attraction to Emma. Another game, for sure—cat and mouse. Macy had been well aware of Emma's feelings for her but crossed the line anyway. She'd led Emma on at every opportunity.

Even though Macy had physically backed away from her desire for Emma, in truth, it had taken root and refused to let go.

Lying on Michael's too-firm mattress, under his plain beige sheets in his plain beige bedroom, Macy didn't regret being with him, she just had major reservations about its rightness. As much as he sometimes angered her with his persistence, she couldn't blame him for wanting more physical attention than she was giving. But she couldn't help thinking about Emma. And she didn't know whether it was worse for her to fake it with Michael or to turn away from him.

Macy didn't want to think about her decisions, or Michael's frustration. She took several deep breaths, banished the negative energy, and tried to relax. Her gaze was caught by the corner of the dictionary, behind the table lamp where she'd left it after she looked up the word *whirligig*. A spinning toy. She focused on the third definition, though—something constantly changing.

Macy rolled onto her back. Staring at the ceiling fan, she focused on the tickle of the breeze. She slid the sheet off slowly and let the air tingle a path down her body. She knew the next day would bring more dreams and more games, and she didn't know how long that would be enough. But for the moment, she only cared about the touch of that breeze. Her hand followed the current down her belly, to the place at the river where whirligigs were action verbs and her dreams waited.

Chapter Eleven

Smashed and Swoled

"If you loved me you'd—"

Dorianne's words sent Kenny's head reeling. He hated it when people said that. His first memory of those words was when he was eight. His mama had an allergic reaction to some poison oak, and her face got all swelled up. It was hideous. She swelled so bad, it made her long hair look shrunk up to her chin.

Kenny could remember sitting at the kitchen table, eating ribs and not being able to look at his mother. Her face seriously scared him.

His mama had asked him to pass the peas, and he tried to do it without looking up. He spilled those peas all over the place. She yelled at him, but he just kept staring down at his plate. That was when she'd said it: "If you loved me, you'd look at me." Kenny behaved himself and didn't tell her that he didn't love anybody *that* much.

His dad had laughed and said, "If you loved *us*, you'd put a bag over your head." Things got real quiet.

Maybe Kenny didn't like his dad saying mean stuff to his mama, or maybe Kenny just wanted to make some points, but he decided to do the right thing. He looked up and was gonna say, "Sorry, Mama." But when Kenny saw her swelled up face, his words slipped out as, "Sorry, Monsta."

His dad laughed real loud, his mama threw what was left of the mashed potatoes at her husband, and Kenny ran to hide in his bedroom.

"Kenny."

He looked up. It wasn't his mama all swelled into a monster; it was Dorianne. Pretty, sweet, Dorianne, who looked like she was about to throw what was left of their mashed potatoes at him.

"I do love you, baby, but I don't want to go see Grace."

"Just show her the proof."

"You already mailed it to her." He stared into his baked chicken and studied the smooth white of the meat. He hoped if he didn't look up, the talking would go away.

"She might not have gotten it."

"She got it." Kenny looked up.

"That's still not the same as face-to-face."

"Then you go see her." As soon as the words were out, Kenny knew it was a mistake. His mind raced back to the scene at the Barnes and Noble, when he'd first laid eyes on Grace. "On second thought, you shouldn't be going anywhere near her."

Dorianne waved the papers from Family Finders. "She's my half-sister, and she can't deny it any longer."

"Okay, say she don't deny it no more. That still don't mean she'll want a damned thing to do with you. It especially don't mean she'll want to carry a baby for us."

"A family member is a logical first choice."

"There ain't nothing logical about anything here, baby."

She took a big breath. "Kenny, if you loved me, you'd take this stuff to Grace for me."

He hurled the plate of baked chicken across the room. It was just like in a cartoon, but instead of Wile E. Coyote sliding down the kitchen wall in slow motion, it was Kenny's dinner. There was half a chicken, leaving behind a long, greasy slug-trail.

As he watched its descent, all he could think was, *Shit, now I got to paint them walls.* He'd told Dori they didn't need any new paint, but now they did and it was all his fault. He deserved getting stuck with Toasted Sunflower or Warm Caramel walls.

"If you wanted your chicken fried, all you had to do was ask," Dori said before catapulting a spoonful of potatoes across the table at Kenny.

He wasn't stupid. He heard the pain behind the joke. He didn't know what else to do, so after he wiped off his arm, he flicked his own spoonful of potatoes across the table. His aim was better—got her right in the cleavage, but he didn't gloat any.

"Okay," he said. "I'll bring the papers to Grace. On one condition."

"What?"

"You'll never use the words 'if you loved me' again."

✝

Kenny pulled up to the vinyl-sided house and wished he could just forget all about his promise to Dorianne. But he knew better. He rang the bell and looked around at the clutter on Grace's porch—little girl skates, a bicycle, a three-legged table wobbling under the weight of a pile of newspapers.

His plan was to only do what he had to, nothing more. He knew if he just put the copies of what Dori had dug up into Grace's hand, he could go back to Dori and say he'd done his part.

Grace answered the door, stepped out, and pulled the door shut behind her, like she was afraid Kenny would try to peek inside. She stood there all but challenging him. For some reason, she reminded him of Jack.

He could hear Jack plain as day.

"You're afraid to go."

"Am not," Kenny said.

"I knew you couldn't be as brave as me," Jack taunted.

"Can, too."

So Kenny went fishing with Jack and Gary, even though Jack was mean, Gary was creepy, and Kenny wasn't allowed near the lake at the chalk mine, no matter how good the fishing was.

Kenny held the papers out to Grace.

"I got enough crap in the mail from you already. You people need to leave me alone."

He waggled the papers, impatient for her to take them so he could get on home. "Dorianne asked me to drop these by."

She didn't take them. She stared at him with eyes lined with the same long lashes as Dori's, but there wasn't anything flirty about Grace's eyes.

Kenny was glad Dori had Macy around to be nice to her when they were growing up, instead of Grace. He had no doubt Grace would have been as big a jerk as Jack, who'd bullied Kenny no end.

Kenny felt the heat of his anger creep up his neck to his face. He got mad at Grace for every time Jack'd had to one-up him when they were kids. He got mad at her for every time he'd felt like other people were telling him in their own way that Jack was better than him. Then he got mad at himself because eventually he'd started believing it.

Once, in high school, Kenny had overheard Lisa Reynolds and Marie Tucker talking about a party Marie was having. Lisa told her to invite Kenny so he'd invite Jack along. Kenny guessed Jack was too far out of their league, and they didn't want to ask him direct. Kenny didn't want to go but went anyway. By the end of the night, Jack and Lisa were making out and Kenny was finishing off the keg.

The next time Kenny went to a party, Jack didn't go, so Kenny got the girl. And except for his one mistake their senior year, he'd been hanging on tight to that girl ever since.

Kenny waggled the papers one last time. Grace didn't reach for them. If she had been Dori's half-brother, he would have punched him. But she wasn't, so he tossed the papers into the air and they floated to the ground. Then he walked down her driveway, watching her out of the corner of his eye as she hustled around grabbing up the papers. He figured she must not have wanted her neighbors to read how she wasn't any better than the rest of them after all.

He felt sick as he pulled away from the curb. There was a nagging going on inside his gut. He thought about high school, and how Jack and Macy were the perfect couple. They were smart, good-looking, and popular. If him and Dori were a perfect match, and he thought Jack was better than him, did that mean he thought Macy was better than Dori?

Kenny shook his head. Nobody—not Grace, Macy, or anyone else—was better than Dorianne.

All he wanted was to get home. And he wasn't gonna think any more, for as long as he could get away without thinking. Instead, he'd paint the kitchen walls Toasted Sunflower. Or was it Sesame?

Chapter Twelve

Even Steven

A bike path snaked along the perfectly manicured shoulder of the road. A stretch of full and lush Bradford pears lined the opposite side. Every time Macy drove through Columbia County, she wondered where the owners of all the big houses worked.

"Thanks again for coming to get me," Cam said.

Macy glanced over at her. "Does it hurt?" She expected Cam to try to impress her by saying no, but she didn't.

"Yeah." Cam sat up straighter, as if that would help her suck it up.

Macy pulled her car to the four-way stop, waited her turn, and went right. "Tell me again what happened." Cam was so busy watching Macy's hands on the steering wheel, for a moment Macy thought she might forget to answer.

"I clamped the press down on my thumb."

"Were you playing around, you know, like y'all play baseball when it gets slow?"

"No, I wasn't playing. I was working."

Cam's words came out so whiny that Macy couldn't resist giving her a look similar to one she often gave Jeremiah when he complained about having to go to bed or finish his dinner.

When Cam blushed, Macy felt bad for the look.

"Things okay with you and Michael now?" Cam asked.

She was caught by surprise. "What's that?"

"You know, when he left in a huff the other night—did you two work it out okay?"

"Oh, that was nothing." Macy gave her a dismissive flick of her hand and rolled her eyes. It was disconcerting for her to know Cam was privy to moments like that, even if she didn't know the full import of them. She changed the subject. "What did Kenny say about your thumb?"

Cam shrugged. "Not much. Not as much as Gary anyway. Gary went on and on about it. Stuff about 'that's why girls shouldn't be in the shop to begin with.'" Cam plucked at a speck of sawdust and faced Macy. "Can I ask you something, just between us?"

"Of course."

"Is Gary kind of—well—slow or something?"

Macy thought about that, about growing up in the neighborhood not far from where Gary sometimes hung out with Russ, but more often where he just seemed to hang out, period. While she was trying to choose her words, Macy's attention spun to the pavement ahead. She jerked her Saturn half off the road, stopped, and put on her flashers.

"Cam, the turtle."

"What?"

"The turtle. Please get the turtle before it gets hit."

Cam looked down at the bulky bandage on her left thumb.

"You can use your good hand. I should stay in the car in case we need a fast exit." She glanced into the rearview mirror. "Please, Cam."

Cam hopped out of the car and trotted over to the turtle. She loitered, contemplating it. When a silver pickup truck pulled up behind Macy, Cam quit dawdling. She snatched up the turtle, apparently surprised by the heft of it. She stretched her hand over the dome-shaped shell, her grip awkward. The turtle wobbled as its clawed feet sliced at the air. She held it away from her body.

Three steps into Cam's excursion, Macy tapped the horn. Cam jumped and fumbled with the now snugly closed turtle before regaining possession with both hands. She winced and looked at Macy. Macy pointed to the other side of the road, and Cam turned around and carried it across both lanes.

She set the turtle down about three feet off the road and jogged past the two lanes of stopped traffic to get back into the car.

"Good recovery," Macy teased as she pulled back onto the road.

"What was with the horn?"

Irritation tinged the words, the first time Macy had ever heard that from Cam. It made Macy curious. She plucked a Wet-Wipe from a dispenser wedged between the seats. She gave it a little flick in Cam's direction—a white flag, even though *she* wasn't surrendering anything to anyone.

Cam wiped off her hands, staying away from her wrapped thumb.

"I tried calling to you, but you didn't hear me." Macy looked quickly at Cam and back to the road. "Always take them in the direction they're going, otherwise they just start right back across."

"You do this often?" Cam asked.

"I don't drive around *actively* seeking turtles to rescue. But if I see one and can get it without killing anyone, I will."

Macy thought about her efforts to teach J-man compassion. The best lessons were learned by example, of course. She hoped she'd struck a balance between being kind and staying safe. It was a struggle.

Cam smiled. "So, do you only do turtles?"

"The squirrels are just too damned fast for me."

Cam smiled again.

They came up to an intersection at River Watch Parkway. Macy turned right and repeated Cam's earlier question. "So, is Gary slow or something?"

"Yeah, is he?"

"Or something." Macy shrugged. "It's always been a sort of don't-ask-don't-tell thing with him. Gary's just Gary, and that's always been pretty much understood."

"Are he and Kenny's Uncle Russ good friends?"

The two were such opposites, it never did fit that they'd be friends, despite being close in age. Russ was so easygoing and quick to smile, whereas Gary wore a perpetual scowl. Sometimes it got so bad that, as a kid, Macy swore one day Gary's face would cave in on itself.

"I wouldn't call them good friends," Macy finally answered. "Don't think I'd even call them friends. Russ has just always looked out for Gary."

"How so?" Cam asked.

"Well, like when Gary was let go from the mine, Russ called Martin and got him a job at the cabinet shop."

"Why was he fired from the mine?"

"I'm not totally sure, but there was some speculation."

"What about?" Cam asked.

"This feels a lot like gossiping." Macy hesitated and placed her index finger near her mouth, in a shhh position. "Something to do with Gary exposing himself to one of the secretaries," she whispered.

"No wonder they let him go."

"Remember, that was just talk."

"I'm just trying to figure the guy out," Cam said. "He doesn't like me very much."

"Don't worry about what Gary thinks. Not everyone likes everyone else. That's just life."

110

"I can't imagine anyone in their right mind not adoring you," Cam said.

Macy shot her a quick look and hoped to find a teasing expression on her face. She was thrown a little off-center when she saw Cam was serious.

"I-I mean—" Cam stammered.

Macy put her hand up, a barrier against explanations or nice words. She didn't know how to take Cam when she made comments like that, but she did seem naïve about it, which made it slightly less troublesome.

Then Cam blurted out, "Do you think the same thing about Sharon—that she might never really like me either?"

"Apples and oranges. Just give her time."

Macy was there when Cam saw Sharon soon after she returned from the mountains. Sharon had acted nice enough but didn't go out of her way. She'd been noncommittal when Cam mentioned wanting to see some of her Aunt Jess's photos and things.

"I want a chance to get to know Sharon."

"I know."

Cam brushed at imaginary sawdust on her pants. "So, you don't think I'm trying too hard with her?"

Macy shrugged. "Maybe you just need to relax."

A train whistle served as punctuation. Macy looked to the left and saw the string of boxcars running parallel to them. Heat rose on her face, much like the friction of the train on the tracks, when she thought about why she'd gone to Whirligig's, and then seeing Sharon there.

Macy sat up straighter. "Want to grab a pizza on our way to pick up Jeremiah?"

"Sure."

When Cam's face lit up, Macy hoped it was just because she loved pizza.

Hitting speed dial on her cell phone, Macy asked, "Is plain cheese okay? J-man is going through a picky stage."

"Sure."

As Macy pulled into the parking lot, Cam offered to run in for the pizza. She got out of the car before Macy could give her any money, but then Macy was glad for it. Maybe Cam needed to have that grownup moment.

When Cam got back in the car, Macy was on the phone with Jeremiah. "Mama loves you. I'll be there in a few minutes. What's that?" She listened and answered, "Yeah, tell your grandpa that's fine. Okay, bye." She hung up and tucked the phone into the sun visor. Backing out of the parking space, she told Cam that Russ planned to take J-man fishing the next day.

"Your ex-father-in-law seems pretty cool."

Macy nodded. "Yeah, Russ is a good guy."

"What type of mine does he work at?"

"Kaolin." The look on Cam's face prompted her to elaborate. "The locals call it white clay, or chalk. It's used in ceramics and a lot of other things."

"They mine it?"

"Yeah. There's a vein of it that runs through the middle of Georgia. It's geology stuff that I don't really understand."

"Hmmm. You know, Russ has come into the shop a few times. He and Kenny seemed close."

"They are."

"What about Kenny's parents?" Cam asked.

"What about them?"

"He never talks about them. I mean, you'd almost think that Russ was his father instead of his uncle. Are his parents even around?" She shifted the pizza in her lap.

"Yeah, they're around. They just aren't close." Feeling less than loyal to Kenny, she stopped. "You know, this really does feel like gossip."

"Sorry." Cam studied her wrapped thumb for a moment and went right on with her digging expedition. "You don't talk much about your parents either."

Macy didn't respond. There was nothing to say about the dad or stepdads she barely knew. And she wasn't in the mood to get on the subject of her mother.

She changed lanes. "Tell me about the info you got from Augusta State."

"It was just stuff about their degrees."

Macy didn't push the discussion. If Cam was going to go to college, it had to be to please herself, no one else.

When they picked up Jeremiah from Russ and Eileen's, he jumped into the backseat and waved goodbye to his grandmother and that silly looking Bella. He was crazy about the dog his grandparents kept for him.

The entire way to Michael's, Jeremiah fussed over Cam's injury, making her blush.

Macy couldn't help feeling relieved that Michael had to work late, and that she and J-man were eating at his house as Cam's guests. Sharon pulled up next door at the same time Macy pulled into Michael's driveway. Macy waved to Sharon as Cam juggled the pizza as she got out of the car.

"Hello," Sharon called over.

Macy knew Cam wouldn't extend the invitation, but that she'd be glad for the chance to be around Sharon. "Come join us for pizza," Macy called.

"No thanks." She held up her briefcase. "Work to do."

"Aw, come on. You can't work effectively on an empty stomach."

"And," Jeremiah added, "it's pizza!"

"Well, then, I guess I better," she said with a smile. She tossed her briefcase back into her car and crossed her lawn.

Macy hoped Cam could eat her pizza one-handed. She knew Cam would be nervous, afraid of looking like a total klutz in front of Sharon, but in the long run, any time they had together would be worth it.

Cam had Jeremiah help her with the sodas, and J-man puffed up with importance as he handed one to Sharon. As Sharon took the can from J-man, Macy eyed the thin gold bracelet dangling from her wrist. Macy tried to recall if she'd always worn it that loose, or if she'd lost weight.

They all settled around Michael's dining room table. Macy handed out napkins, doing so with a slight wrist action. Again, the white flag flickered, and she wondered who would surrender. She hoped it'd be Sharon, that she'd actually give Cam a chance to peek into the life she'd shared with Jess.

Looking across the double-cheese pizza, Macy decided to help Cam and Sharon find some common ground. Surely she could mold a relationship of some sort between them. It might be another game, but she figured it was okay, since her intentions were admirable.

"Mama, where do you think Spider-Man is right now?" Jeremiah didn't give her a chance to answer. "If I could have a superpower, I'd want to be able to walk through walls."

"Really?" Macy asked.

"Yeah, then I wouldn't have to touch germy doorknobs." He crinkled up his nose and swiveled toward Cam. "And if Mama needed rescuing, I could get to her faster." He took a bite of his pizza and, with his mouth full, asked, "Cam, what superpower do you want?"

Cam set down her slice. "Time travel."

"Cool!" J-man's eyes grew wide. "In a special car or a spaceship?"

"It wouldn't matter, as long as I could go back and make things right. You know, take back the mean things I said when I was younger." Then she was speaking to her pizza, but Macy knew the words were intended for Sharon. "At the very least, I would have been there for Aunt Jess. She should have had some family with her in the end."

Sharon was staring at Cam. The concentration on her face told Macy she was trying to decide if Cam even knew what she'd just said. Macy's guess was that she didn't, but she couldn't take her eyes off Sharon long enough to look at Cam to figure it out herself.

Sharon got up and carried her plate into the kitchen. Macy glanced at Cam, who looked oblivious, and followed Sharon.

"She didn't mean anything by that," Macy said.

Sharon's face sagged, and the circles under her eyes seemed darker. "I know you mean well, but please, don't." Then she left.

Macy stared at the door through which Sharon disappeared, disappointment mingling with a slight ache in her chest. She went back into the dining room. She'd explain to Cam the mistake she'd made in defining family so narrowly.

"Mama, what superpower do you want?"

When she looked at Jeremiah, the ache in her chest intensified. Standing behind him, she wrapped her arms around his thin body and wished she could keep him safe in a cocoon forever. She took a deep breath. "Whatever it takes," she whispered and kissed the top of his head.

†

Macy recognized Dorianne's voice as soon as she heard the words. "But you're my sister, Grace."

"Half-sister. Look, I just don't think of you that way. All the documentation in the world won't change that."

Macy was waiting outside the café in the Barnes & Noble for Cam and J-man to return from the restrooms. Dorianne hadn't seen her yet.

Tomato Florentine took its place as soup of the day, competing shamelessly with the aromas of a latte, cappuccino, mocha-this, and morning-blend-that.

Grace's voice drowned out the background jazz. "Even if I did think of you as family, what makes you think I'd carry a baby for you and what's-his-name?"

"Kenny," Dorianne said.

"Listen, you're a data entry clerk and he's a mechanic, not quite the caliber of people I'd want raising a baby I gave birth to."

Macy felt like she'd been punched in the stomach and couldn't do anything about it. She was thankful not to see Dori's expression.

Dori's voice wavered. "Kenny's not a mechanic, he's a—"

Macy stepped into the café just as Grace held up her hand to quiet Dorianne. "I don't care what he is. You two just aren't ideal parent material. Face the facts. I will never consider being your surrogate."

She imagined the rejection catching in Dori's throat and threatening to strangle her. It all but did that to Macy, sneaking out of her throat as a low, guttural protest.

At the sound, Dori reeled around and came face-to-face with Macy for the first time in years. She whispered, "Macy."

Macy quickly turned away from her to address Grace. "I think Dori and Kenny will be fantastic parents."

"Wonderful," Grace shot back. "Then you carry their baby."

"Mama, are you gonna have a baby?" Jeremiah asked as he walked up behind her.

Macy's discomfort level shot up. "No, J-man, I'm not."

"Who's having a baby then?"

"I want to have a baby," Dorianne said.

"She's Uncle Kenny's wife!" J-man sang out.

Macy smiled. "Yes, sweetie, she is."

"Aunt Dorianne gave me Bella." His eyes shone black as onyx. "So if you give her a baby, we'll be even-steven."

Grace laughed. "Now this is getting good." She turned toward Macy. "Who are you?"

"Macy Stokes. Who are you to—"

"I'm— Wait a minute," she said. "You are *her*?"

"Her who?"

"Her. Macy. Michael's new girlfriend."

"Yeah, I'm her." Macy recalled then that Michael had dated a woman named Grace not long before they started going out.

Grace let out a nervous laugh. "This is weird." She wheeled around and almost ran into Cam.

Grace stopped and stood stock still when Cam blurted out, "You."

Macy looked at Cam. "Her?"

Dorianne shook her head. "Does everyone but me know every freaking person in this town?"

"Grace gave me a ride when I first got here," Cam said.

Macy remembered Cam telling her about a ride she'd accepted from a woman in town. Apparently she'd driven Cam everywhere except where she wanted to go.

Grace cleared her throat. "How is your aunt, Cam?"

"You're Cam?" Dori seemed to fit the last piece into the puzzle. "Kenny's new coworker hangs out with Macy and knows my half-sister?"

Macy almost laughed, but the reminder of Grace's rejection of Dori kept it lodged in her throat. "Cam, could you take J-man to the kids' books?"

Cam gave J-man a big smile. "C'mon, sport, let's get while the getting's good."

"Stay right with Cam, Jeremiah," Macy called after them.

Macy turned her attention back to Grace. She wanted to ask her who she thought she was, treating people the way she did, but Grace theatrically looked at her watch and announced that her break was over. And just like that, with a toss of her hair, she sashayed away.

Smiling at Dorianne, Macy said, "This place is exhausting."

Dori laughed and twisted her wedding band around on her finger.

It dawned on Macy that they were standing within feet of each other, and there was no violence, no cursing, no... anything. She was afraid to let this strange moment pass. "Would you like to get a cup of coffee?"

To her surprise, Dori nodded.

It was more than a little awkward sitting across the table from Dori after all those years. "That woman's your half-sister?" Macy asked.

"Yeah. Can you believe it? I always knew I had a sister. I think I was born knowing it."

Macy remembered. Dori frequently commented how cool it would be if they were sisters. The thought had always made her queasy, and it wasn't just the idea of being named Macy Mason. Young and confused, she hadn't wanted to be Dori's sister; she wanted to be her boyfriend.

Now they talked about their jobs and people they once knew. Macy told her about her promotion at the accounting office and her sporadic night classes at Augusta State. She held Dori's gaze briefly as she claimed, "I still don't know what I want to be when I grow up."

"I remember you wanted to be a veterinarian."

Macy stared into her coffee. "I was eight."

"A very smart eight." Dori smiled.

Dori's mom didn't think Macy was so smart, especially not when she convinced Dori that they should rescue all the neighborhood cats they could round up. Macy had no idea of the ruckus and the mess a dozen unfamiliar cats would create in Dori's bedroom. Mrs. Mason never trusted her again after that, which was one reason they hid the comics at Macy's house and played the secret hero games in Macy's bedroom.

She tried to imagine the quickened pulse and sweating palms that she'd felt for Dori back then. It didn't happen. She thought about the rush of the hero saving the beauty, the scent of grape gum, the pretend kiss that always followed. Nothing. Instead, J-man's term, even-steven, kept playing over and over in her head. She hated when words got stuck and forced her to think about what it meant that they wouldn't go away. Even-steven. She fiddled with her coffee cup and did her best to distract herself.

Dori fiddled, too, with her wedding band.

"I'm sorry about your mom and Brian."

Dori nodded.

"I was at the funeral."

"I know. I saw you. But you didn't come say anything to me."

"I didn't think you wanted me to."

"I didn't." Dori smiled. "But I wanted you to try, so I could tell you to go to hell."

Macy couldn't imagine how hard it must have been on Dori. Her father had died when they were in the eighth grade. Then she lost both her mom and her brother soon after high school. It amazed Macy that Dori would want to love anyone else, let alone a child, after all that loss. But maybe that made more sense than the alternative of not having anyone.

"Tell me about Michael."

"Well, he's from the Midwest, went to medical school at MCG, and stayed in Augusta to open a family practice."

"How did you meet?" Dori asked.

"At the Partridge Inn."

"He sounds like a great guy."

"He is, and J-man really likes him."

"I'm happy for you."

Macy believed her. And she kept to herself her conviction that Michael could do so much better than her.

Dorianne twisted her wedding ring again. "When we were little, I couldn't believe you wanted to be my friend. Remember when we were in the second grade and you slugged John Dawson for saying the n-word? I thought you were all it. When you wanted to be friends, I was just crazy happy."

"But?" Macy studied the wall.

"But then things got uncomfortable the older we got."

"Uncomfortable?"

"Yeah. Sometimes I felt like you didn't like me at all, like there was some big joke and I was the butt of it."

"That was never the case. There was never a joke, and I never *not* liked you." She couldn't tell Dori it was just how she tried to deal with the roller coaster of hormones and emotions she didn't understand.

"When you went out with Jack, it got even more uncomfortable. I kept imagining you two laughing about my crush on him, and I was terrified Jack would tell Kenny. It was just easier to steer clear of you two."

"I never told Jack anything about us or the comics. And I never understood why you pulled away like you did."

"I didn't know what else to do." Dori sighed and shifted away from the table. "And, well, we both know the death blow to our friendship."

"You and I were so far past being friends when—" Macy stopped. She would not say the words.

"When you slept with Kenny." Dori paused for emphasis. "That's when I knew we were never really friends, that you'd never really liked me. I mean, how could you have, if you'd do that to me?"

"I have no excuse, nothing logical anyway."

"Had you always faked being my friend?"

Tears streaked Dori's cheeks, and Macy knew she had thought a lot over the years about asking that question.

"I never faked anything with you. I always liked you." Macy looked away. "I always liked you too much."

"What's that supposed to mean?"

Macy braced herself for Dori's realization, for the disgust that would surely follow.

"You liked me so much that you slept with my boyfriend?"

"I liked you so much that it killed me when you got together with Kenny," Macy said.

"You were jealous?"

"You were playing more than hero with him." She'd hated it when Kenny would walk Dori to third period history, and she'd see them kiss before Dori would come in and sit two rows away, wearing the blushy glow that made Macy want to hurl her textbook against the ugly cinder block wall.

"You could've had any guy. You already had Jack, why did you have to have Kenny, too?"

"That's just it. I didn't have to have Kenny. I didn't want to be with him as much as I wanted to *be* him."

"I guess I'm just not getting this."

And why should she? It had taken Macy years to finally get it. And lately she'd been wondering what would have happened if she'd just moved her hand from between their mouths and kissed Dori, like she'd considered doing so many times.

But what-ifs didn't count. Besides, had things been different with Dori, Macy might not have ever been with Jack, and then she wouldn't have her J-man. No outcome could possibly be better than her son.

J-man came into the café with Cam. They went to the counter, and Cam got them each a bottle of juice.

Dori wiped away the last of the dampness from beneath her eyes. "Jeremiah is getting so big."

"He is."

Macy waved them over. J-man leaned against her side, holding a book close to him. She put her arm around him and pulled him in for a hug. Macy had made a conscious effort not to skimp on physical contact, not to raise him on stiff, half-hugs like those she'd known as a kid.

Cam leaned against the top of the chair between Macy and Dori and smiled awkwardly.

"Now for a proper introduction. Cam Webber, meet Dorianne Brewer."

Cam extended her hand. "It's great to finally meet you."

Dori smiled and shook her hand. "Kenny's not giving you too hard of a time, is he?"

"Of course he is," Cam teased. "That's Kenny."

She laughed. "Yes, that is Kenny."

Macy motioned to Cam. "Sit with us."

Holding the black thumbnail she was sure to lose out of the way, Cam pulled the chair out.

Dori winced. "Kenny told me about your run-in with the pneumatic press."

Macy knew Cam was embarrassed about the incident and upset with herself for not responding better. She'd sheepishly told Macy about how she panicked and forgot she could just take her foot off the pedal and it would release itself. She felt like an idiot just standing there, trying not to scream as she asked Kenny if he had a minute, if he could come give her a hand.

"A lot of people don't think right when they're in that position. Look at Kenny. He's been at it for years, and even he has panicked."

Cam gawked at Dorianne. "Kenny forgot to take his foot off the pedal?"

Dori laughed. "Even worse. He pulled away with it still clamped down on his finger. Left a chunk of himself behind, too."

"Yuck," Jeremiah said, finally distracted from his book.

"Kenny didn't tell me about that," Cam said.

Macy smiled at how Dori seemed to relish telling tales about her husband.

"So, Kenny is in the restroom running cold water over his finger," Dori said. "Blood's all over the sink, and Tank comes in with a screwdriver, waving it around. He says, 'Dude, you want this back?' and there's a chunk of skin dangling from the end of the screwdriver."

"Yuck," Jeremiah repeated.

Macy could tell by his enthusiasm that he was actually enjoying the theatrics.

Dori laughed. "I'm surprised Tank or Eddie didn't tell you about that."

"They'd already left for the day. It was just me, Kenny, and Gary. Of course, Gary got all mad. You'd think I'd caught *his* thumb in the press."

"Don't pay any attention to Goof—I mean to Gary," Dori said.

"Mama, can we go now so I can play with Bella at Grandma's?"

Even-steven. Even-steven.

Macy checked her watch. "Yeah, we need to get going." She looked at J-man's book, a picture book of backyard birds. "That's your final choice?"

"Yep."

"Tell Aunt Dorianne goodbye."

"Bye." He leaned a little closer to her. "I'll tell Bella you said hi."

"Thank you, Jeremiah."

Macy straightened J-man's collar. "Can you head toward the cash register? I'll be right there."

As he took off, Cam said to Dorianne, "It was nice meeting you," and followed him.

"This has been, well, nice." Macy waited a second, giving Dori a chance to respond, then went on. "To be honest with you, I expected a shouting match if we ever spoke again."

Dori leaned forward and rested her elbows on the table. "I guess I'm too tired for shouting." She sighed. "And yes, this has been nice."

They said their goodbyes, and Macy went to meet J-man and Cam. The words ricocheted through her mind. *Even-steven, even-steven.*

Chapter Thirteen

Molting

"The chalk company might have took my granddaddy's land, but I got me a good job at one of the mines."

Turning away from the saw, Cam looked at Gary, unsure whether Gary was talking to her.

He kept on. "I thought I was finally getting my due, but the chalk people got the last word. They filled my lungs and veins with silica and took away the best job I ever had."

Cam just stared at him. That was the most Gary had said to her since she'd started working at the shop.

"Me and Kenny used to be friends. That was before he gave up fishing for football and girls," Gary said.

Cam glanced toward Kenny on the other side of the shop. She had to admit she was curious about Gary's claim. She thought about her conversation with Macy, how she'd said Russ took up for Gary. That day Macy hadn't said anything about Gary and Kenny ever being friends.

"Same old story," Gary muttered. "Use me until something better comes along."

Staring at Gary's heavy brow, made weightier by his scowl, Cam felt a pang of guilt for her next thought. *The 'something better to come along' was called evolution.* She turned away so Gary wouldn't see her smile as her guilt melted into amusement. Her friends in Maryland, Ryan and Travis, would have appreciated the humor in that. Sometimes she missed the guys—and girls, even Courtney—but she didn't give any real thought to going back.

Cam couldn't imagine moving away from Macy. She smiled as she anticipated the cookout. She was looking forward to spending more time with Macy, especially since Michael would be busy playing host and grilling the food. It was great that Michael was letting her stay with him, but Cam preferred it when she didn't have to share Macy.

When she turned back, Gary had come up behind her. She didn't like Gary so close to her, especially with a hammer in his hand.

"I deserve better than this crap," Gary said.

Cam looked around. Kenny was helping Tank with one of the rush jobs that had required them to work the last couple of weekends. Cam faced Gary. If the freak was going to pummel her with a hammer, she wanted to see it coming so she could at least try to dodge it.

"I should have gotten my granddaddy's land, then I wouldn't be stuck working here with you punks. But the chalk company—"

"Hey, Cam, quit screwing around, and let's get going."

Thank God for Kenny, Cam thought. Even driving with Kenny was better than listening to Gary go on and on. Besides, the sooner they got out of there, the sooner they'd get to the cookout. And it wasn't just the prospect of spending time with Macy that had her psyched. Sharon was going to be there, too.

Kenny pushed his old Maverick pretty hard. A few times Cam could have sworn she heard the engine moan when Kenny started out after a full stop. There wasn't much Cam knew about cars, but that sound didn't seem like a bad one. It just sounded tired.

"Piece of junk, huh?" Kenny asked.

Cam shrugged, thinking about how much she wanted her own vehicle. "It's better than what I have."

"You gonna get you something?"

"Once I get more money saved."

"There's a guy I know selling his old pickup truck. You might could afford that."

"Yeah, I might could." She tried out Kenny's dialect. The words felt wrong in her mouth, like getting to the bottom of hot chocolate and finding it much too thick.

Kenny made a left turn and headed a different way to Michael's than Cam was used to. Even though she knew there were several ways to get from any point A to any point B in Augusta, it still caught her by surprise.

To the right, a swath of land had just been cleared. Huge piles of brush and stumps smoldered in the middle. Beyond that was Phase I of the same development, where mammoth houses huddled close to one another. The homes dwarfed newly planted Bradford pears and Japanese maples, which were mere twigs sticking out of fresh green sod.

Across the street was a nursery. Cam imagined they'd be plenty busy as new homeowners rushed to put their thumbprints on their yards. Now that Cam knew where the nursery was, she had every intention of checking it out herself.

As they passed groupings of bushes and saplings for sale, Cam tried to figure out what each was. She liked having the luxury of noticing things around her. Well, until it got to be the same-old, same-old. Baltimore had become that way. She'd lost interest and no longer noticed. And that got her thinking. If she wasn't driving, and she wasn't paying attention, then what good was she?

At Michael's, they parked at the curb between a Beemer and a Benz. Cam guessed that the cars belonged to Michael's friends. She didn't see Sharon's Miata next door in her driveway. Maybe she'd made a run to the store.

Voices drifted from the backyard, and Cam hoped no one was stepping in her flowerbeds. She couldn't wait to hear what Sharon would say about what she'd done in the back. She'd started working in Michael's yard to give Sharon the opportunity to walk over and say hello or even just wave through her car window. Sharon didn't do either, but before Cam knew it, she had Michael's yard looking so good that sticking with it became a matter of pride.

Kenny walked around to the back of the house where Dorianne and the other guests were gathered. Cam went in through the front door, jumped in the shower, and changed into a clean shirt and cargo pants before joining the party.

Showered and sawdust-free, she grabbed an orange soda from the fridge. A makeshift bar was set up on the kitchen counter. She eyed the rum and wondered whether it might taste good with her soda.

She went out the back door, and the sight of Macy squatting down in front of Jeremiah stopped her in her tracks. Macy was telling her son something as he nodded, obviously only half paying attention. She leaned toward him, kissed his forehead, and cut him loose. She hadn't even finished straightening up before he was off playing with his dog.

Macy's mom stood by the picnic table. Cam assumed the man with her was Harold. Dorianne took Kenny by the hand and pulled him over. He went reluctantly. Macy's mom introduced Harold to the couple, and it dawned on Cam that she didn't know the woman except as "Macy's mom."

Macy glanced in their direction and looked over at Sharon's house. Cam's gaze followed hers. Sharon's car still wasn't there. Turning, Macy saw Cam and smiled. Cam perked up. Macy was so beautiful.

Macy approached her. "I love what you've done with that retaining wall."

Cam's face grew warm. The muscles in her shoulders stiffened at the memory of hauling all the blocks.

"It looks great," Macy added.

"I'm glad you like it." Cam looked away, a little embarrassed and still wondering about Sharon.

"She'll come," Macy said, as if reading Cam's mind. "She said she would." They both looked to the driveway next door, almost like they could will her to come home.

Cam couldn't get over how sweet Macy was about trying to help her with Sharon. That was what she loved about Macy—such a kind heart. Add that to the perfect smile and those incredible dark eyes... No wonder she thought about Macy constantly.

Michael called out to Macy from the grill, "Can you please grab more paper plates?"

Cam sighed. Michael would do anything to reclaim Macy's attention.

Macy placed her hand on Cam's back for a moment before going off to assist Michael. Cam stared over at Sharon's, not moving, so as not to dissipate the lingering warmth of Macy's touch.

"Cam, come see what Bella can do."

She smiled at Jeremiah and made her way over to him.

"Look." He turned to the dog. "Bella, sit." The dog stood, wagging her tail. "Sit." Wag. "Sit." She cocked her head to the side. "Sit, sit, sit."

Jeremiah crossed his arms over his bony chest and marched away. Bella sat.

Cam patted her head. "Good girl," she said.

Cam chugged half her orange soda and went inside and helped herself to a hefty amount of rum. She swirled the can carefully, trying to mix it without sloshing.

Back outside, Cam hung on the periphery and watched Michael's friends. They seemed nice enough. An older man was talking to Macy. Cam thought he was the anesthesiologist but wasn't sure. What Cam was sure about was that she didn't like the way the guy was looking at Macy. He also touched her arm way too much as he spoke.

The wall Cam had engineered around a group of three skinny pines changed the dynamics of the yard. She wondered if anyone other than herself and Macy appreciated it. Sharon maybe? She glanced over at Sharon's driveway. Still no Miata.

Taking several chugs of her drink, Cam watched Jeremiah with Bella. From the look of his gesturing, Jeremiah was trying to get her to roll over.

Cam went inside for another soda. She poured most of it down the kitchen sink and added rum. The last time she'd been drunk was at Courtney's. Her girlfriend's parents came home unexpectedly, broke up the party, and kicked them all out. As usual, Cam's buddies stuffed her in the backseat of the car. Just "one of the guys." Travis drove, and Ryan sat up front with him.

Travis always took the turns rough, trying to send Cam to the floor of the car or make her puke. His plan never worked, because Cam was never as drunk as they thought she was. Until that night. She was drunk and, once again, just along for the ride. Since she'd just picked herself up from the floorboard, Cam didn't know what they were up to until Travis and Ryan threw their arms up and yelled, "Score!" They'd driven right through old man Gibson's yard, taking out his three row garden and decapitating his scarecrow.

Cam shook off the memory and took a long drink. Things were going to be different. Cam had grown up, she was a woman, and was really liking the warm and confident feeling she was getting from the rum. She was sure other things would be different now, too. If she had a chance to be with Macy, she wouldn't blow it. Not like with Robyn or Courtney.

Cam looked next door, and it became clear. Cam didn't care what Sharon had told Macy, Sharon wasn't coming.

Cam found Macy looking toward Sharon's a few times, too. Then Macy caught Cam catching her. At first Cam looked away, like she hadn't been staring at Macy, but then she didn't try to hide it. It was liberating not to care if Macy knew she was looking at her.

Macy's mom and Harold left right after some of Michael's important doctor friends. It didn't matter to Cam; their faces had all started to swirl together.

Kenny hung out with his wife, standing behind her and watching as she talked to Jeremiah, or watched Bella not sit.

"Hey there."

Cam spun around at the sound of Macy's voice. She must have moved too quickly, because she almost lost her balance.

"What's going on?" Macy asked.

"Sharon stood us up."

"I'm sure it wasn't intentional."

"She hates me," Cam said. "Aunt Sharon hates me."

"Aunt Sharon?" Macy sighed. "You can't replace Jess with Sharon."

"I'm not trying to." She looked at Macy for a long time. "You are so beautiful."

Macy gave her a funny look, took the soda from her hand, and sniffed it. The intimacy of the act almost choked Cam up. Macy's face twisted. "What's in here?"

"Orange soda." Cam slurred the word *soda*.

"Tell me the truth."

"Okay, I'll tell you the truth." Cam took a deep breath and pointed to where Michael stood by the grill. "He's not good enough for you. You should be with me, because I love you so much. There it is—I love you so much."

Cam realized she was sobbing, and all the remaining faces were swirling in her direction.

Macy was asking her not to say things like that, so she decided to kiss her instead. Cam took a clumsy step toward her.

"Okay, that's enough." Michael was suddenly there. He handed the long spear-looking fork thing to Macy and herded Cam into the house.

Cam could barely see Macy through the screen door. Macy stood in the yard with her hand to her mouth. "The truth hurts, huh?" Cam asked Michael, as she fell against the kitchen counter.

The next thing she knew, Michael had her jacked against the wall. She figured Michael would tell Macy it was because she couldn't stand on her own, but Cam knew it was really about Michael being jealous of her.

Michael's face was close to hers. "Don't forget where you are."

Like I could, Cam thought. Then she puked on Michael's expensive shoes.

Michael backed away, and the next thing Cam knew, Kenny was taking her to the bathroom. Once the walls quit throbbing and messing with her head, she confided in her coworker.

"He's always been jealous, because he knows me and Macy are perfect for each other." She tried to get up but went right back down on her butt. "Macy and I have so much in common. Neither of us really knows our fathers, and we aren't close to our mothers."

Cam could tell Kenny still wasn't convinced, so she added, "And I'll be a good co-parent for Jeremiah."

"You mean a good playmate for Jeremiah."

"No." Cam's chest heaved. "I love Macy so much."

"You'll get over it."

"I won't." But her protest ended when she started puking again. The bathroom spun around and around, and Cam had a fleeting thought that it was like she was back at Courtney's.

But it wasn't Courtney's house, it was Travis's car.

Cam looked out the back window, making brief eye contact with Mr. Gibson as the man stood in the rubble of his zucchini and scarecrow. But then the pieces of squash became a mangled yellow dog, and it was Cam standing over it.

"I didn't do it," she blubbered. "I was just along for the ride."

"Sure you were, kid," Kenny said, standing behind her. "That's what you keep saying."

†

Something squeezed Cam's head. Crushing pain. Her face felt warm. "Shit," she whispered. "Where am I?"

"In bed."

The sound of Macy's voice made her jump. Cam looked down. She was in a wife-beater tank but still had her pants on. "What the hell?" She felt her head and was surprised to find that no one was sitting on it. *Oh yeah... hangover.*

"Here." Macy held out her hand.

Cam couldn't look at her.

"Take the aspirin. I promise it'll help."

She took the two tablets and the glass of water Macy offered. After forcing down the pills, she set the glass onto the bedside table and stuck her head under her pillow. "Sorry," she said from beneath the cool cotton. She waited a few seconds for Macy to reply, but she didn't.

Cam peeked out. She recognized the look of disappointment on Macy's face from the many times she'd seen it on her mom's. Cringing, she repeated, "Sorry." A rush of memory ambushed her. "Does Michael want me to leave?"

"He did, but he's over it now." Macy reached for the glass. "We aren't making a habit of that sort of behavior, are we?"

"No." Cam felt like she was twelve years old and had just been caught sneaking a cigarette.

As she started to put the pillow back over her head, a wave of nausea catapulted her out of bed. She barely made it into the bathroom.

When Cam came out, Macy was at the table with Michael and Jeremiah—a perfect, happy little family eating Sunday morning breakfast. She didn't make eye contact on her way back to bed. Not that it mattered. She was pretty sure there wasn't a place set for her at the table.

†

Michael took Macy to Antonio's Broad Street Bistro for a romantic, jazz-flavored birthday dinner. The exposed brick walls and colorful art worked well with the casual ambiance, which complemented the seared scallops and soft music. But a tension headache had threatened Macy all evening, so, when they got to her house, she didn't ask Michael in.

He wasn't thrilled, but he understood. "Put an ice pack on your head. That usually works wonders." Then he kissed her quickly and left.

As Macy walked in the front door, J-man rushed her. "Mama, Mama, Emma called."

"What?" She swept him up in her arms and hugged him. "Tell me what she said," she whispered, knowing her voice would set the tone for his.

134

"She said to tell you happy birthday," he whispered back.

Her heart thudded, and she held him tighter. "What else did she say?"

"She misses me. And she got a dog, too."

"She did?" Macy kept her voice light, hoping her cardio-acoustics wouldn't give her away.

"Yeah, and I told her all about my Bella."

Macy felt the beginning of a squirm from J-man, but she wasn't ready to let go of him.

"Mama." J-man giggled.

"Yeah, baby?"

"Too tight. I can't breathe."

He giggled some more as she let him go. She gave him a little tickle for good measure.

Macy grabbed a Diet Coke from the fridge to wash down some aspirin. She'd wait on the ice pack, give the drugs a chance first.

Her mother was in the den, cross-stitching. Seems there was trouble in paradise, so she'd volunteered to sit for J-man as a way to get out of the house for an evening. Macy got the idea that Harold was keeping her on a pretty tight rein, which was not the way to keep her mother's interest.

She looked up when Macy walked into the room. "How was dinner?"

"Very nice."

"Good." She held her project away from her, giving her no longer perfect vision a little help. "You know, you didn't tell me how your lunch went with Dorianne yesterday."

"It was good." Macy sat on the other end of the sofa.

"How's she doing? I'm so glad you two are friendly again. I always liked that girl."

"Yeah," she answered, distracted by the red blink of caller ID on her phone.

"I can remember when you two started experimenting…" Macy's heart lurched before her mother finished, "with makeup."

Macy laughed with relief.

Her mother shot her a look over her cross-stitch. "She was a lot better with it than you were. I guess she still is."

She knew what was coming—the foundation and blush lecture, how mascara and lipstick weren't enough.

"You were such a natural beauty, more so than Dorianne, but she always knew how to work with what she had instead of just letting herself go."

Macy ignored the dig. She no longer cared what her mother thought about her makeup or wardrobe. There were things in life much more important, and Macy contemplated spoon-feeding the idea of one such thing to her mother. There was no reason to admit she had been thinking nonstop about wanting to be Dori and Kenny's surrogate, so she just asked her mother what she thought about a couple having a friend or relative carry a child for them.

"You're talking about Dorianne and Kenny?" Macy gave her a puzzled look, so she added, "Not much gets by me, young lady."

"Well, what do you think?"

"I think they'd be good parents, and it's a shame things haven't worked out for them." She put her cross-stitch down.

"Do you think they should do *in vitro*?"

"I think it's not my say. They've got the right to do whatever they wish. I'm a very tolerant person, you know."

It wasn't lost on Macy that she wouldn't be so tolerant if it had anything to do with Macy. She wanted to raise that issue, but the pounding at the base of her skull told her to quit while she was ahead.

After her mother left, Macy colored with J-man. It wasn't long before he lost interest and cozied up to the TV.

Macy scrolled to the latest number on her caller ID and jotted it down.

She waited until after J-man went to bed to call Emma. She dialed slowly, fearful that her shaking finger might hit the wrong buttons.

Emma answered, and it was awkward for the first several moments. Then Macy decided she'd give herself a birthday present and just get to the point. She took a deep breath and blurted out, "I think about you a lot."

"I think about you, too."

"I mean *think* about you, like in a very intimate way."

"You shouldn't. You aren't like that, remember?"

"Ouch," Macy said.

"Sorry, that was a cheap shot. I thought it'd make me feel better."

"Did it?"

"No."

All at once Macy found herself telling Emma, "I'm sorry I hurt you. I wanted to call, to see you, but I was just too damned scared."

"It's okay to be scared," Emma said, "but it isn't okay to turn your back on a friend. Above all else, I thought we were friends."

"We were. We are. God, I miss you."

Emma didn't respond.

Macy went on. "I have dreams about us, together. I mean like really together. Do you ever think about that?"

"Should I lie so we can stop this conversation?"

"You think about making love to me." Macy was surprised when it came out sounding more confident than it really was.

After a slight pause, Emma said, "I have in the past."

"Describe it."

"Don't do this," she whispered.

"Come on, tell me all about it, Em." Her hand drifted between her breasts, down to her belly.

She didn't answer, so Macy continued. "In my dreams, it's about your hands and your mouth, all over me. Then it's my hands, my mouth, how sweetly you yield to me, how much we need each other."

"Macy."

She remembered the last time Emma had said her name in that half-pleading, half-needing way. "I wish you were here right now."

Emma sighed. "Why?"

"Because I'd like to know if your eyes are more blue or more green at this moment."

"I'm guessing blue," Emma said.

"I'm hoping blue." Macy smiled, thinking of the conversation they'd had about Emma's wardrobe not being the only influence on her eye color. They'd been walking along the river when Emma had admitted that the more passion, the more blue.

"We have to stop this," Emma said, not particularly convincingly.

"No, we don't. I shouldn't have stopped us before either."

"This can't help anything," Emma said.

Macy's heart pounded. "I can't stop thinking about you. I want you so much." She almost choked on the words then wished she had.

"Why this now? What's changed in your life that makes this okay now, when it wasn't before?"

All Macy could do was repeat herself. "I can't stop thinking about you."

"Where's Jeremiah?" Emma asked.

"Sleeping."

"What would you do if I walked through your front door this very second?"

"I'd—"

"Be truthful with yourself," Emma said.

Macy glanced toward J-man's bedroom door. She couldn't answer.

"See? When we kissed, it was just the moment. You aren't a lesbian."

"But I'm pretty sure I am," Macy said.

"Okay. Tell me about being a lesbian."

"What?"

"At least tell me that you are one. You know, actually call yourself the L-word."

Macy looked again at J-man's door. "I really do want you."

Without the least hesitation, Emma said, "If you want me, it's because I'm unobtainable."

"Are you?"

"I'm three states away. I'm not coming back, and you won't leave Georgia. That's pretty unobtainable."

Macy was thrown by how decisive Emma's words were. The image she'd had in her mind when she'd dialed Emma's number now mocked her. There would be no heavy breathing into the phone as they whispered how much they wanted to touch, to taste... How could Macy have expected anything different? Who did she think she was, to think she could fix it all with a phone call?

The hand Macy had imagined as Emma's still rested on her belly. She stared at it, feeling foolish. Once her body and brain were back in synch, she didn't know if she wanted to cry or to laugh. She did neither. Taking a deep breath, she said, "Jeremiah says you got a dog."

With relief clear in her voice, Emma accepted the more comfortable topic. She told Macy how she'd rescued Layla, a Great Dane, on her way up to Virginia.

Macy listened, sort of, but couldn't concentrate.

She wanted to tell Emma about how she'd been contemplating being a surrogate for Dorianne and Kenny, but she started focusing on the word "unobtainable" and couldn't get past the ache of it. She decided if Emma wasn't going to be in her life, she didn't need to know any of that.

They said goodnight and hung up. Macy grabbed the ice pack from the freezer and went to stretch out on the sofa. She wondered if she'd hoped to find Emma living with someone, or not willing to talk to her at all. Had she wanted to find there was no way to be with her, so she could better focus on Michael? Emma said herself that she was unobtainable. But for some reason, Macy only half believed her.

If nothing else, Macy mused, she should be relieved. With things going nowhere with Emma, she wouldn't have to give any serious thought to the ramifications of being "like that." She wouldn't have to worry about losing J-man to Jack because of it, or about how to eventually tell her son.

She draped the ice pack across her forehead and thought about Emma's note that had accompanied the pictures she'd forgotten to thank her for. The note said Emma had found what she was looking for. Macy should have asked her to be more specific. Again, she found herself wondering, *Have I found something in my life?*

Macy closed her eyes and knew she had indeed found something. She'd thought about it and thought about it. And she knew that carrying Dori and Kenny's baby was the natural, logical thing to do. She just had to convince Dori and Kenny.

Part Four

Nesting

Chapter Fourteen

A Done Deal

"I haven't been here in so long," Dorianne said.

"I love the French Market. And I'm so glad we're doing these lunches." Macy opened the menu, even though she already knew what she was having.

"Me, too."

The waitress approached their table. "What can I get you ladies to drink?"

Macy ordered water with a lemon. "I'll take sweet tea," Dori said.

Macy smiled. Emma had always ordered unsweetened tea. She got what she ordered about half the time. Afterwards, guarding her tea from well-meaning wait staff armed with sweet tea became a full-time job for Emma. Macy figured that at least in Virginia, Em could get her iced tea how she liked it.

"A guy two tables away is staring at you," Dorianne said.

Macy didn't bother to look. She'd seen the familiar face as they were waiting to be seated and had refused to make eye contact. She still didn't plan to.

"That hasn't changed much," Dori added, smiling.

Macy shrugged. She wanted to enjoy Dori's company without interruptions. The past few weeks of getting reacquainted with Dori had meant a lot, and the fewer distractions, the better. She couldn't believe she hadn't realized how very much she had missed their friendship.

Dori sat back from the table when the waitress set down her sweet tea.

"Thanks for the water," Macy said. "I'd like the Crepes Louisiana, please."

"I'll have the same," Dori said. After the waitress went to put in their orders, Dori said, "You know, Jeremiah's going to be a heartbreaker one day."

"I just hope I raise him to respect people."

"You will. You are. I just know you're a good mother."

Macy shrugged. She knew Dori would have been a great mother, and she hated how things had turned out for her. The words started again—even-steven, even-steven. "Have you talked to Grace lately?"

"No. She's made it perfectly clear that she doesn't give a hoot about me."

"I'm sorry." Macy sipped her water. "It's probably for the best, though."

"Oh?"

"I hope I'm not out of line," Macy said, "but when I saw y'all at the bookstore, there was something about Grace that didn't sit right with me."

"Kenny's been saying that all along. I was just convinced that she'd eventually feel a connection."

"Maybe she will one day."

"Not enough to carry my baby. That much I know for sure."

"Well, maybe she wasn't the best choice anyway. Maybe someone else would be more appropriate, someone you've known longer and better." She felt a flutter in her belly.

"I don't think I could ever put myself out there again to ask anyone else. Besides, I don't really know anyone of childbearing age *that* well."

"You know me that well." Macy waited for Dorianne to respond. She didn't. "Ever since Jeremiah said that thing about making us even-steven…"

"Trading a dog for a baby? Only a six-year-old would think that was normal."

Macy looked away. She wanted to say that was because he hadn't been corrupted by the world yet, that maybe adults should listen closer to what six-year-olds had to say.

Their salads came, and they busied themselves fussing with them. Dori's fork stopped a few inches from her mouth. "Besides," she said, her voice low and measured, "I couldn't ask you to do something like that for me."

Macy's heart raced. "Let's say you could." She spoke quickly, not wanting to lose her nerve. "Let's say you did ask, and I said yes."

Dori stared at her fork for several moments before using it to separate the tomato from the lettuce. "Okay, let's say I'm asking then."

"And let's say I'm saying yes." Macy shoveled parmesan-laced salad into her mouth.

For several long moments, they ate without talking. Catching each other stealing glances, they took turns looking quickly away from one another.

The waitress took away the salad plates and left their lunches. Neither had started eating when she came back to top up Dori's tea.

"This looks great," Dori said. She teased the side of her crepe with her fork. "Yes, it looks great," she repeated.

The casualness of Dori's words confused Macy. Had she misunderstood their exchange just moments earlier? Had Macy been so focused on wanting to carry Dori and Kenny's baby that she'd not understood what they'd said to one another? Her heart pounded. How horrible if they weren't talking about the same thing, if they weren't making the same agreement.

"You are white as a ghost," Dori said.

Macy swallowed hard but was unable to dislodge the lump growing in her throat. "I think someone needs to say out loud what we just agreed to."

"Okay," Dori whispered.

"And I think it should be you to say it."

Dori reached for her tea, her hand shaking. "I don't think I can."

"You don't think you can do what we were talking about?"

"No, I don't think I can be the one to say it out loud. What if I didn't hear you right? God, I'd be so..." Her hand covered her mouth for a second and dropped into her lap.

Macy looked at Dori and saw the same vulnerable girl she had known in the eighth grade, when Dori's father's liver finally gave out. She was the same scared girl who'd cried into Macy's neck, worried that she should have been sadder over her daddy dying.

"You are sad," Macy had said. "Look at those tears. You're just as sad as Penelope was in *Stony-faced Sea Urchin* when she thought her hero, Count Paulo, was dead. Remember?"

Dori had sniffled and nodded. Macy cleared her throat and said, "That's better, my beauty," in her best hero voice, making Dori smile through her tears.

She looked across the table at Dori, all grown up but still vulnerable. Macy took a sip of her water. Her heart pounded so hard she couldn't believe the entire restaurant didn't hear it.

145

"If you would like for me to carry a baby for you and Kenny, I would be honored to."

Dori sipped her tea. "Thank you so much." She reached across the table just long enough to lightly touch Macy's hand, then she took a bite of her crepe. "This is delicious."

"Yes, and so light." Macy glanced around the room to see if anyone had overheard, if anyone had registered the moment. No one seemed to have noticed how lives were about to change.

Dori smiled. "And the rice is the perfect balance to it."

"Yes," Macy agreed.

✝

Kenny came home from work to find Dori cleaning the house. It wasn't the ferocious housekeeping she did when she was upset; it was more like the excited, hummingbird kind she did when she was real happy. He hadn't seen that kind of cleaning since she won tickets to see Brad Paisley in Atlanta years earlier.

Dori dusted the owl and the glass sea turtle and plucked some lint from the sofa. Kenny braced himself. He had no idea what could possibly have her feeling that good.

She reeled around, a huge grin plastered on her face. "Kenny, you're home!"

Oh, Lord. He was nervous about what she could possibly be up to but not so nervous that he didn't notice how pretty she looked, red cheeks and all.

"Come sit down. I'm making your favorite—meatloaf."

He didn't know where she got the idea that was his favorite. Hell, he'd have to douse it with a ton of Texas Pete just to get it down. "What's up, baby?" he asked, more than a little scared.

She set two placemats on the oak table. Those mats were eggplant-colored, not purple. He'd made that mistake when she was buying them at Target, called them purple, and got a twenty minute lesson on different hues.

"Sit and eat, then we'll talk," Dorianne said, putting their plates of meatloaf and butter beans onto the table.

She was smiling so big, Kenny thought she was fixing to bust. Kenny sat, tried to eat, and begged her to quit staring at him. "Okay, out with it."

"I love you so much, Kenny." She all but crawled into his lap, kissing his cheeks and mouth.

"Oh shit, how much did you spend?" Visions of eggplant-colored furniture danced in his head.

"Stop kidding."

"I ain't kidding."

The next thing he knew, she was telling him about her lunch with Macy. He listened, staring at his meatloaf that was like a wedge of cake, only frosted with hot sauce. The sauce was a cool color orange, but he'd bet Dori would say it was something else, another fancy color right out of a box of crayons.

Dori told him about how she and Macy had been meeting over lunch and coffee. She spent a few minutes about what a wonderful kid Jeremiah was, but Kenny already knew that. Seems she and Macy had done some major talking. In a matter of weeks, Dori managed to forgive Macy, and a whole lot more.

"How in the hell did you go from I-hate-Macy to thanks-for-the-uterus?"

Dori crossed her arms over her chest. "Of course you wouldn't, couldn't understand. You're a man."

"Jesus H. Christ, Dori. Listen to you."

He didn't think Dori listened to herself, or to him. She just went on.

147

"So, we were at lunch, and we got to talking about women of childbearing age."

He waited for her to let on that she knew he and Macy had talked that day at the hospital. She didn't. She just went on about their lunch. "Macy told me that ever since Jeremiah said that she should give me a baby in trade for Bella, that she—"

"What?"

"At the bookstore. Never mind." She waved him off. "Macy said she's been thinking about what Jeremiah said. I said I could never ask her to do something like that for me. Then she said that if I did ask, she'd say yes."

Like so many other times, Kenny sat there staring at his wife, wondering when she'd flipped all those pages, because he sure as hell wasn't reading along with her.

Dori kept on. "So then I said, 'Let's say I'm asking,' and she said, 'Then let's say I'm saying yes.'"

Kenny almost dropped the soda he didn't remember picking up.

"Next thing I know, we're talking about it like it's a done deal."

"A done deal?" His shock wore off real quick. "Is it a done deal?"

"Well, of course not, Kenny. Why are you getting so mad? I thought you'd be happy."

"I thought this whole thing was over when Grace said she wouldn't be our surrogate."

"You were willing to let Grace be our gestational carrier, why not Macy?"

"Our what?" he asked.

"Gestational carrier—since the eggs will be mine and the sperm yours. I learned that online."

"Of course you did," he said, more than a little ticked.

"What's that supposed to mean?"

148

"Nothing." But then he went on to tell her he'd only gone along with the Grace thing because he never figured in a million years it would really happen.

"You weren't all right with it, but you still let me go through the humiliation of asking Grace?"

He hated it when she twisted things around like that. "No, that ain't what I meant."

"So when you said you were okay with it, you lied to me?"

"I didn't lie. I was okay with it then, but now it's different. Now it's Macy. Hell, Dori, Macy? What are you thinking, girl?"

"Why wouldn't I think of her? You like her—you can admit that you do—and we know her. We know she'll take care of herself while she's pregnant."

"But you just started talking to her again. You spent all them years hating her."

"I've forgiven her. That's all in the past."

"You've forgiven her?"

"Yes, I have. Come on, think about it. She's healthy, she—"

"Yeah," he agreed.

"Strong and sincere."

"I guess."

She put her hands on her hips. "So, what's really bothering you?"

"It's you I'm worried about."

"What?" He didn't answer, so she went on. "I've never wanted anything more, Kenny. You know that."

"Yeah, but—" Kenny raked his fork through the hot sauce. He didn't know how to tell her that he really did want a kid and was okay with it happening this new way, but that he had serious doubts about Dori's choice of people. The idea of Grace was just plain crazy, but Macy? All he could think of was that with all the history there, things could get way too complicated.

"But what? Just say what's on your mind."

"But what if you unforgive her? What if you wake up one day while she's fat and happy carrying our kid and just as quick as you forgave her, you unforgive her?"

"What kind of flaky twit do you think I am?"

He had never seen such anger on his wife's face. Not once before in his life. He wanted to get her unmad at him, so he did the only thing he could think of. He ate every bite of that damned meatloaf, even kept eating after she'd left the room without saying another word to him.

Then he went into the spare room where she kept her computer. He stood close but didn't dare touch her, just looked over her shoulder. Wanting to score some points with her, he tried to act interested in what she was doing. She was looking at info about clinics. It seemed there were clinics that did nothing but make people like him and Dori into mamas and daddies.

"Costs a lot, don't it?" he asked.

She just shrugged.

"I don't think you're flaky, and I know you ain't no twit."

He figured she'd at least say thanks, but she just kept on clicking that computer mouse all over the place.

"Okay, Dori, what I gotta do to make this up to you?"

"Agree to at least sit down, the three of us, and talk about this. We don't have to decide right away, but we should soon."

"We'll just sit down and talk?"

"Yes."

Kenny shrugged. "Okay."

Then Dori set it up with Macy for the next evening.

†

When he got home from work, Kenny jumped right into the shower. He couldn't go meet their possible *gestational carrier* with sawdust in his hair, could he?

As he was drying off, thinking about what shirt to wear, he started feeling weird, almost like he was getting ready for a first date or something. To make matters worse, he was sporting a hard-on when Dori came waltzing into the bathroom. He tried to hide it under his towel, but she saw it.

"Looks like you and me were thinking about the same thing."

He was nervous when he asked her what she thought he was thinking about. Then she touched him, and he knew it was all about her and there was nothing to feel guilty about. They backed up, kissing and laughing, until they tumbled onto the bed. When he moved himself against her and then slid in, he imagined they were making their own baby right then and there.

†

They got to Macy's early, because Dori didn't want to be late. Kenny was a little surprised when they went inside. He guessed he was expecting the place to be littered with kid stuff: toys not put up, report cards stuck to the refrigerator door. But it wasn't like that. Everything was either put up or in neat piles on the kitchen counter or on the coffee table in the living room.

While Macy was getting them sodas, he nosed through a coloring book on the counter. Macy handed him his drink, and he gestured toward the picture and said, "Jeremiah sure is good."

She let out a nervous laugh. "I did that one."

Kenny had to smile at the image of Macy coloring.

"Jeremiah's not really interested in that. He only does it to make me happy. Pretty pathetic, huh?"

"Where is Jeremiah?"

"I let Cam borrow my car to take him to play Putt-Putt."

Macy put a stack of brochures on the table. When Kenny and Dori both raised eyebrows, Macy shyly said, "A friend of Michael's gave me the information."

"Michael knows?" Kenny asked.

"I told him y'all were thinking about your options, but I didn't say anything about my involvement... or possible involvement. I thought it would be premature to say anything else."

Well, at least Macy didn't act like it was a done deal, Kenny thought. As he was thinking about how much he appreciated that, he started checking out Macy's kitchen table. It was oak—good—but wasn't put together too well. He figured he could secure the legs better if—

"Kenny?"

"Huh?" He didn't know why they were both staring at him.

Then Dori whispered, "Pay attention, please."

Oh, I'll pay attention all right. "How much is this gonna cost?"

"Kenny," Dori started to say.

"Anywhere from six to ten thousand a cycle," Macy answered.

"What cycle?" Already he didn't like the sound of it.

Macy rummaged through a few brochures. "Here." She slid one closer to Kenny. He pulled away when he saw a drawing of a female's insides. Macy kept on. "A cycle is the whole process of hormone treatments, egg retrieval, and transfer."

"Damn," he interrupted. "It'll cost a fortune."

"Michael says some specialists and clinics offer financing."

Kenny looked at Macy. "Yeah? So what about Michael?"

"What do you mean?" she asked.

"I mean, what's he gonna say about all this? No man I know would want to put up with something like this. What if he says you can't?"

Things got way too quiet, and he realized right away he'd committed a big sin. It was one thing to say something like that in front of one stubborn woman, but two?

Dori's expression shifted from "almost mad" to something different. She looked smug, like when she got the answer right to a question on *Jeopardy*.

A secret girl-smile passed between them, and Macy politely said, "This isn't about Michael. He'll accept it or he won't. Either way, it's not an issue."

There was no way Kenny was going to argue with that.

Dori turned to Macy. "While I take hormones for egg production, you take them to build up your uterine wall?"

Macy leaned forward and put her elbows on the table as she answered. "Yeah. If we synchronize our cycles, they won't have to freeze the eggs."

"Great," Dori said, like she knew all about that stuff.

Kenny sat back as the women talked about hormone injections and embryos. He looked at them and thought, *Wow*. If he focused hard enough, blocked out the table of brochures and the wedding band on Dori's hand, he could swear they were all in the ninth grade, sitting in the library. Well, Dori and Macy would be sitting, Kenny would be standing just out of sight. He'd spied on them one day in particular, sitting next to each other at a big, smooth, library table. They leaned into each other every now and again while they talked. It was so different for girls. Boys didn't sit huddled like that, not unless they were sneaking a peek at a titty magazine or comparing notes on which friends had the hottest sister or mother.

It seemed like no time had gone by since high school, and Kenny thought maybe things wouldn't get messed up again, maybe Dori wouldn't unforgive Macy after all.

He stared at a chart on the table and wondered about their chances of pulling it off. He knew him and Dori would need to pay for everything. Maybe they could get a loan from Martin. Or Uncle Russ.

"You okay, Kenny?" Dori asked.

He looked from one of them to the other, and it hit him like a ton of pressboard. It really was a done deal.

Chapter Fifteen

Mama Bear

Macy stood at her front door and stared at her uninvited guests—her mother and Jack. She took mental notes on her ex. He was still good-looking but getting a little thick around the middle. Ironically, Kenny seemed to have gotten better with age, but Jack was just a diluted version of the old Jack.

It had only been two days since Macy told her mother of her plans to carry Dori and Kenny's baby, and there she was already bringing in Jack for battle.

They steamrolled into Macy's living room. She was too mad to even worry about her mother noticing she still wasn't the best housekeeper in town. At least things were picked up, and she had vacuumed sometime in the not too distant past.

"I need to get going. I have to pick up Jeremiah," Macy said.

"Don't worry, I already told my mom you'd be late."

"Who do you think you are?" she asked.

"Jeremiah's father, for starters."

"When it's convenient." She noticed then that she'd picked up a throw pillow and was squeezing the imaginary life out of it. She fluffed it before setting it back on the sofa.

"That ain't what this is about. This is about you going around telling people you're going to have a baby for Kenny."

"For Kenny and Dori."

Jack made a snorting sound. "You're crazy."

Her mother just stood behind him with her hand covering her mouth. Macy was so mad, she couldn't even look at her.

"This ain't natural, Macy. It ain't moral," Jack said.

She'd heard enough. "Who are you to talk about morals?"

"I'm moral enough to know God doesn't intend this crap."

"How do you know what God intends?"

Jack's face turned crimson. "I know well enough that God would say don't fuck around where you ain't got no business fucking around."

Her mother cringed. "God wouldn't say that word."

"Oh, she could drive even Him to say it." Jack glared at Macy. "This cheapens your pregnancy with Jeremiah."

"They are in no way connected."

"Are you charging them rent?"

"Don't be absurd."

Jack paced the length of the living room. "And what kind of message do you think this will send to Jeremiah?"

"A message of doing for others. A message of love."

"Even if that wasn't a load of crap, he's not going to understand it."

"He does understand."

"Does? You told him without my permission?" He puffed up like a wild turkey putting on a display.

"Your permission? Whoa, back up, buddy. Since when do I need your permission for anything?"

"Since he's my son."

"Again, when it's convenient." The air tasted stale. She knew her home wasn't the culprit, mediocre housekeeping or not. Jack and her mother were depleting its quality, robbing Macy of the security and solace she should have felt.

"You just want the attention that goes with being pregnant."

"Thank God this time I won't have a husband obsessed with my swollen breasts. That was the only attention you gave me when I was pregnant. Your interest deflated right along with them."

"Hey," her mother said, "don't talk like that. I don't need to know what—"

"You're right. You don't need to know what went on between us. It's not your business. And neither is me being a gestational carrier for Dori and Kenny."

Jack blew air out from between closed lips, making that adolescent noise he'd always been fond of producing when he didn't get his way. "Big words, Macy. But big words won't change you being Kenny's whore."

She reached to slap him, but his reflexes were better than hers, and he grabbed her arm.

"Oh dear," her mother murmured.

Still grasping her arm, Jack spoke through clenched teeth. "Listen up." He squeezed tighter. "If you do this, I'll see you in court, and you can kiss Jeremiah's ass goodbye."

She twice tried pulling away before Jack released her arm. Then she stepped closer, close enough to see the pores of his skin, where he'd obviously just shaved. "Go to hell," she said. "Now I want you both out of my house."

Jack laughed and stomped out the door.

Her mother didn't move. "Macy, I—"

"Please leave."

"Don't be mad at me. I didn't know what else to do."

"You didn't have any right to be talking to Jack about this." Macy started to shake. She hadn't been that angry at, or hurt by, her mother in a long time. Not since the incident in the fifth grade, when her mother got her several pair of dark-tinted sunglasses for Christmas that year.

"Wear these every chance you get," her mama had said. "They'll help hide how unnatural your eyes look." Then she'd shaken her head and muttered, "Where you got those black eyes is beyond me."

Macy had learned two very important lessons that year. First, not to hold eye contact with anyone long enough for them to see how unnatural her eyes were, and second, she'd never be good enough for her mother.

"Macy, don't be mad. Jack has a point about this, you know."

"Look, I need to think about a couple of things. I'll call you in a few days."

"A few days?"

"Mama, please, I'm begging you."

†

Macy walked across Michael's front yard and into Sharon's. She studied the bruise on her arm. She should never have taken a swing at Jack. What was she thinking? Oh, yeah, she was thinking, *Don't mess with the mama bear.* Maybe she needed a different approach with Jack, maybe teeth and claws were not the answer. She could be a killdeer, the noisy bird that creates a ruckus, faking a broken wing to lead predators away from its young. Of course she'd learned that from Emma. Her face grew warm at the thought of Emma and then caught on fire with renewed anger toward Jack.

As she took the three steps up to Sharon's front door, a courthouse scene flashed through her mind. Did Jack really think he could win custody of Jeremiah? Then little Timmy Jones came to mind. Maybe the speculation was right—maybe his father had decided to skirt the legal system and just snatch his son after all. But Jack wouldn't consider that route. Would he?

Macy knocked on Sharon's door. Michael had suggested she talk to Sharon right away. Macy knew Michael was right, but the idea of airing her past to the woman she admired so much, no matter how good a lawyer she was, made Macy uncomfortable.

Sharon opened the door and smiled as she let Macy in. "I'm glad you're letting me help you."

Macy picked at a rough edge on her thumbnail. She didn't want to tell her friend how weak she'd been. She didn't want Sharon to know the things she'd done in the past and what a wreck she was. "Thanks," she murmured.

Sharon led the way into her living room. They sat on the sofa, and Macy told her how she planned to be a gestational carrier for Dorianne and Kenny, and how Jack had taken a sudden interest in their son because of it.

"I need to know anything Jack might use against you in court."

Macy hesitated. "I've slept around a bit." She waited, but lightning did not strike and no look of disgust transformed Sharon's face.

"Anyone Jack knows?"

"I'm not sure. Maybe."

"Okay, we'll just have to be prepared for the possibility of that coming up. Anything else?"

She hesitated again but knew if Sharon was to help her she'd need to know everything. "I kissed a woman once."

Sharon raised an eyebrow. "Does Jack know this woman?"

"No." The idea of him corrupting her friendship with Emma was intolerable.

"Would she have talked to anyone who knows Jack?"

"Absolutely not." Macy couldn't have been surer of that.

"Okay, then that shouldn't be an issue." She smiled. "At least not in a legal sense."

Macy sat back and tried to relax a little but knew she wouldn't until things were fixed.

"Look, I can't imagine Jack having a leg to stand on based solely on your decision to carry the baby. I'll look up some cases and try to see if any precedents have been set."

"Thank you, Sharon." She nodded and Macy went on. "About that woman, Emma…"

Sharon pushed her hair behind her ears. "I won't say anything."

"I know. I just wondered if I ever needed someone to talk to about her if I—if I could talk to you?"

She gave Macy's hand a squeeze. "Yes, of course."

"Thanks again." Macy exhaled long and hard and went on. "You know, every time the four of us got together, I was sure that would be the night you and Jess would see through me. I kept waiting for y'all to see I was some kind of fraud with Michael." She fiddled more with her thumbnail, picking at it until it peeled painfully close to the quick. "Your gaydar didn't go off when you met me?"

"No. But it's interesting that you would use that term." She pulled one leg up under her on the sofa.

"Emma taught me that. She taught me a lot of things." At Sharon's raised eyebrow, Macy quickly added, "About poetry, but mostly about birds. She called herself a bird-geek."

Sharon laughed.

"What?"

"You're blushing." She pulled her other leg under her. "Emma sounds wonderful."

Macy wanted to tell her yes, wonderful *and* unobtainable, but she didn't have the energy to say any more.

†

Cam hung up the phone with Macy and wandered out into Michael's front yard. No matter how much work Cam did, it would always be Michael's yard. But that didn't matter. Macy had invited her to lunch the next day. The invitation inspired confidence, which, although laced with some apprehension, was energizing.

She looked next door. The shift in color where Michael's thick, green lawn bordered Sharon's made Cam feel a little boastful.

Taking a deep breath, Cam walked into Sharon's yard. Halfway to her front door, she registered the crunch of the grass under her feet. Sharon needed to water more.

She rehearsed possible openings to a conversation with Sharon. "Hi, just wanted to say hello." No, too lame. "Hello, just wanted a chance to talk to you." Still no good. Before she could come up with something worthy, she was standing on Sharon's front porch. She knocked before she could chicken out.

Sharon opened the door, and Cam took her in with a glance. Her eyes rested on Sharon's bare feet. They were small and pale, and so vulnerable.

"Hi." Then Cam had a brain fade and couldn't think of anything else to say.

Sharon stared at her.

"I'd like to talk," Cam blurted.

"So talk."

Cam tried to look past her, over her shoulder and into her house. "Can I come in?"

"I'd rather you didn't." Her face showed no emotion.

Cam thought about how Macy had once told her to relax, to give Sharon some time and space. Well, she'd given her plenty of room, and it wasn't getting her anywhere. The time had come to take a chance. "I'd really like to get to know you."

Sharon didn't say anything.

Cam's face grew hot. "Come on, help me out here. I'm trying to—"

"I'm sorry, really, but I'm just not interested." She started to shut the door.

"Why are you so angry?" Cam asked, a little too loudly.

Sharon stopped. "I'm not angry, I'm indifferent."

"And I'm Jess's niece. If you really cared about her, you'd honor her—"

"If I cared about her? Who do you think you are? And don't give me that niece crap, or anything about honor."

"I—"

"She was crushed by how you treated her. She'd done so much for you, just to have you be so hateful and ugly."

"It was complicated. You don't know what it was like for me."

"I know exactly what it was like. I was there, I saw how you turned on her."

"You were there?"

"See? You were so self-absorbed. You still are."

Confusion clung to Cam like ice crystals on the mile-high bridge. When she was nine, Aunt Jess took her to Grandfather Mountain in North Carolina. Seeing the swinging bridge disappear into the icy fog had scared her, and Aunt Jess had to use the promise of hot chocolate to coax her across.

162

"We hid our relationship for years. Anything to spare poor Cam any discomfort. I stayed in the background while you took and took and took from her. Then who was there when she was devastated by having to give you up?"

"Devastated?" Cam fought off an inappropriate smile at the thought of Aunt Jess being emotional over her.

"Who was there when you showed your appreciation by calling her names and telling her you never wanted to see her again? I was. And I was there when she got the news about the cancer. I sat up nights with her when she was vomiting and shitting all over herself. Where were you?"

Sharon's voice rose with each question, and Cam found herself looking around to see if anyone was listening. Shame chased away her confusion, melting into the sweat of embarrassment, stunning her. Unable to say anything else, she whispered, "I'm sorry."

"Of course you are. Now if you'll excuse me, I've got laundry and other grownup things to do." She turned on her heel, went inside, and closed the door behind her.

†

Cam crossed the graveled parking lot of the cabinet shop and saw Macy talking to Kenny between his company truck and Gary's installer's van. Cam slowed down, curious about a sense of familiarity that she hadn't noticed between them before. It made her uneasy, but she didn't know why.

Dusty rocks ground together under Cam's work boots as she approached Macy's car. She watched Macy inspect Kenny's right hand and wondered what she knew about the swollen knuckles Kenny had showed up with that morning.

And Cam wondered what her lunch with Macy was about. Something was up, she just couldn't figure out what.

She hoped Macy wasn't going to tell her that she and Michael were engaged, or anything horrible like that.

When Macy saw Cam, she left Kenny and met her at her car.

"Next time I can drive," Cam said, trying not to sound nervous.

"Yeah, you'll have your truck soon." Macy's smile was beautiful but distracted.

Then it hit Cam. What if this was a delayed reaction to what she'd said and done at the cookout? What if she and Michael had decided Cam needed to be out of their lives?

As they got into Macy's car, Cam reminded herself that Macy hadn't shown any signs of discarding her friendship in the time since Cam's drunken screwup.

"Where would you like to eat?"

"Doesn't matter." And it didn't, since she wasn't convinced she'd even be able to eat.

Macy drummed her fingers against the steering wheel as she pulled her Saturn out of the parking lot. She did that when she was deep in thought. Cam knew her habits and her signs of discomfort. She was almost as nervous as Cam was. Cam could tell by the way she used her index finger to pick at the nail of the thumb she'd stopped tapping against the steering wheel.

Outside her window, a car wash and strip mall and countless restaurants drifted by. Since Washington Road had almost every conceivable dining option, they could have been going anywhere.

Macy steered into the parking lot at a Red Lobster. That was Cam's favorite but not Macy's, so Cam figured things must be serious. She heard a low ring and saw the glow of Macy's cell phone that was tucked into the sun visor.

"Hey, Eileen. Yeah. The lake tomorrow? I don't see why not." She parked the car but left it running. "Oh, Gary's going, too?" She looked at Cam, carefully, as if she'd find an answer scrawled across her face. "You know, I just remembered, we have plans with Michael. Yeah, maybe next time."

Macy turned off the ignition, and Cam wondered if she had any idea how bad of a liar she was. "What are you and Jeremiah doing with Michael?" she asked. Macy didn't answer, and Cam smiled. "I wouldn't let Jeremiah go anywhere with that freak, Gary, either."

Cam made a point of not looking at the death row lobsters when they went in. It was still early, so they were seated right away. Cam slid into the booth and started fidgeting with her menu. She didn't need to open it. She already knew she'd order the fried shrimp. Whether or not she'd be able to eat it was a whole other matter.

When the food came, Cam ate a few bites but mostly just fussed with her food. She wished Macy would say what was on her mind and get it over with.

"You aren't hungry?" Macy asked.

Cam looked at Macy's mostly uneaten broiled flounder. "You aren't either?"

Macy took a deep breath. "There's something I need to tell you."

Cam dunked a shrimp into the cocktail sauce and left it stuck there. "I've known for a while that something's going on."

"I wanted you to hear it from me." She stabbed at her fish with her fork and looked up. "Do you know what a gestational surrogate is?"

That didn't sound even remotely like "pack your bags, loser." Cam looked at her. "What?"

Macy sat back a little. "Do you know how sometimes a woman will carry a baby for someone else?"

"Yeah, but—"

"I'm going to carry a baby for Dorianne and Kenny."

Since Macy was studying Cam's face, Cam was sure her confusion was evident.

"You're going to get pregnant by Kenny?" Cam couldn't wrap her brain around what Macy was saying.

"*In vitro.* An embryo belonging to Dori and Kenny will be implanted, and I'll carry it for them." She took a bite of flounder and another one, real fast, like she was trying to get nourished for Cam's reaction.

"You're going to be pregnant."

Macy held her gaze and nodded. "Yes."

Jealousy jabbed at Cam's breastbone. She attacked her potato with her fork, working the butter in. She didn't want to share Macy with some baby, or have her spending all of her time with Kenny and his wife.

Cam wanted to beg her not to do it, and she wanted to ask how this would affect their relationship. Would it bring Macy and Michael closer? Would it make them start thinking about having kids together?

"Cam?"

She stared into her cocktail sauce and concentrated on the flakes of horseradish. "What did Michael say?"

Macy let out a nervous chuckle and tore a biscuit in half. "Michael didn't say too much about it, at least not near as much as Jack."

"Jack knows about this?"

"Yeah, but that wasn't my doing. My mother dragged him into it."

Ex-husband or not, Cam hated that Jack knew before her. Didn't Cam's friendship with Macy count for more than that? A sense of betrayal rose up from her feet, left behind a tingling in her toes and settled in her gut. The sensation reminded her of being up too high, like on a roller coaster or that damned mile-high bridge in the mountains. "Who else knows?"

"Of course Dori, Kenny, and Michael." She paused and continued when Cam nodded. "Russ, Eileen, Sharon, and Jeremiah."

Cam put down her fork and let it clank, not caring if people stared. "Everyone but me."

"My mother told Jack, and Jack told Russ and Eileen." She sighed. "Then Kenny and Jack had a blow up at Jack's parents' last night. One thing led to another, and Kenny decked him."

A half smile stole onto Macy's lips. It almost made Cam smile, but she was still too irritated. "Sharon knows?" The memory of Sharon's anger the day before did not help the churning in Cam's stomach. She fantasized about free-falling off the mile-high bridge, allowing microscopic ice particles to embed in her on the way down.

"I needed legal advice."

"Legal advice?"

"Jack threatened to take Jeremiah away if I go through with this."

The anger jolting through Cam displaced the self-pity. Unlike her initial jealousy, it was primal. The idea of anyone threatening Macy over anything infuriated her.

"Sharon doesn't think Jack has a chance to take Jeremiah away," Macy said.

Cam took several slow breaths and sat, not moving, thinking about doctor appointments and baby stuff that wouldn't include her. She didn't even know how to act around pregnant people.

"I would appreciate your support in this." When Cam didn't respond, Macy tapped her fork against the edge of her plate. "Please?"

"I wouldn't figure you'd care. You didn't care enough to talk to me about this earlier."

"It's not like it was up for debate."

The words stung.

Cam thought about Sharon, about standing in her doorway. Her small, bare feet looked vulnerable, but nothing about her was. Instead, she was powerful. Sharon was in control because she knew the truth and wasn't afraid to throw it out there. Sharon's words slammed into Cam: you are so self-absorbed.

"I wanted to work out the details before telling you or anyone else, but my mother got hold of it, and it took on a life of its own."

Cam fished the soggy shrimp from the cocktail sauce and stuck it into her mouth. It was several moments before she could make herself swallow it. "This will change everything, won't it?" Yes, she was self-absorbed.

"It won't change the fact that you're like family." When Cam looked up, Macy's black eyes held onto her, not letting her look away. Macy smiled. "I'm serious, Cam."

That was the last thing Cam had expected to hear. And the one thing she needed the most. Tears threatened, so she looked away. Even if they were like family, she still didn't want Macy to see her cry.

A smile snuck onto Cam's face, and she found herself once again on the swinging bridge, a mile up, looking down through a fog of ice crystals. Terrified—yet not.

Chapter Sixteen

Commissioning Couple

Sharon opened the door, smiled real big at Kenny and Dori, and said, "The commissioning couple has arrived."

"Commissioning couple? Wow, Kenny, we have a title now." Dori walked to Macy, who stood behind Sharon, and gave her a quick hug.

Kenny rolled his eyes, not really wanting a title. But he didn't want to not be nice, so he used a teasing voice and said, "Oh, goody."

Kenny rubbed his sore knuckles, the ones that told his cousin Jack he didn't have any say in what they were doing. Jack had told Kenny that his wife being barren wasn't his problem, and Kenny needed to stay the hell away from Macy. Kenny reminded him they weren't married anymore. Then Jack reminded Kenny that he and Macy had a kid together, one that came the normal way. Jack said he didn't want his son around their screwed-up situation. Kenny didn't know what else to say, so he punched Jack.

Macy sipped from a glass of water. Kenny knew if anyone could take on Jack and win, it was her. Especially with Jeremiah involved.

Sharon offered them something to drink—soda, wine, beer, water.

169

"Diet soda, please," Dori said.

Kenny saw that Sharon had some wine. "How 'bout a beer?"

Dori held out her hand. "And I'll take the car keys."

Watching Sharon as she got his beer from the fridge, Kenny couldn't help but think she didn't look like a lesbian.

"Should we get started?" Sharon led them into the dining room, where they settled at a fancy table. "I have to tell you, I haven't found a lot of legal information," she said.

"Isn't this pretty commonplace now?" Macy asked.

"I seen it on Montel," Kenny said. "Or was it Springer?" Dori shrugged.

Sharon said, "Some states have very specific laws governing all aspects of this procedure."

Macy looked at Sharon. "Let me guess. Georgia's not one of them."

Kenny eyed the peanuts and the chips with salsa Sharon had set on the table. He got to wondering if the snacks would be any different if Sharon had gays over instead of them. Then Dori nudged him under the table, so he quit thinking and started paying attention instead.

"So," Sharon said, "here's what I would recommend. We'll draft the contract to follow the guidelines from the 1996 bill. The bill never went anywhere, but it's a good place to start." She looked around, but only Macy nodded.

"What would be in the contract?" Dori asked.

"Here." Sharon slid a typed page across the table to Dori and Kenny. "This is just to give you an idea."

"What's that mean?" Kenny pointed to the first thing on the list.

"The gestational surrogate, Macy, has sole consent with respect to management of the pregnancy."

"Yeah," he said, "but what does it mean?"

"The bottom line is that while the baby is inside Macy's body, Macy calls the shots. She does have to follow this next one, though." Sharon pointed at the second item on the list. "She must get all reasonable medical care before, and during, the pregnancy. But whether or not there's any testing—or even discontinuing—that's up to Macy."

Kenny knew he looked shocked, no way around it.

Macy was quick to speak up. "We just need to be sure that we agree on things before we get started."

"On what things, exactly?" Dori asked.

Sharon said, "Genetic testing for one."

Kenny scooped up a handful of nuts. He was pretty sure he didn't like where things were going. "Testing for what?"

"Health issues," Sharon said.

"We've all had physicals. We're all healthy." Dori looked at Kenny, then at Macy, waiting for full agreement.

"Then there's the issue of multiple pregnancy," Sharon added.

Kenny about choked on a nut. "Multiple?"

"They are going to implant three to five embryos in a cycle—to increase our odds," Macy said.

Dori sighed. "But it also increases our chances of twins or triplets or—"

"That's how them people on Montel have all them babies," Kenny said.

Dori shot him a look before turning back to Sharon. "What you're saying is that if Macy ends up pregnant with triplets, it'll be up to her whether or not to go through with all or any of them?"

"Yes, and you and Kenny will be responsible for them once they're born."

"We can't afford no triplets." Kenny popped a chip into his mouth and washed it down with a swig of beer.

"You can reduce the number," Sharon said.

The color drained from Dori's face as she stared at Sharon. "We would have to pick one and abort the others? How could anyone choose?"

"Your doctor would decide which embryo, or embryos, would have the best chance of making it. He'll talk to all three of you about this when you see him next." She sipped the last of her wine. "There are still some legal things to be worked out."

Kenny looked around at how serious everyone was. He wished someone would lighten things up. Hell, he would, if he had any lightening up left in him. But he didn't. He guessed it'd got buried under that heap of paperwork the lesbian lawyer had piled in front of them. He wasn't knocking her. It was great that she was helping. Good thing Macy had a lawyer friend, lesbian or not.

"Okay," Kenny said. "Give it to us like you're reading Sur-ro-gating for Dummies."

Sharon sat back. "In a nutshell: Macy has rights and responsibilities while she's pregnant with the child or children, but after giving birth, her say is done. Then all the rights and responsibilities are Kenny's and Dori's."

Dori nodded and stared at Kenny until he gave in and nodded, too.

Macy asked Sharon, "What about the birth certificate?"

Sharon leaned forward. "I'm still trying to get a definitive answer, but here's what I have so far." She shuffled through some papers. "The ideal situation will be to get a pre-birth order. That would mean Dori and Kenny's names go directly onto the birth certificate."

"Since we're the genetic parents," Dori said.

"Yes," Sharon replied.

"How hard is it to get that order?" Dori asked.

"I don't know. It'll depend a lot on the judge."

"There's lots you don't know." Kenny's words came out harsher than he'd meant. He didn't want to sound like he didn't want her help. It was just all so much to take in.

"Yeah, there is," Sharon said. "This isn't the easiest subject to get information on. And this state that we live in isn't the most progressive, either."

"I used to like that about Georgia," Kenny said. He finished his beer and wanted to ask for another, but after looking over at Dori, he figured he better not.

"Sharon, what happens if the judge doesn't let us do that?" Dori asked.

"Then the child will be considered born out of wedlock, and the birth certificate will list Kenny and Macy as the parents."

Dori's face was white as caulking.

"But that doesn't change the fact that you two will have your baby," Macy quickly added.

"With you as the legal mother." Dori looked like she was going to cry. Kenny almost couldn't stand it.

"Not necessarily." Sharon ran her finger along the bottom of her empty wineglass. "If that's what happens—and it may very well not be—then we'll petition the court to have your name substituted on the birth certificate. And then we'll also have to petition the court to have the baby legitimated as Kenny's."

Kenny's head spun. "It sounds hard."

"Yeah, but, Kenny, remember that's the worst-case scenario. And I'll be handling all of that. At that point, you two will be busy with your baby."

"Our baby," Dori whispered to Kenny.

"I know this is a lot of information to digest. Let's call it a night, and everyone sleep on it. I'll draw up the contract, and if everyone is still interested—"

"Of course we're still interested." Dori turned to Macy, panic obvious on her face. "Right?"

"Absolutely," Macy answered without hesitation.

Kenny's finger traced a trail along the grout between two squares of cream-colored tile and gathered his chip crumbs along the path. People with kids didn't have tables this nice, or this hard to keep clean.

Everyone turned to Kenny. He looked up and nodded. He thought about how he'd have to go home and look again at their furniture, see if it was okay for a kid. Then he thought about how he could make the crib himself.

"Okay," Sharon said. "I'll draw up the contract. Then you'll be ready to start with the medical side of things."

"I have my psychological evaluation on Tuesday," Macy said.

Kenny didn't even want to think about his own shrink appointment coming up right after Macy's. Besides, he was busy wondering if he should make Dori a rocking chair. He could surprise her with one that matched the crib. Dori would like that. He hadn't done anything that cool for her in a long time.

Chapter Seventeen

Breaking

Macy was building up the courage to go talk to Michael when Dori called.

"Macy, it's me."

"What's wrong?" She sat on the edge of the sofa and leaned forward to slip her shoes on.

"I had to tell you about an article I read. I know the next time we meet with Sharon, I'll freak out about it. It's a case where everyone ends up fighting for the baby, but no one gets it. It says these things often turn into pure chaos."

"I read it. But it was a hired surrogate and anonymous egg donor—a group of people who didn't know one another." Macy tied her shoelaces into double knots and asked, "Where are you?"

"I'm still at work. But I can't concentrate on anything. In the beginning, their intentions were good, too."

She made her way down the hall to the bathroom. "Okay, Dori, let's break it down. First, what are the chances of you and Kenny ever splitting up?"

"That's not an issue."

"And what's the likelihood that I'd run off with your baby?"

"Won't happen," Dori said.

"See? We all want the same thing—for you and Kenny to have a baby. I trust you two to do your part. You trust me to do mine." Peering into the mirror, Macy swiped dark red lipstick across her lips.

Dori lowered her voice. "I'm just all jumbled up inside, even though I know all this legal stuff is just a formality."

"We'll jump through whatever hoops it takes. And we'll get through this. Don't worry."

"My boss is coming. I better go."

"Relax, Dori. It'll be all right."

†

Michael's calendar was stuck to the side of his refrigerator with freebie pharmaceutical magnets pushing the latest drugs for high cholesterol and impotency. His tiny print told him who to see, when, and where. He was the most organized person Macy had ever met.

Macy took a deep breath. This wasn't about closure or having a grand epiphany. There was no ah-ha moment, no sense of long-awaited calm. There was only her admitting she didn't know what she was doing.

"What's wrong?" Michael asked.

Macy hoped that enough time had passed since the cookout that Michael wouldn't think Cam's stunt had anything to do with her decision. She got angry at Cam all over again when she thought about her getting falling-down drunk and professing her love for Macy in front of Michael and everyone else. Then she reminded herself how angst and alcohol could combine to make people do stupid things. She knew that firsthand, in the form of past adventures with strangers.

Michael waved a hand in front of her face. "Macy, hey, where's your head?"

"Sorry."

He put his hand on her back and steered her out of the kitchen and into the living room. "Just say what's on your mind."

Macy felt the tears building. "I've been thinking a lot lately and—" She hesitated and tried to organize her thoughts. "I'm so confused. I just can't do this."

"Do what?"

The tears started down her face, and she couldn't answer him.

"You want out of the surrogacy? It's not too late. Just stop taking the hormones. Dorianne and Kenny will understand."

"No, that's not it." She couldn't look at him, didn't want to see his face if she finally did get the words out.

"Look at me," Michael said.

Macy shook her head.

"Come on, you always do that. You always turn away from me when you should look at me the most."

She did that with everyone. It was easier than letting them see the eyes her mother had disliked so much when she was growing up—the same eyes Macy loved on Jeremiah, but had such a hard time accepting on herself.

Emma had, however, brought her one step closer to appreciating her eyes. *Hematite*. Just having someone care enough to write a poem about them had done wonders for her.

The idea that she was thinking about that, instead of telling Michael about it, drove home how ill-fitted they were to one another. Macy wanted to be with someone she could tell things like that to, or not be with anyone at all.

She looked at Michael. "If you had to write a poem about any part of me, what part would you choose?"

"I'm not a poet."

"Pretend."

"Your heart."

When he said it, Macy wasn't convinced that he was looking that far inside her chest. "Okay, but if you were to write a poem about my eyes, what would you title it?"

He looked at her face, and she had to force herself not to look away. Then he said, "Black."

"Black as…?"

"Macy, just tell me what's going on."

"Humor me, Michael. Black as what?"

He shrugged. "I don't know. Night?"

She knew what she was doing was wrong. It epitomized everything not right about them being together. He was not like Emma, and all the stupid word games in the world wouldn't change him. He would never write a poem about her eyes and call it *Hematite*. He would never be Emma, or any other woman, and either Macy accepted that or she moved on.

"Michael, I think we should stop seeing each other."

"What?" His eyes went wide, and his face drained of color. "Where in the world did that come from? Macy, our relationship is going great. Except for this surrogate thing, it couldn't be better."

"Now the truth comes out."

"Okay, I admit I hate this pregnancy idea, but I love you and I can deal with it." He reached for her hand. "This is just the hormones talking. You'll feel more like yourself in no time."

Macy didn't say anything, just stared at the nondescript beige wall.

"What's this all about?" Michael asked.

She took her hand from him. "My doubts started before the hormones. I think I need to be single for a while."

"You need to be single?"

She knew she owed him the truth; she just couldn't look at him when she said it. "And I think I'm attracted to women."

"Oh God."

Macy did look at him then. He was smiling, but his grin was way too big.

"What?" she asked.

"Isn't this classic? And I can't get pissed at you, can I, with one of my best friends being a lesbian?" He crossed his arms over his chest. "This is bullshit. I can't believe you'd be this lame, to make up something like this because you haven't the guts to be honest with me."

"I'm trying to be honest with you, Michael. I'm sorry. I hoped if I ignored the feelings they'd go away, but they haven't."

"I know damned well this isn't about that. At least give me the consideration of being honest with me."

"I am."

"Is this about Cam?"

"This has nothing to do with Cam. It's about a woman I knew before I met you. But more than that, it's about being honest with myself."

"And all of a sudden you can't be with a man anymore?"

"I just need to concentrate on the surrogacy and getting my feelings sorted out."

"But you know you don't want me?"

"I'm so sorry, Michael."

"You need to leave. Please, just go."

†

Macy didn't want to pull her car out of Michael's driveway and right into Sharon's, so she drove around for thirty minutes before taking Sharon up on her earlier offer of a visit. As Macy pulled up, she was very conscious that Michael's car wasn't next door. But Michael's whereabouts were no longer her business.

Sharon let Macy in and offered her some wine.

"Thanks, but no. I already quit drinking in preparation for the pregnancy." What she didn't say was that she'd already quit a lot of things in preparation.

She followed Sharon into the kitchen.

"You look beat," Sharon said.

"I am."

"Want to talk about it?"

"Not really." Her head was starting to throb, an almost daily occurrence since she'd started taking hormones. But headaches and hot flashes were a small price to pay.

Sharon pulled the refrigerator door open, and the note Macy had read right after Jess died swung toward her: Milk, bread, Pop-Tarts, I love you!

"Michael called about fifteen minutes ago. He told me about you two breaking up." She held up a bottle of water. Macy nodded and Sharon handed it to her.

Macy's eyes returned to the note, and she stared at it until the refrigerator door closed. "Did he say anything else?"

"I didn't push for details. I figured he'd tell me if he wanted me to know." She poured her wine and set the bottle on the immaculate white counter.

"Or that I'd tell you." Macy smiled.

She laughed. "Whenever you're ready."

Macy leaned against the counter and watched the play of light off the coffeepot. She was convinced that Jess had picked out all the red accents and equally sure Sharon would keep them around indefinitely. She took a closer look at Sharon. "How are you doing?"

"Fine."

"Really?"

180

"Well, I still can't sleep in my own bed." She sighed. "Maybe I'm not fine. Maybe I'm almost fine." Her mouth shifted, an exhausted, unconvincing attempt at a smile.

At least Sharon had been brave enough to be with someone one-hundred percent. At least she wasn't a coward. Then it went into perspective. This woman was grieving the loss of her lover, and Macy was jealous. The heat of shame warmed her face.

Sharon said, "I don't want to talk about me."

Macy resisted the urge to reach for her, to take her hand. Instead, she said, "So, let's go ahead and talk about Michael."

"Okay." Sharon perked up a little, making Macy laugh. She led the way into the living room.

"I just decided it was time to be honest, both with him and with myself." Macy sat on the blue leather sofa and let its suppleness cradle her.

Sharon sat at the other end and placed her wine on a sandstone coaster she slid across the coffee table toward her.

"You told him about..." Sharon's voice trailed off, an invitation for Macy to finish for her.

"I told him I needed to do this surrogacy alone. Well, not alone—obviously there's Dori and Kenny, and now you. Have I thanked you lately for all you're doing to help us?"

"You have. And I'm happy for the distraction. But what about Michael?"

"I told him I need to be single right now." She drank some water before going on and tried to get her words organized. "I'd been thinking. Obviously I wouldn't have sex with Michael while I was trying to get pregnant with Dori and Kenny's baby."

Sharon nodded.

"Then I figured it'd be weird to have sex with Michael while I was pregnant with a child that wasn't ours." Macy shrugged. "All I knew was that the prospect of not having sex with him for a prolonged time didn't bother me in the least."

"How much of this did you tell Michael?"

"Only the part about needing to be single." She sighed. "But then there was the part about being attracted to women, too."

"You didn't."

"I did." Macy blew out a breath. "You think maybe I should have kept that part to myself?"

"No, it's good that you were honest." She sipped her wine. "Did he freak?"

"He didn't believe me. He accused me of making it up as an easy way out of our relationship."

Sharon gave an exaggerated grimace.

Macy thought about how, as she was telling Michael it was about a woman she'd known before him, she'd realized it wasn't about Emma specifically. Macy was attracted to women, but she'd also been using that moment with Emma as a crutch.

"So, here we are," Macy said.

"What now?"

"What do you mean?"

Sharon chuckled. "Do I fix you up with my single lesbian friends?"

"No, nothing like that. Hmm, do you have single lesbian friends?"

"Actually, no, I don't. What about Emma?"

"I've known for a while that wasn't going anywhere. I guess I've been using thoughts of her to help me walk away from Michael. You probably think I'm the most screwed-up person ever."

Sharon shook her head. "No. I think it's good that you've got such insight into your motives. Some people never know why they do the things that they do." She got up and went to the kitchen for a refill.

When Sharon returned with her wine, she sat on the floor with her back against an overstuffed chair, facing Macy. The rug under Sharon mapped out the living area with earthy tones in jagged lines and geometric shapes.

Macy studied the muted colors and looked up and caught Sharon giving her a funny look. She realized she was fanning herself. "Hot flash."

Despite the fact that Sharon was still sleeping on the sofa, she seemed more like the woman Macy had first met, before she lost Jess. There was something less distracted about her, less like she was waiting for Jess to come back from running some errand. Macy wondered if having this surrogacy research to engage her really was helping. She couldn't help thinking that Sharon looked good when she was engaged.

Macy was still hoping that Sharon and Cam would spend some time together. Cam wanted more than anything to develop a relationship with Sharon. Both of them having loved Jess, and both being lesbians, they at least had a foundation to build on.

She decided to meddle. "Cam told me she talked to you the other day."

"Yeah." Sharon gave a sheepish grin. "I know I was rough on her. There's just something about her that rubs me the wrong way." Her eyebrows furrowed. "Smugness? No, it's more like she acts entitled."

Macy decided to risk overstepping boundaries. She figured sometimes you had to take risks in friendships. "Can I make an observation?"

Sharon smiled and nodded slowly.

"Is it possible that your dislike for her is about lashing out? That maybe you're taking your anger over losing Jess out on Cam?"

"You sound like my shrink."

"You have a shrink?"

She smiled. "No. But after hearing that, maybe I should."

"Cam's a good kid," Macy said.

"Even after she got drunk and made a pass at you?"

"Okay, maybe not her finest hour."

"I know Jess wanted to mend things with Cam, but I can't do that for them, at least not at this moment."

Macy picked at the label on her water bottle.

"I don't mean to come off as heartless or cold," Sharon said.

"Trust me, no one thinks you're either." Macy was the cold one in the room, the one who didn't know how to have an adult relationship. "I've never been in love."

"You've loved but have never been in love?" Sharon asked.

"Maybe not even that." Macy slid off the sofa onto her own section of rug and pulled her knees up to her chest.

"What about Emma?"

Macy shrugged. "I always loved her as a friend. Then our kiss and her leaving happened so fast, I think it became more about loving the idea of her."

"Don't get caught in that trap. That'll just hinder finding a real love when you're ready for it."

"You think I'm just not ready?"

"If you were, we wouldn't be sitting here talking about it. You'd be off loving someone, and I'd be here alone, getting very drunk." She raised her glass in a toast.

Macy stretched her legs out on the rug, across a circle and a square—terra cotta on mustard, laced with cornflower blue—until her toe touched Sharon. She nudged Sharon's foot. "I'm glad I'm here with you, even if it means having a conversation about how unready I am for love."

Sharon nudged her back. "When you're ready, there will be someone perfect for you, who's also ready, and you'll be so glad everything led you to that moment and that person."

"Is that the wine making you so eloquent?"

"No, it's wisdom making me eloquent. It is the wine adding that slight slur, however." She drained her glass. "Eloquent is a great word. Maybe even my new favorite word."

"My new favorite word is whirligig."

"Ah-ha." Then like a whirligig, Sharon's attention shifted, and she studied the stem of her wineglass, then the point on the rug just to the left of where Macy's leg bisected a yellow circle.

Macy started feeling anxious to get home to her J-man. Jack's threat about taking their son constantly threaded in and out of her mind. He hadn't moved forward with fighting for Jeremiah, though, and Macy felt pretty confident he wouldn't do anything, not with his dad on her side. But she wouldn't know for sure until things were in motion. "I should get home to Jeremiah."

"I'll walk you out." Sharon flipped on the floodlight, illuminating the driveway, Macy's car, and the strip of her side yard that abutted Michael's.

Macy turned to her to say goodnight and thought she'd just give Sharon a little hug or squeeze her hand. She froze, though, when she saw the intense way Sharon was staring at her yard.

"I've been thinking about planting grass in that landscaping area," Sharon said. "It's nice when it's kept up with flowers, but I haven't had the time."

Macy nodded.

"I hate mowing around it—it disrupts the perfect rectangular order of things. Jess used to say it reminded her of a woman, the way it curves."

"I can see that," Macy said.

"I missed a spot," Sharon whispered, leaning her head toward the left. "When Jess was our official grass cutter, I'd redirect her towards any area she missed."

She stared into the yard, perhaps trying to conjure up an image of her lover, or maybe fighting it off, Macy wasn't sure which.

"When the cancer came, I took over the mowing." Sharon laughed. "I got so defensive the first time Jess pointed out a place I'd missed. I thought she was telling me my lawn care was lacking, or maybe my care of her was."

Macy wanted to say something brilliantly compassionate but couldn't think of anything. So she just listened.

"Once when she pointed out a thin ridge of uncut grass that sliced through the yard, I thought maybe it made her think of the angry red scars crisscrossing her body. Or maybe it was just me thinking about them."

Sharon looked at Macy. "When Jess died, there was no one left to point out my sloppy spots." Tears coursed down her face. "And then Cam was here—cutting Michael's grass next door in the same perfect pattern that Jess did. With the same blondish hair, same darker eyebrows and lashes, and the same care. I hate how she cuts Michael's grass right before I get around to ours—I mean mine—making me look inadequate, saying to Jess, 'Look, look how much better blood-relatives are.'"

"Cam doesn't..." But Macy knew nothing she could say would help, so instead of finishing her sentence, she stepped toward her. Sharon moved into her arms. Macy held on, feeling the heat of Sharon's tears on her shoulder. Then

Macy's temperature rose, and she pulled away, ashamed of her body's involuntary reaction.

Chapter Eighteen

Balance

Kenny had been working on the baby's cradle at the shop after hours and on weekends. He wanted it to be a surprise for Dori, so he told her everyone had been working overtime to get some big jobs out the door. He couldn't wait to see the look on her face when she saw the cradle. It was early in the game to be making baby things, but he thought it might bring them good luck if he got it started.

Dori was under the weather from the surgery to retrieve her eggs. Right after that, Kenny's sperm and her eggs went on a date in a dish at the lab. He hoped they were playing nice. Their stuff had to incubate for a few days, and then it'd be Macy's turn for her procedure.

At least Dori didn't have to take any more hormones. It'd been rough for a while. Kenny gave her the shots, and all she gave him was hell, like he couldn't ever do it right. Her mood swings meant that one minute she was bitching, and the next she'd get way too excited about things moving along so good. He sure hoped she wasn't getting her hopes up for nothing. There were still all kinds of things that could go wrong, and then they would have to start all over again.

Kenny had given Dori shots of one thing twice a day for ten days. After that, he had to give her a shot of something else one night at midnight. The needle for the middle of the night shot was huge. That stuff was called hCG. The human-gonadot-something, as Kenny called it, was to mature her eggs. Once upon a time, he never would have guessed he'd know so much about this stuff. Sometimes lately, he even felt sort of smart.

Kenny knew a cradle wasn't especially practical, but it would be like a family heirloom. That was why he wanted it to be perfect. He didn't care if it took a lot more time to make it balanced so it would swing just right. It didn't matter how careful he had to be to keep the temperature and humidity steady to be sure the wood didn't warp. He didn't care about all the extra work, because it was going to be worth it.

Kenny was using maple for the cradle. It was no secret that was his favorite. Maybe it would be his baby's favorite, too. "My baby." He laughed out loud. He was dying to say something like, "Hey, look at this picture of my kid." He just wanted it to hurry up and be there.

For her surgery, they gave Dori drugs so she'd sleep and not remember anything. Then they did something in there with a needle that Kenny didn't want to know the details about. It might not have been as bad as her hysterectomy, but it was bad enough. While they were doing that, Kenny was in a little room on the other side making his deposit. Some guys can't do it in that sort of situation, but he didn't have a problem. He just closed his eyes and thought about Dori doing him in the old Maverick. With memories like that, who needed girly magazines?

Kenny pulled out several maple planks and put them on the workbench. He was going to match the grain and plane them to dimension, to be sure the opposing parts were exactly the same. For the cradle to move right and be safe, it had to be exact. Balanced. He felt one of those metaphors sneaking up on him, but he fought it off with a big whiff of the wood.

He knew Jack had never done anything like that for Jeremiah. Kenny was gonna love being one up on his cousin. Hell, in the being there for his baby department, Kenny was gonna be a bunch up on the jerk.

Kenny thought he heard something at the back door. It was Dori. Damn it, that girl just had surgery and sure as hell isn't supposed to be driving.

Dori walked in and started looking around. She was clutching something in her hand. "Where's everyone else?" she demanded.

"Ah, they, ah..." He saw his pay stub in her hand and knew he was busted.

"You lied to me? You aren't allowed to lie to me, Kenny Brewer."

The words roared out of her, and he could only think maybe those hormones weren't all out of her yet after all. "Sorry," he said.

"Sorry? Did you think I wouldn't notice there's no overtime on your check? What the hell have you been up to?" She started nosing around, craning her neck to look toward the break room.

Kenny wanted to tell her what he'd been up to was bending over backward so far that he thought he'd either snap in two or stay bent like a sapling after one of those unexpected ice storms. He wanted to remind her that he'd been as happy as a pig in shit until she started this baby crap. What he didn't want to tell her though, was now that she'd got this thing started, all he ever thought about was having a kid. And he was scared shitless that if something went wrong, he couldn't go back to being happy like they were before.

Kenny didn't say any of that. Instead, he said, "Well screw me for wanting to surprise you with something nice. I don't know why I even bother."

"A surprise?" She ran her hand along one piece of the maple, and he had to keep himself from being defensive and pulling it away from her. "What are you making?" she asked.

He kicked at a scrap of oak. "A cradle."

"Oh, Kenny."

He took a big breath. "I hadn't thought about there being no overtime on my check. You're probably scared to death that our kid's gonna be stupid just like me, huh?"

"You're not stupid."

"Any idiot would have known," he said.

"Yeah, but you're not just any idiot. You're my sweet, handsome, loveable idiot." She saw the blueprints for the cradle and picked them up. "I love it."

"Look here." He pointed to the base. "The trestle design will make it real safe."

She smiled and glanced around. "Is there anything else?"

He thought about the rocking chair he'd decided not to make. Would she always expect more from him than he could actually deliver? He forced a smile. "Maybe."

†

Macy carried J-man into his room and tucked him into bed with a kiss and a whispered goodnight. He'd drifted off on the sofa after Sharon helped him draw his dog, Bella, and a horse he'd named Buster. He was sound asleep, and Macy knew nothing short of a tornado would wake him once he was out.

Sharon had come over to help distract Macy from worrying about her procedure the next day. When Sharon had asked if she was excited, Macy reminded her that the stats weren't in favor of the embryo implant taking the first time.

Macy had been giddy waiting for her to arrive, and she found herself unable to keep her mind and eyes off Sharon once she did get there. Macy couldn't deny that she'd been thinking about Sharon more and more.

She paused in the hallway and watched Sharon pick up a framed photo from the bookshelf. It was Macy's favorite one, the one of her holding Jeremiah just after he was born. Sharon ran her finger along the edge of the frame, similar to the way she often outlined the base of her wineglass.

Her glass stood almost empty on the coffee table. Macy had bought a bottle of Sharon's favorite red wine, but she'd only had one glass. She told Macy she was on self-imposed restriction, limiting what she would allow herself each night.

Sharon spoke without looking away from the picture. "You were such a beautiful new mother."

"Ah, past tense?" Macy's audacity surprised even herself.

Sharon gave Macy a puzzled look from over her shoulder. "You know what I mean." She set the picture down and glanced at the others nestled between paperback mysteries and a field guide to regional birds.

Next she picked up the picture of Macy sitting under the overpass by the canal. Surrounded by graffiti, Macy sat with her arms around her knees, which she'd drawn up to her chest.

Macy walked across the living room and looked over Sharon's shoulder at the picture. Her black eyes gazed back, and she saw herself, saw the content of the photo, not the photographer. Emma flitted through her thoughts but did not take root.

Sharon still wasn't looking at her. "When you told me about Grace offering to be Dori's surrogate after all, you didn't give me details about Dori turning her down."

Earlier, Macy had changed the subject because her emotions had threatened to get the better of her. "It seems Grace thought there was an income involved in the deal."

"Ah-ha."

"But the best part was when Grace said she thought Dori wanted family to carry her baby." Macy took a deep breath, determined to keep her voice steady. "And Dori said, 'Macy is family.'"

Sharon turned and took Macy's hand. The gesture was meant to comfort her, but it did much more than that. Sharon must have sensed it, because she quickly let go and returned her hand to the picture.

Macy was left staring at Sharon's back and arms. Her heart was pounding its way to her throat. Blood surged through her and pooled just under her skin and beneath her nipples. Her hormones caught a ride with the current. They raged.

Desire had crept up on Macy. She couldn't remember exactly when her thoughts had crossed the line from pure admiration to something less cerebral. Sometime after the surrogate contract and breaking up with Michael, Macy had started looking for any excuse to see Sharon. Shared glances and accidental touches sparked responses from more than one body part.

Urgency coursed through Macy. Each heartbeat, marking time, reminded her that her body would soon not be totally hers. If all went well the next day, she would share herself with a part of Dori and Kenny; she would be host and guardian to a precious life.

But for this moment, this blood, this skin, this ache was hers.

Sharon put down the photo and smiled. "Hot flash?"

"What?"

"You're bright red," she said.

"Oh." Oh, indeed.

Macy wanted her so much. She wanted to feel her inside her. She wanted to taste her. To be on the receiving end of those fingers, that mouth...

"Are you okay?" Sharon asked.

"Yes." The word came out breathy, and Macy was immediately embarrassed. Had she really presumed Sharon would be with someone like her? After having such a romance with Jess, why would she settle?

"Macy, you don't look well."

Blood, like minutes, passed through her. One pulse at a time.

Macy could smell the fruitiness of Sharon's earlier glass of wine. She was glad that Sharon had decided to cut back on drinking, though not necessarily that night. She blurted out, "Have you ever wanted someone to the point that you felt you'd burst?"

Sharon's eyebrow cocked.

"Of course you have. With Jess."

She nodded.

Her entire life, Macy had been a fraud about anything that even resembled passion. Worse than faking an orgasm, she'd faked intimacy—with Jack, Michael, even Emma to a large degree. She'd never wanted anyone in such a complete, all-consuming way. And in wanting Sharon like that, she didn't know how to react, or where to place the blame. Was it hormones? Karma?

"And now?" Macy asked.

"Now I remember all that I can without getting to the point of losing it."

"Losing it?"

194

"Control. Sometimes remembering can be physically painful. Sometimes memories aren't enough, or they're too much."

"Do you fantasize about Jess?" Macy asked.

"Oh, yeah. My biggest fantasy is to have the chance to be with her one last time, to be over-the-top passionate like we were before she got sick."

Macy leaned against the wall for some much-needed support. Her lower back, just above her tail bone, rested against the chair railing.

"Let me help," Macy said. "Let me be your one last time, your over-the-top."

"What?" Sharon looked only half-there, half-aware.

Macy put her hands on Sharon's hips and guided her closer. "Let me be Jess." She brought Sharon's hand to her breast. Surely she could feel how much Jess wanted her, needed her?

"Jess is gone." Sharon lowered her hand.

Macy pulled Sharon against her. Sharon closed her eyes, and Macy felt encouraged enough to take the risk. She lightly touched her mouth to Sharon's and sucked her top lip into her mouth. "One last time," she whispered. "You and Jess…"

With her hands entangled in Macy's hair, Sharon pulled her closer. Her tongue found Macy's and engulfed her with tingling and need.

With both hands, Sharon tugged at Macy's waistband, clawing until the silver disk slipped from its buttonhole. She slid her hand inside Macy's jeans, pushed aside her damp panties, and found where her desire had pooled.

Macy's breath rushed out. She clutched the chair railing, its bottom edge digging into her fingertips.

"Jess," Sharon whispered.

"Yes, yes."

Her fingers sank into Macy, and Macy melted into the wall.

Then Sharon stopped. "Oh God."

She started to pull out of Macy, but Macy grabbed her hand, holding it to her, begging her without words to take control from her, for her.

"We can't do this," Sharon said. "This isn't right. Jess is gone and—"

"Sharon, I'm sorry, but please don't stop."

"*You* want this?" The question was asked into Macy's neck. Her breath was hot, and Macy's neck was wet with her sweat, or Sharon's tears, or both. "*You* want this?" Sharon repeated.

"I want this. I need this."

"Let go."

Macy released her grip on Sharon's hand and braced herself for the emptiness Sharon would leave behind when she pulled her fingers out.

Sharon pushed deeper inside, causing Macy to whimper. "You're sure?" she asked, her voice ragged.

"Yes," Macy begged.

Sharon whispered Macy's name, and Macy knew it was no longer a game. Sharon's mouth found hers, and her tongue echoed the searching, probing movements of her fingers.

Macy reached for the button on Sharon's jeans, but as Sharon took Macy's hand and held it hostage against the wall, Macy understood.

Sharon's fingers twisted inside, and her hand flattened against Macy, smearing her with wetness, scrambling her thoughts, buckling her knees. She came hard against the palm of Sharon's hand and relished that precious balance between control and the lack of it.

Macy would have sunk to the floor had Sharon's body not held her up. The contrast between the wall at her back and the softness of Sharon pinning her there was almost more than Macy could take.

Sharon stood very still and pressed her body against Macy's until Macy stopped shaking. Then Sharon whispered, "This can't happen again."

Macy could think of so many reasons why Sharon wouldn't want them to be sexual again. A stronger woman might have asked why, but all Macy could do was choke out, "Okay."

Chapter Nineteen

Implant

The paper liner crinkled under Macy. When she put her feet in the cold stirrups, her thighs, buttocks, and lower back tightened. The memory of her muscles contracting the night before with Sharon sent a wave of heat sweeping over Macy's skin.

She steadied her breathing.

Dr. Benson draped a sheet over her legs. Macy crossed her arms just under her breasts, and thoughts of Sharon crept in. Nothing could have prepared her for the longing she felt as Sharon sank deeper into her, or for the surge of feeling, physical and emotional, at the precise moment when—

But Macy was familiar with the consequences of crossing that line in a friendship. This wasn't the first time she'd felt guilt festering in her gut, or the aftershock of regret threatening to choke her.

"Slide down farther," Dr. Benson said.

She did as she was told, and the sound of the paper became a hissing voice. Why can't you leave things alone? First Emma, now Sharon. And what about Dorianne? Why are you really doing this for her?

Macy squeezed her eyes shut. *Leave me alone*, she pleaded. *Just leave me alone.*

Then she made a choice. No negative thoughts. She only wanted positive energy during the implant. She stared at the white-tiled ceiling and wondered what Jeremiah was doing at that moment. Her precious, sweet J-man, the one person she could trust not to pass judgment on her. She imagined holding him, smelling the sun in his hair.

"When you get home today, you'll need to take it easy, but you'll be able to resume your normal activities in three to four days." Dr. Benson's voice drifted from behind the tent made by the stark, white sheet draped across Macy's knees.

She closed her eyes again.

"I'm now inserting the catheter," he said.

Cramps wracked her abdomen, and she arched up off the table a couple of inches. She took a deep breath and lay back flat.

"This procedure sends some patients through the roof. Others barely know I'm there."

Macy was well aware of Dr. Benson's presence. She took several more deep breaths. Once the surprise of the unexpected cramping wore off, she felt better. It wasn't much worse than the bad menstrual cramps she had when she was younger, before having Jeremiah.

"The uterus is a funny thing," said Dr. Benson, almost to himself. He raised his voice a little and added, "It doesn't like having something in it, so it rebels. Seems counter to—"

His words were lost as Macy tensed and gripped the side of the padded table. She squeezed her eyes shut until the wave of pain subsided.

"We'll use progesterone to continue building the uterine wall, and you'll have a pregnancy test in two weeks."

Macy whispered, "Okay," but she wasn't paying attention. She was thinking that when it was all over, she'd take Jeremiah somewhere special. Maybe the beach. Or to pan for gold up in the mountains. She knew he'd like that.

"All done," Dr. Benson said. He left the room, but the nurse stayed behind.

Bearing down on her hands for leverage, Macy slid back. *Why?* The voice started again, before she could even get out of the gown and into her clothes. *Why are you doing this?*

†

Just as she'd done the day before, Cam shut the door behind her and watched as Jeremiah ran to his mother on the sofa. Cam tensed for a moment, hoping he wouldn't jar Macy too badly with his enthusiasm to be home.

"Hey, big guy," Macy said, her voice a half whisper.

"Cam let me pick the radio station in her truck again."

"She did?"

Macy smiled at her, and Cam's heart jumped.

Jeremiah knelt beside his mother. "Are you pregnant yet?"

"I don't know, sweetie." She looked at Cam. "You come bearing gifts. I guess Jeremiah ate at Eileen's?"

"Yeah," Cam said. "Eileen sent dinner again. She made me a plate, too." She lifted the foil covered plates for Macy to get a better look.

Macy scooted to one end of the sofa, and Jeremiah quickly jumped up beside her.

"Homework?" she asked him.

"Just to practice my letters."

"Let's go ahead and start working on that." She nodded toward Jeremiah's backpack, a bumpy lump of canvas by the door.

"I'll heat this up a little." Cam walked toward the kitchen.

"Thanks. For everything," Macy said.

Cam grinned. It was her pleasure to help out. Really.

When she took the warm plate to her, Macy swung her legs around and sat up.

Cam said, "Eileen made me promise to make sure you ate. She said to at least eat the meat, that you need the iron and protein and crap."

"Crap," Jeremiah sang out.

Cam twisted her mouth, showing her distaste over slipping with her language in front of Jeremiah.

"Mama can't eat crap," he said, giggling.

"That's enough." Macy pushed the food around on her plate. "Show me how you write your name."

He sighed. "My name is so long. My friend Joe finishes his work the fastest."

"Well, look at all the extra practice you're getting. Your letters will be fantastic by the end of the school year." She ruffled his hair.

Cam noted how tired Macy looked. And it was pretty obvious that she'd been crying. She watched Macy push her green beans to the side and fought the urge to feed her herself.

Cam wasn't going to be shy about her own dinner. She was starving, and Eileen Stokes was a great cook. She stuck a piece of steak in her mouth and chewed.

Jeremiah finished spelling out his name, first and last, and leaned closer to his mother. "Now are you pregnant?"

Macy smiled. "We won't know for another week or so, baby."

"When you're pregnant, then have it, I won't be the baby. The new one will be. And I'll always be older. And the boss."

"Write my name."

"M-a-m-a," he said, giggling.

She laughed. "My real name."

He giggled some more. "I'll write your name and our address. Then I'm gonna write Cam's name." He looked thoughtful. "What's your last name?"

"Webber."

"That's going to be hard to write."

"You can handle it." Cam winked at him.

Jeremiah whipped out a new piece of paper and started writing oversized, lopsided names. After doing his mom's and Cam's, he wrote "Uncle Kenny" and "Aunt Dori."

Cam glanced from Jeremiah to Macy and saw that she was putting a piece of steak in her mouth. She relaxed a little.

"More, Mama?"

"Yeah, baby," Macy answered and ate a forkful of green beans.

Cam figured if she could keep Jeremiah writing, Macy would stay distracted and eat most of her dinner. "What other names?" Cam asked.

"Emma," Jeremiah said. He slowly wrote the name Cam was unfamiliar with.

"Good," Macy said. "Who else?"

Jeremiah leaned against her side. "Help me with Sharon's name."

She put her fork down and pushed the plate away. "Why don't you let Cam help you with that one?" She swung her legs around and twisted into a lying position.

Cam watched Jeremiah form the letters and showed him how he'd written the "N" backward. She glanced in Macy's direction. Macy had buried her face into her pillow and shifted toward the wall.

Jeremiah practiced writing his numbers while Cam cleared the plates. She covered Macy's leftovers and set them in the fridge, hoping she'd get hungry later. She washed her plate and both forks and knives. As Cam walked back into the living room, she clapped her hands together and said, "Hey, buddy, it's getting late."

"I can take a bath all by myself," Jeremiah said.

Cam looked at Macy, who looked up from the pillow and nodded.

"Okay." Cam sat down on the chair. "Shout if you need me." She picked up a book and opened it to the middle. Big, bold letters jumped out at her. STRETCH MARKS. She closed the book and looked at Macy. She was again facing into her pillow. Cam would have done anything to make her feel more like her old self.

She looked into the index of the book. Depression. She flipped to the section on depression during pregnancy. Then she remembered the brochure Macy had brought home from Dr. Benson's. She snooped around in the kitchen until she found it on the counter by the phone.

Jeremiah came barreling in from the bathroom, hair damp around the edges, toothpaste smeared on his chin.

"Tell Cam thanks for the ride home from your Grandma's."

"Thank you. Will you pick me up tomorrow, too?"

She looked at Macy and then said, "Yep."

Before Cam left, she carefully spread open the brochure and placed it at the end of the coffee table, closest to Macy's head.

Chapter Twenty

Leveling the Playing Field

The paper under Macy sounded exactly as it had two weeks earlier when she'd had the embryo implanted. It was even tinged with the hiss of the voice, the one obviously trying to drive her crazy. *Why are you doing this?* it demanded.

"You okay?" Dori asked.

"Yeah. Thanks for coming in with me today." It was nice to have Dori there while she waited. Macy hoped it would keep her from obsessing over Sharon. And maybe even quiet the accusing voice in the back of her mind.

Macy realized Dori was talking, but the words hadn't registered. "I'm sorry, what did you say?"

"Kenny was so hyped up this morning. He's probably driving everyone at the shop crazy."

"I'm sure he is. You told him we'd call as soon as we were done, right?"

"Yeah."

Dr. Benson came into the small room wearing shiny black shoes, brown slacks, and a white lab coat over a gray button-down. Macy hoped his fertilizing abilities were better than his fashion sense. She squelched the negative thoughts. Michael had set them up with Dr. Benson, and she was glad the specialist hadn't backed out after she and Michael broke up.

They were given the rundown again.

"If the pregnancy test is positive," Dr. Benson said, "I'll do an ultrasound in two weeks to confirm and to count heartbeats. If the test is negative, you will have to decide when to start the process again."

Macy had been watching Dori's face as the doctor was speaking. She felt Dori's pain when she winced at the mention of starting over. Macy wanted to assure her it wouldn't be necessary. J-man had kissed her belly before she left for her appointment, telling her it was for luck. At that moment, Macy knew she couldn't lose.

"I'll be back with a nurse, shortly, to examine Macy and draw blood." When there were no questions or comments, he went out and left them alone.

Dori twisted the ring on her finger. "Macy, can I ask you something?"

"Sure."

"The other day something popped into my head. Remember at the bookstore when you said you once liked me too much?"

Macy studied the waffled texture of her paper gown.

"I feel stupid for just now catching on to what you meant," Dori said.

Macy held her breath.

"I need to be sure that you're clear the comics were just a game for me—practice even," Dori said.

"I know."

"It was never real for me."

"I know," Macy repeated. She smoothed the gown over her legs. "This is a weird time and place to be having this conversation."

"Yeah, it is, but I need to understand some things."

Macy pulled at the bottom of her gown. "Dori, I'm feeling a little vulnerable here."

"Sorry." Dori stood and walked toward the door. Staring at a poster of fetal development hanging on the wall, she went on. "I've felt vulnerable for years. And now with me needing help with something this natural and basic, well— that's real vulnerability."

Dori turned, and Macy saw no malice on her face. "Okay," Macy said, "maybe the time and place is a karmic leveling of the playing field." Dori paced the length of the room a few times, and Macy asked, "What do you want to know?"

"Are you a lesbian?"

Macy felt the blush creep from her face to her neck as the memory of Sharon inside her came crashing back over her, as it had so many times the past two weeks. "Yes." The word came out much weaker than she'd intended.

"Do you still like me that way?"

"No." This time Macy's response came out much stronger than she'd wanted. She didn't want to sound like she was protesting too much, or like she was suggesting that Dori shouldn't flatter herself.

But to Dori, it was apparently just a word. "Okay." She walked back to her chair.

Macy thought about how she'd kept the secret of their romantic comics—*Love Me,* Volumes 1 through 4, and *Real Romance,* aka Stony-Faced Sea Urchin. She hadn't told Emma, or Sharon, or anyone else about them. She thought about how she had been denying her feelings for so long and about overcompensating by sleeping with men she didn't have any feelings for. She'd cheated herself, by not having the courage to be with Emma and by not having what it took for Sharon to want to be with her again. Macy didn't want to be cheated out of having this baby for Dori, and Kenny also, but she had to know Dori still wanted it, after learning the truth about her.

"Do you want to change your mind?" Macy asked. Anger stabbed at her chest. "Because if you do, two weeks ago would have been the time to say so, not now."

"Change my mind? About this?" She gestured around the room with her hands.

"Yeah, about me carrying your baby."

"No." She sniffled. "No way."

"What is it, Dori?"

She started crying. "This is the sweetest thing anyone's ever done for me."

Macy cried, too. Had Dori rejected her—on top of Sharon's declaration that they'd never be intimate again—it would have been too much for her to bear.

Macy had cried a lot right after the implant. Curled into a fetal position, she'd lie around wishing Sharon would call and say she wanted to come over. She had called several times but only to check on how Macy was doing, not to ask to see her.

Cam had been great, coming over to Macy's house in the evening after work. Since Kenny had helped her find an inexpensive pickup truck, she wasn't relying on other people for transportation anymore. Macy had become the one relying on her. And of course Jeremiah was quite the man of the house. He brought her drinks and snacks and even read to her from his Spider-Man comics.

While Macy had been camped on the sofa crying, Cam left a brochure on the coffee table. It was opened to the section about it being normal for the patient to be depressed following the implant phase of the cycle. That reminder got Macy's butt off the sofa and back to being J-man's mama and Cam's friend.

When she and Dori both jumped at the knock on the door, Macy guessed Dori had been in her own little world also.

The doctor came in with a nurse. "Are you ready?" he asked Macy. When she nodded, he turned to Dori. "You can wait outside, Mrs. Brewer. The nurse will let you know when we're finished."

She glanced at Macy, and Macy nodded. Dori gave her a quick smile and left the room.

Macy knew the routine, so she scooted down when the doctor pulled up his stool.

The voice returned. *Selfish*, it hissed.

More and more, Macy worried if her motivation to have the baby was as altruistic as she'd made it out to be. Maybe it was an issue of control, like the voice in her head claimed. She shut the voice out. She would not ruin this precious time in all of their lives by questioning herself.

"Slide down a little farther," Dr. Benson said.

During the exam, Macy mentally left the room to be with her son. J-man had a thing for the sound of the water at the Savannah River rapids. She took him along the path between the canal and river a few times when he was a baby. This was the other end of the path from where they went with Emma. One day, three cyclists rode by, rowdy and loud, and J-man started crying. Macy tried everything to hush him. Nothing helped, not rocking, not even playing his favorite game, kissy-face. Finally she held him with his back against her chest, looking out over the water. He stopped crying and started giggling. Every time she tried to turn away to leave, he'd start crying again. She held him facing the white-laced water until her arms and legs ached and J-man breathed with the rhythm of sleep.

Dr. Benson's voice ripped her away from the rushing water. "Everything looks good. Now we'll take some blood. How do you feel?"

"Fine," she answered.

He motioned for the nurse, who helped Macy sit up. Then the nurse came at her with a needle, and Macy did what she knew would divert her attention. She closed her eyes and relived the moment when J-man gave her belly the good luck kiss. It just had to have worked.

†

"You swore you'd never drive a station wagon, Kenny." Dori turned away from the computer screen and looked at him.

"Did not."

"Yes, you did." She swirled the mouse around on the table. She did that a lot, and Kenny hated it. The arrow moving fast on the screen like that made him seasick.

He looked away from the computer. "What, when I was twelve?"

"Seventeen, actually."

"That was a long time ago. That was before we had a bun in the oven. Well, a bun in Macy's oven. Besides, now they ain't station wagons, they're sport wagons."

"Oh, you want a sport wagon. Why didn't you just say so?"

"You ain't acting so sick now," Kenny said.

"I feel better."

"Better enough to be a smart-ass," he teased.

"Yeah, but you love me." She paused. "Now would be a good time to tell me that you do."

"I do what?"

She punched his arm.

"Okay, okay, I love you." Kenny was relieved to see she wasn't as pale as before. "You are feeling better."

"Yeah." She sighed. "I hated missing Macy's appointment today, but with the morning sickness, I just wasn't up to it."

Kenny had been putting up with that nonsense for four long months. "Dori."

"Don't look at me like I'm crazy. If a man can have sympathy symptoms, why can't I?"

The phone rang. They looked at each other, and Dori picked it up.

"Macy." She paused and nodded a few times. "Yeah. Yeah, I'm feeling better, how about you? Good." Dori was quiet for another few moments. "Oh? Wow. Yeah, he's right here. Macy, thanks."

When she hung up the phone, she had a dreamy look on her face. It was even spacier than her after-sex look.

"So, what did she say?" Kenny asked.

"Two distinct heartbeats."

"In English, Dori."

"Twins."

Kenny sat down. Actually, more like fell down. "Twins." The thought flashed through his mind: *twice the cost, twice the worries.* But all he did was repeat, "Twins."

"Are you okay?" Dori asked.

"Yeah. Hell, yeah." He smiled a big, goofy grin.

"I guess that settles it." She rolled her chair closer to the computer. "We go with the sport wagon."

She clicked the mouse a few times, and the next thing Kenny knew, there was a picture of one on the screen.

"Can we get one with a CD player?" he asked.

"Oh no." Her eyes got wider.

Hell, it was just a CD player. "What?"

210

"I've read somewhere that twins sometimes means double the morning sickness."

Here we go again. But then he started to feel a little queasy himself. It was probably just all the excitement. To settle his stomach, he thought about the materials he would need to make the second cradle. Thankfully, the flathead wood screws, cross dowels, and Roto hinges helped him relax some.

†

Kenny and Dori dropped Macy off at her house and were trying to decide where to eat lunch before they both had to get back to work. Dori was driving. She'd been feeling better. In the two weeks since they had learned Macy was carrying twins, Dori's morning sickness had disappeared right along with Macy's.

The sun reflected off the slick surface of the sonogram picture. Kenny stared into the black and white murkiness, not seeing what Dr. Benson saw. But it was good enough for him that the doc saw it clearly. One boy, one girl—their babies.

Dori glanced over at him. "Macy's already four-and-a-half months along. We need to talk about names."

"It ain't too soon for that?" He knew it wasn't. He'd been thinking about names ever since this started. "You know we're never gonna agree on no names."

"We can't even agree on Taco Bell or KFC," Dori said. She reached over and touched the edge of the picture.

"We could write some ideas on scraps of paper and draw them out of a hat."

"That's kind of lame. No offense." She smiled.

Kenny shrugged. "Then you name one, and I'll name the other."

"Really?"

"Why not?" Kenny pivoted in his seat to face her.

"Can I name the girl?"

"If you want." He gave a silent thanks that he wasn't gonna have to fight to name the boy. "This could be pretty cool."

"Promise—no naming the baby after race car drivers or baseball players."

He faced forward again, crossed his arms over his chest, and pretended to be mad. "Damn, I had my heart set on Earnhardt Brewer."

"Kenny."

He laughed. "Relax. I done gave it lots of thought already."

"Really?"

"Sure. I've known for weeks what our son should be named."

Dori took a left onto Washington Road. "Well, tell me."

"You tell me yours first."

"I'm not sure yet. Come on, what's the boy's name?"

"Mason Kenneth Brewer." He held his breath.

"Oh God, I love that." Dori's tears welled up. She slapped her hand against the steering wheel. "I can't match that."

"You ain't got to match nothing, just come up with a girl name you like." He patted her leg. "We got time, you know. Ain't no hurry."

"Not that much time. Besides, I want to have names to call them both when we start talking to them."

"What?" he asked, pretty sure he didn't really want to know.

"Macy and I discussed it, and we think it's time you and I started talking to the babies."

"You're kidding, right?"

She shot him a hell-no-I'm-not-kidding look from the corner of her eye.

"You mean we're going to talk to Macy's stomach?"

"Yeah. We can read to them, tell them stories, tell them how much we love them."

"I ain't talking to Macy's stomach." He said it slowly, so she'd know he meant it.

"Fine. But don't come crying to me when they're born not knowing your voice."

"You really are serious."

"I am." She flicked on the turn signal.

"And Macy don't think that'll be weird?"

"No." Dori glanced at him. "I meant to tell you—Grace called again yesterday. I actually feel sorry for her."

"She don't care nothing about us. She just saw a way to make a buck. I wish I could buy her for what she's worth, and sell her for what she thinks she's worth."

Dori didn't say anything to that. She just kept on driving until she pulled into Taco Bell. "I think I've decided."

Kenny nodded toward the big bell. "Good. I could eat a Burrito Supreme, or two."

"No, I mean I've decided on a girl name."

"Oh?" It seemed to him she'd been giving it some thought over the last few weeks, too.

"Mya Elizabeth Brewer."

"Hmm. I like that just fine." *Mason and Mya.*

"I had a doll named Mya when I was a little girl. She had this beautiful emerald green dress that matched her eyes. I adored that doll."

Kenny nodded.

"Elizabeth is Macy's middle name," Dori said.

As they crossed the parking lot, Kenny looked back at the old Maverick. He tried to imagine a green sport wagon with two car seats in the back.

Dori pulled free from his grasp, and he realized he'd been squeezing her hand.

"It's gonna be fine, Kenny."

She'd only half read his mind. If she'd read it all, she would have seen that as much as he wanted that to be true, he knew from the boiling in his gut that it might not be

Part Five

Survival

Chapter Twenty-One

Overburden

Jack walked in, chalk-white. When his parents called Macy, searching for Jeremiah, she thought Jack had pulled a sick prank. Looking at him, she knew he wasn't the one who'd taken Jeremiah from Russ and Eileen's.

"Oh, God," Macy said and sobbed as Jack crossed the living room.

"What have you done?" Jack asked.

Russ stepped between them. "Come talk to me, son." It wasn't a request. The two men went into Macy's kitchen and spoke without looking at one another.

Macy couldn't watch. She felt the heat of a thousand accusations, spoken and unspoken. She was probably guilty of them all, deserving of their collective burn.

Her mother stood beside her. It was the first time she'd seen her mother—or Jack—in the months since she'd started the surrogacy. "Macy, if God—"

"Don't you say it, Mama. Don't you say a word about God or vengeance or messing around with His plan."

Macy was doing a thorough job of beating herself up; she didn't need any help. Her mother had taught her well.

Eileen pushed a mug of hot tea into Macy's hand. "Here, take this."

She didn't need lectures or tea. What she needed was for someone to teach her how to breathe, to retrain her heart and lungs.

The police detective approached from her right, with Jack in tow. "Mrs. Stokes, we'd like to talk to you now."

Dorianne was on the other side of them, clutching her list of all the gas stations and truck stops off I-20. Dori had faxed and emailed flyers to all the numbers with a recent photo of Jeremiah and the heading, "Have you seen me?"

Dori had already researched what to do if one of her children was kidnapped. She'd follow the structure of the Amber Alert, but old school, without the delay of the proper agency deeming it necessary. Dori was good at stuff like that. She was going to be a great mother.

"Macy." It was Russ talking to her. "This is Detective Durell. He wants to ask you and Jack some questions."

She nodded and put the tea on the coffee table, briefly resting it on J-man's Spider-Man comic before she picked up the cup and used a coaster instead. She let her hand linger a moment on the glossy cover of the comic.

Detective Durell sat across from her and Jack. It was the first time in a long while that they'd sat on the same piece of furniture at the same time. She hated him. She hated herself.

Russ stood behind the detective, his massive arms across his chest.

"Tell me about Jeremiah's friends," Durell said.

Macy named his closest ones: Billy, Joey, Ricky, Connor. "I've already talked to all the parents."

"Has Jeremiah been behaving lately, or has he started acting out, acting differently?" Durell asked.

"No," Macy said. "Everything has been normal, great."

"Do you have anything to add?" Durell asked Jack, who shook his head.

"Has he ever run away before?"

"No, never," Macy answered without hesitation.

The detective looked at Jack. "What kind of things is he interested in?"

Jack looked at Macy and glanced toward his father.

"Video games, sports, typical boy stuff," Macy said. "He likes to read and watch TV, especially Animal Planet. He loves the funny animal videos. And the crocodile specials. During shows about bugs, J-man makes crawlies on my arm with his fingers, pretending he's a spider. He loves it when I act like I'm scared."

She stopped talking when she noticed Jack studying her like she was the pin-riddled frog in high school biology.

The detective looked toward Jack, as if to ask if he wanted to add anything, but Jack wouldn't look at him. Instead, he picked up the Spider-Man comic, fidgeted with it for a moment, and set it back on the table. He rocked forward and backward, his elbows digging into his knees. "I can't contribute anything. Why am I even here?"

"Because you're his father." Macy knew it was her voice, but the words were foreign.

"Yeah, but that's all I am. His father. I want to be his daddy. I should have been his daddy."

"He called you daddy. Maybe not lately, but he has." Then Macy laughed, too loud, too painful in her own ears. "J-man cracks me up with the things he says. Just last week he said the neatest thing. Russ had joked about how ugly Bella is. Bella is J-man's dog, the one with the huge head and short legs. So, J-man says to me, 'God must have put Bella together in the dark, because he got some of the pieces wrong.'" She took a deep breath, gasping when the air pierced her lungs. "J-man's only six years old," she said and sobbed.

†

218

Kenny narrowed his eyes, focusing. Cam was leading for the first time ever in their nail-gun contest, and he sure as hell didn't want to be beat by a girl. The phone was closest to him when it rang, so he snatched it up.

"Jeremiah's gone missing."

Dorianne's words stunned Kenny, and he repeated them out loud for Cam's benefit. When he hung up, he thought for sure he'd be sick.

"I have to go be with Macy," Cam said.

"They said for us to stay put." But Kenny had serious doubts about that being possible. "Get Gary on his cell phone. Tell him to drive around and look."

Kenny couldn't believe Jeremiah had disappeared right out of his aunt and uncle's backyard. It was the same yard where Kenny had played as a kid, where he and Jack had fought so many times, under the big, messy magnolias.

He pulled out the phone book. He would call every person he knew and get them to help in the search for Jeremiah.

"I can't get through to Gary," Cam said, sounding panicked.

"Wait a few minutes, then try again."

"Then what?" she asked.

"We wait to see what they want us to do next," Kenny said.

"Just wait?"

"Find something to keep you busy. You don't know anyone in town, and you don't know your way around. Ain't nothing you can do but wait here for Gary to call back."

The next thing Kenny knew, Cam was in the front office. She was cussing, crying, and scrubbing at the carpet, all at once. Kenny went in there, too, to use that phone, since it wasn't attached to the wall like the one in the back. Kenny knew there was no way he was gonna be able to stay still and just wait. He looked up Freddie Miller in the phone book. Freddie had kids, all younger, but Kenny was sure he'd drive around and look for Jeremiah.

Cam was mumbling something. When Kenny got Freddie's answering machine, he just hung up. Cam was still groaning, so Kenny asked her what she'd said.

"I said..." She slammed down a wet wad of paper towels. "That goddamned Gary's always tracking this crap in." She scrubbed at the clay that streaked the carpet.

"You give Dori a run for her money with your bitching." He flipped through the phone book. "Better yet, you sound like Aunt Eileen complaining about us tracking clay through the house when we were kids."

Cam was on her hands and knees, attacking the dirt. It looked to Kenny like Texas Pete with mayo mixed in. Hot sauce, mayo, and what? Eye shadow. The purplish-blue eye shadow Dorianne wore to their prom. Did he actually remember that?

Then it dawned on Kenny that he was remembering that combination from another time. His Aunt Eileen was bitching about the dirt, but she wasn't scrubbing at it. She always let it dry, then she could just vacuum it up. Kenny was about to tell Cam to leave it be, to let it dry, but then he remembered something else.

The day Timmy Jones disappeared and everyone was at his Uncle Russ and Aunt Eileen's, waiting to hear something, there was a mess just like that one on the carpet. The same mess of red and white clay that his Aunt Eileen yelled at him and Jack for when they'd go fishing at the lake by the chalk mines. With Gary.

"Cam, when's the last time you seen Gary?"

"This morning. He came in here for a few minutes while we were finishing up the Cooper job."

His hands shaking, Kenny dropped the phone book onto the front desk.

Cam was babbling. "That's probably when the jerk dirtied up the carpet."

It all made sense. Gary was there when Timmy went missing, too. He was right there with Uncle Russ when Aunt Eileen bitched about the clay tracked in. And Gary was the one who always snuck Kenny and Jack out to the lake. He knew the chalk mines better than anyone, even better than Uncle Russ.

Kenny started digging through his pockets, looking for the truck keys. "Shit."

"What?"

"Where are my freaking keys?"

Cam stood up and reached across the desk for the keys behind the phone book. "Where are we going?" Cam asked.

"*We* ain't going nowhere. I'm going. You stay here and wait for me to call you."

Cam's eyes narrowed. "No way. I'm going with you."

"All right, just give me the damn keys."

She did, and they bolted out the door.

Kenny had never driven so fast in his life. Past the south side of town, he jumped onto Highway 25, toward Burke County. He made a couple of turns onto paved roads he'd never known the names of and then made a right onto a dirt road. The red clay was a little slick in some areas, bumpy with ripples in others.

He rounded a corner and suddenly stomped on the brakes. They slid to a stop right at the edge of a huge pile of discarded topsoil that had been moved to uncover a vein of chalk. The overburden rose up in front of them, blocking the old road into the mine.

"Shit." Kenny pounded his fist against the steering wheel.

"Are we lost?"

"We ain't lost. The road's just gone. Happens all the time around here." He knew he sounded defensive, and he was. He didn't want this punk-ass kid to think he didn't know how to get where they were going.

To their left, rows of pine came right up to the edge of the overburden. Kenny hated the unnatural neatness of land reclamation. Pines weren't meant to be in such skinny, even rows. He jerked the wheel to the right. There was a steep ditch on the other side of the mound, but he figured they could pass if he hugged the side as tight as the truck would let him.

The truck was all but on its side, but it worked. The red clay road started back up on the other side. Kenny floored it and they fishtailed, but he quickly regained control.

Ahead, Kenny saw more rows of trees to one side and the long pond collecting water on the other side. The water was its typical unnatural turquoise, thanks to the minerals that settled at the bottom.

"What the hell is that?" Cam's mouth hung wide open.

Chapter Twenty-Two

Duct Tape

When they rounded the corner, the landscape caught Cam totally off guard. A huge crater spread out in front of them. Striations of color layered its sides—red and brown at the top, then gray, purple, white, a layer of rust, more white. At the bottom was a pool of the most intense blue.

Cam knew then what Kenny meant when he said he used to swim at a blue hole. "It's beautiful," she whispered.

"No, it ain't."

Ignoring him, Cam studied the colors of the crater. They were all shades like the clay smeared into the carpet at work. "What do you think is going on?"

"I think that freak Gary is up to no good," Kenny muttered.

One side of the orange-red road was lined with clumps of long grass that made Cam think of a vacation at the beach where Aunt Jess took her one summer. The other side of the road had some regular-looking grass and a spattering of frilly purple flowers. Cam thought she saw dog prints around the plants.

"What is this place?" Cam asked.

"Chalk bed." Kenny looked from side to side as he spoke. "Ain't been mined in a while, though."

Chalk. White clay. Kaolin. All the terms Macy had used rolled around in Cam's head. *Macy. God, I hope she's holding up okay.*

She checked out the mocha-colored mud that led toward the mine from beyond the grass with the flowers. They hit a rut in the road, and her head banged against the roof of the truck.

Focus, Cam told herself. For once, she wasn't just taking in the scenery, going where everyone else was going. For once, she was participating. "What do I need to look for, Kenny?"

"Any sign that someone's been out here—tire tracks, footprints, anything."

As he sped forward, Cam saw something move ahead to their left.

"There he is," Kenny shouted.

When Kenny got to where Gary had ducked into the pine trees, he stopped the truck. He looked from left to right and back toward Gary.

I am not along for the ride, Cam reminded herself. "You go after him. I'll go back the way he came and look for Jeremiah."

She barely had the words out before Kenny leaped from the truck and took off after Gary. Cam got out and ran to the other side of the road. In the mud, she saw a set of elongated footprints, like someone had been slipping and sliding as much as walking. Not far from those prints, she saw a set of two more heading away from her. One smeared path was made by much smaller feet. *Jeremiah.*

When Cam ran into the mud to follow the double prints, she immediately found out how slick it was. She half-stumbled and half-ran. The mud sucked at her work boots and coated them and her in its thick coolness. Bile burned its way from her stomach to her throat.

Please, Cam begged. *Please let Jeremiah be okay.* Her feet grew heavier as the mud caked her boots. She thought about stopping to take them off but didn't dare take the time.

The prints turned toward a clump of weeds and brush and followed the outer ridge of the mine. Cam did the same. As she stood up on the highest point, she could see a creek below. The prints slid in that direction.

She lost her balance halfway down and ended up sliding on her back, the sting and burn of gravel and dirt biting into her.

"Is someone there?" The voice was tiny but distinct.

"Jeremiah? J, is that you?"

"Help me. I'm slipping down."

Jeremiah clung to a branch, midway down the embankment. The flow of water below him wasn't fast, but it was more than Cam figured a six-year-old could fight against.

"Hang on," she yelled, hoping Jeremiah wouldn't hear the panic in her voice.

Cam took a couple of steps down the bank, but the ground sucked at her feet and threatened to swallow her. She figured she could get down to Jeremiah but didn't know what she'd do once she got there. Without some rope, she'd just end up stuck alongside him.

"I'm getting help, Jeremiah. Just hang on. Okay?"

"Hurry," he cried.

"I will, buddy." Cam ran along the edge of the ridge, figuring she could make it back to the truck faster that way. She ran until her legs screamed. The whole time she thought there was no way she could let anything happen to Jeremiah.

She searched the bed of the truck and behind the seats for some rope. Finding nothing remotely useable but a roll of duct tape, she jumped into the truck and drove along the ridge until she worried she'd disappear down the red and white sides of the crater. She grabbed the duct tape and sprinted the rest of the way back to Jeremiah.

When Cam looked down, she could tell Jeremiah had slid another few feet. "I'm here."

"I'm tired. I can't hang on."

"Just a little longer. I'm almost there."

Cam grabbed the end of the tape and started winding it around the sturdiest tree she could find. It wasn't a big tree, but it would have to do. At first the tape slipped off the bark, but when it started sticking to itself, Cam knew it would work. She kept unwinding it, hoping it was as strong as everyone said it was, using it to make the best rope she could.

When she had a good length pulled out, she stuck her hand through the cardboard center of the roll and started down the embankment. She locked her fingers together and held her arms close to her chest, knowing she couldn't let go for any reason. With every inch of tape that freed from the roll, the cardboard dug into her arm. It cut and slipped and scraped and threatened to slide off.

Please. Please let this work.

By the time she had almost reached Jeremiah, Cam was shaking with exhaustion and the duct tape was losing its stickiness because of the blood and mud and sweat on her arm.

Jeremiah slid another foot down the embankment. Cam reached down and grabbed onto his arm. Just when she thought she couldn't hang on any longer, she thought about Aunt Jess.

When Cam was young, she'd fallen off her bike and knocked a baby tooth loose. At the dentist office, Aunt Jess held her hand through the entire thing. Cam had never felt safer. Remembering her aunt's strength, she knew she could do it. She heaved Jeremiah up to her and held him tight against her chest.

Cam dug her feet into the mud and wrapped the tape around Jeremiah's waist. Just before she could tape him to her, the roll ran out. Cam took several deep breaths. Knowing she had no choice but to make the tape rope work, she started inching them up the embankment.

✝

Kenny chased Gary through a section of pine trees. Gary cut sharply to the right and headed to the upper ridge of the mine. Suddenly he stopped and swung around to face Kenny, holding something behind his back. Kenny couldn't see what it was, but it worried him, so he stopped, too, about fifteen feet away.

"Where's Jeremiah, Gary?"

Kenny took a step forward; Gary took one backward. Kenny didn't remember Gary ever saying anything about owning a gun, but he didn't know for sure.

"Where is he?" Kenny asked.

"He's okay. I took him fishing." Gary put his left hand behind his back with the other one. "He already knew how to swim," he said.

"Tell me where he is."

"I learned how to swim in a blue hole."

Kenny's face grew hot. "Who fucking cares? You told me and Jack that a million times when you brought us out here fishing."

"You don't understand," Gary yelled.

"Where's Jeremiah? Do you have any idea what this is doing to his mama? Hell, what it could be doing to my babies?" Right away Kenny wished he hadn't brought that up. He knew Gary knew about the surrogacy, but it still wasn't any of his business.

"What makes you so special that you have to have kids? What makes you better than other people who can't have them?"

"That ain't your business," Kenny said.

"You think it was worth it to Russ, getting a second mortgage on his house to help you out? And what about Martin—putting his business on the line for you? What a waste."

Kenny's hands flexed in and out of fists. He got more and more pissed as he thought about what the stress of all of this must be doing to Macy.

"You are a waste of a human being." Kenny took two steps forward; Gary took three back. "Where's Jeremiah?" Kenny demanded.

"Sometimes I can feel the silica from the mines. It's clogging every vein and every organ in my body. One day I'll be a pillar of chalk."

That side of Gary was scaring the crap out of Kenny. He would have rather had the scowling, grumpy Gary he'd been seeing at the shop for so many years. "I'm sorry you're so screwed up and pissed off, but you ain't got no right taking it out on little kids. Now, where is he?"

"I'm not taking anything out on anyone. I never meant to hurt that boy. I wasn't gonna hurt Jeremiah either," Gary said.

The hair stood up at the back of Kenny's neck. "You never meant to hurt what boy?"

"Timmy didn't know how to swim. I was doing him a favor."

"Timmy Jones? What did you do to Timmy?" Kenny's stomach churned. "Where's Jeremiah?" He swore to himself that if he had to ask Gary one more time, he'd kill him.

"I took Timmy swimming at one of the chalk ponds. I knew that hole, knew it'd be okay. But then he wanted to swim here." Gary nodded toward the pond to his left. "I told him he couldn't, that there was equipment they'd left sunk at the bottom, and it'd be dangerous. Then as we were leaving, he got too close to the edge up here on the cliff."

Gary was so involved in telling his story, he didn't notice Kenny inching closer to him.

"I told Timmy to be careful. I swear I told him to be careful."

"What happened to Timmy?" Kenny asked, taking another step.

"He fell in. He got stuck between two pieces of rusting metal junk. I tried to unstick him, but I couldn't." He started to blubber.

"So you just left him there?"

"There was nothing I could do for him. He hit his head. I couldn't save him. I liked him. I wanted to help him."

Gary brought his left hand forward and Kenny held his breath, still not knowing what was behind his back. Gary used his hand to swipe at his dripping nose, and Kenny saw the hand was empty.

"I didn't hurt that boy. I'd never hurt that boy or any boy. Don't you see?" Gary asked.

"See what?" Fear for Jeremiah flashed through Kenny.

"I just wanted you kids to like me. I wanted you and Jack and the others to like me. I wanted to be your friend, for you to stop calling me Goofy Gary behind my back. I wanted to be just *Gary*." He wiped at his face again. "When I took you and Jack fishing, you liked me. We were friends."

"We were never friends," Kenny said, losing patience.

"Me and Timmy were friends, too. And me and Jeremiah. And I'll be friends with your son, if you have a boy."

Kenny wanted to puke at that man mentioning his son. "You ain't going anywhere near my kids. And you're gonna tell me right now where Jeremiah is."

"He's such a beautiful boy. His daddy was a beautiful boy, too. Jack was always good at stuff. Remember when he caught that huge bass?"

Kenny flexed his fingers.

"And Jack had his son the real way."

That was all Kenny could take. He rushed at Gary with long strides. A few feet from him, Kenny put up his arms, blocking like a football player. He caught Gary across the chest, and they both tumbled to the ground. Whatever Gary had behind his back was knocked away, and it rolled several feet.

Gary's laugh was loud and distorted, like some B-movie madman. It pissed Kenny off even more.

"Where's Jeremiah?" He sat on Gary's chest, his knee pressed hard against Gary's breastbone. "Tell me right now, or I'll kill you. I swear, I will fucking kill you."

Gary stopped laughing. "I didn't hurt Jeremiah. I'd never hurt him."

"Tell me," Kenny screamed. When Gary didn't answer, Kenny raised a fist. "Tell me," he demanded.

Kenny didn't wait for an answer. He brought his fist down into Gary's face, but his hand was muddy and slipped to the right of Gary's nose. Kenny's blow glanced off of Gary's cheek, and then his knuckles slammed into the ground.

Gary bucked and threw Kenny off him. He got up and started toward the rows of pine trees. Kenny got back to his feet and caught up to him in no time. He grabbed the back of Gary's shirt.

Kenny spun him around until Gary was facing him. Gary teetered on the edge of the mine. Kenny's next punch caught him on the chin. Kenny hit him again, square on the nose, and blood spurted.

Gary raised his arms to protect himself, stumbled, fell, and clawed at the ground.

Kenny hesitated for a second before trying to grab his arm. When he did reach out, it was too late. Kenny landed on his knees at the edge as Gary cartwheeled down, bouncing off the carved layers of colors, sending clumps of brown and gray and white down with him.

When Gary hit the water, it was like the wind was knocked out of Kenny. For a few seconds, he was catching his breath. Kenny tried to see if Gary would come up. He didn't. Kenny knew it'd be too late now, even if he could get to Gary. There wasn't any way Gary would come out of that alive.

Kenny started back the way they'd come, along the edge of the mine. At the place where he'd first tackled Gary, Kenny saw a fishing reel on the ground. He almost laughed. He'd been afraid of a fishing reel?

When Kenny finally made it to the edge of the water, he stared, watching for bubbles or something. He didn't see anything, nothing but the reflection of white clouds turning gray. He heard a rumbling in the distance and figured he better help Cam find Jeremiah before the sky opened up, before something awful happened.

Chapter Twenty-Three

Cellular Waste

The walls of the living room throbbed and threatened to crash in on Macy. She looked around, and it seemed no one else noticed how the pale green paint fed on her growing panic.

All the voices grew louder. *Shut up.* Oh, God, she knew they meant well—the police, Russ, Eileen, Dori. Even Jack and her mother. But she needed them all to just shut up.

Then there was the voice in her head. The one that had started months earlier and made her doubt every little thing about what she was doing. *Selfish*, it reminded her.

Macy moved to the far corner of the living room, but still all the noise pierced her eardrums, like in the eleventh grade when Jack talked her into water skiing. She'd taken a spill, and water was forced into her ear. She didn't know she'd busted her eardrum until later, when her mother put in drops and the alcohol sent searing pain through Macy, not stopping at the ear but shooting into her head and radiating down her neck.

That's how it felt when cells exploded. And that's how she felt waiting for news about Jeremiah. Her body vibrated. Every cell was going to explode; there was no way around it.

She looked toward the kitchen. Jack was leaning against her refrigerator. Emma's photos were on the fridge, directly above him, in their manila envelope. Macy thought about the image Emma had captured down at the river—J-man's cocked head, Macy's stiffness. Yes, she remembered. Fear had skewered her when she thought about his curiosity, the same inquisitiveness she tried so hard to foster, to encourage. Before that moment at the river, she had been thrilled at her little man's need to know. Then she became acutely aware that curiosity is simultaneously a gift and a curse. Just like motherhood.

The noise grew. It would demolish her every cell, not ceasing until she was senseless mush. Without her J-man, she was broken cell membranes, confused nuclei, spewed cytoplasm.

"How many cells need to burst before I'll be numb?" she asked her mother.

She stared back at Macy and shook her head.

Then Dori was holding Macy's hand. Sweet, sweet Dori. She'd be a great mother. She wouldn't mess up like Macy. Maybe she knew. "Dori," she whispered, avoiding her mother's accusing stare, "how long until I'm a puddle of nothingness?"

Jack was walking toward Macy, and she wondered if he had the same questions. It'd be just like him to not let on.

Tears burned her face—salt in the open wounds of her shattered cells. She looked at Jack, and the tears flowed harder. In Emma's poem, her eyes were hematite, now they were liquefying, a black river of lava scorching a path down her cheeks.

As she cried, the look on Jack's face shifted. He looked bewildered. Yes, that was it. She'd marveled at that same expression when he'd held Jeremiah for the first time. He started talking to her, but she couldn't hear him clearly. She had to strain just to barely make out what he said. He didn't want to take Jeremiah from her, he just wanted to be a bigger part of his son's life.

Macy believed him. She nodded. Moving her head released some of the pressure. So did letting out a low moan.

Tears filled Jack's eyes, and he quickly rejoined his father in the kitchen.

The voice returned. It's all about control, it screamed over the volume of the other sounds. You like the power of having someone else's baby growing inside you.

Macy had to convince the voice that she was only having these babies to help friends; it had nothing to do with power or control. There were no games. There hadn't been in a long time. The voice could just ask Sharon. She hadn't tried to do a thing to manipulate Sharon, to try to change her mind about them being together again.

Hot shards coursed through Macy's swollen belly. The heat was beyond fire, beyond raw flame. Was her body destroying itself, or just the precious lives inside? Was biology telling her not to bring these babies into a world where little boys disappeared and their mamas dissolved?

She hugged her belly. The fire of cellular waste corroded her from the inside out. The acid burn of her becoming a puddle was just too much to bear.

Scream, she told herself. It was the only way, even if the sound of her own roaring would surely kill off whatever cells remained in her head. It had to come out, had to go somewhere. *Just scream.*

Dori knelt beside Macy and held her hand tightly. She whispered over and over that it'd be okay. Since the scream had released some of the pressure, Dori's voice no longer threatened to tear Macy's eardrums.

Where's the control now? She put her hands over her ears. Where's the mama bear, the mama killdeer?

Squeezing her eyes shut, she imagined J-man in his
Levi's and T-shirt that morning. She took the image of him
and wrapped herself around him; she put him inside of her. J-
man and the twins swam in a sea of liquid hematite, safe
from the world, safe from harm.

Biology wasn't telling her anything about these babies,
and neither would she allow the voice in her head to. She was
a good mother and a good friend. She would not let doubts
tell her otherwise.

But then, hot and viscous, the hematite began to seep
out. Macy put her hands in her lap, trying to hide it. No, no,
no. There had to be enough room for all three of them inside.
She had to keep J-man safe. And she did want to bring those
babies into this crazy world, where Dori and Kenny and
everyone else in their mixed-up families could love them.

Pain ripped through her. Would keeping all three safe
kill her? Was she strong enough to accept that?

Dori looked down into Macy's lap. Macy could tell Dori
wanted to say something, but she didn't. Dori wanted to
swallow, but she couldn't. She just stood there, growing paler
and paler.

"It's okay," Macy tried to reassure her. "J-man's safe."
She patted her belly to prove it. "They're all safe."

"We need to get you to the hospital," Dori said.

Macy closed her eyes and wrapped her arms around her
belly. Hugging J-man and the twins, she felt movement
against the soft undersides of her arms. She smiled. Waves of
hematite carried through her the rhythm of three priceless
heartbeats.

†

Cam held on to Jeremiah until her arms ached, and she
realized with a start that they were safe at the top of the

embankment. The mud and clay coating them was thick and oddly warm. Insulating. She felt protected, as if by a liquid armor.

Jeremiah pulled at the tape Cam had wrapped around him, and Cam helped him unwind it, tugging against what adhesive had survived the muck.

"You were just like Spider-Man," Jeremiah said.

Cam looked past the dirty face into his black eyes and saw Macy. If Cam were Spider-Man, she would send Macy a high-frequency arachnid signal to let her know her son was okay. Cam had sworn to Macy months earlier that she was over her feelings for her. She'd lied. She'd had to. She didn't want Macy to feel self-conscious around her, or worse, to feel sorry for her.

Cam wasn't an idiot. She knew she didn't stand a chance with Macy, but she also couldn't help how she felt about her.

"Uncle Kenny!" Jeremiah ran to Kenny. "Cam saved my life—just like Spider-Man."

Kenny looked Cam over. "Duct tape?" He laughed. "Damn, girl, I guess you are one of us after all."

"A living, breathing cliché," Cam said, and she laughed, too, a sobbing, painful laugh.

Cam yanked the slick, bloody tape from her arm. Clawing at the mud, her hand hit something small and hard. She rubbed it between her thumb and index finger until the shiny black surface was revealed.

"What is it?" Jeremiah asked.

"I don't know." She held it up for them to see.

"Shark's tooth?" Kenny suggested.

"Cool," Jeremiah sang out.

Cam studied it closer. "Here?"

"I guess this place could have been beachfront property a gazillion years ago," Kenny said.

"Where's Gary?" Jeremiah's voice was small, hesitant.

The question overrode Cam's own about sharks' teeth, the alien landscape, and what else Kenny knew about it.

"Gary's gone."

Something flashed across Kenny's face, and Cam wasn't sure if she wanted it identified or not.

Kenny squatted in front of Jeremiah. "You okay?"

Jeremiah nodded. "Mama's going to be mad at me, isn't she?"

"No way," Kenny said. "She can't wait to see her big man."

"You can tell her how brave you were," Cam said.

"Yeah!"

As they walked away, Cam looked down. Several sets of dog prints were visible in the dirt. She imagined wild or abandoned dogs forming a pack to survive the harsh environment. They had the right idea.

They climbed into the truck with Jeremiah between Cam and Kenny. They sat, unmoving, staring straight ahead for several moments. Cam plotted how to not fall apart when she saw Macy. For beginners, she wouldn't look her in the eyes for more than a second at a time.

Cam looked at Kenny and wondered what he was thinking. Kenny had so much riding on Macy, on how well she'd held up through the ordeal. Kenny was gripping and releasing the steering wheel. Cam didn't know what else to say, so she joked, "Can you find your way out?"

Kenny smiled, and Cam could feel some of the tension lifting. Then Kenny covered Jeremiah's eyes with one hand and made an obscene gesture at Cam with the other.

Kenny started driving, and Cam glanced back over the mine. On the far, pine-studded ridge, she saw two dogs. As she watched them get farther and farther away, Cam thought about another dog, almost left on the side of Highway 278. She knew the scenario with the old man and the yellow dog could have played out differently. From then on, Cam promised herself, she wouldn't ever let anything around her get that close to destruction again.

On the ride out of the mine property, Cam checked the cell phone for a signal several times. She didn't get one until they'd turned from one paved road onto another. She dialed Macy's number.

"Hello," the deep voice said.

"Is Macy there?"

"Who's this?"

"It's Cam. Kenny and me found Jeremiah. He's okay." Cam had never heard such a heart-wrenching sob in her life.

Kenny held out his hand. Cam didn't argue. She handed Kenny the phone.

"At the hospital?" Kenny asked. "She had some spotting," he said, glancing at Cam. Kenny listened for a few moments and hung up.

"What else?" Cam asked.

"Russ said to go to Macy's. We'll talk to the police there and get cleaned up so we can go to the hospital."

†

Kenny's statement to the police only took a few minutes. He told the detective how he and Gary had fought, and Gary had fallen into a chalk pond. He told him where they could find him. And Timmy Jones.

After quick showers and a change of clothes, they were ready to head out.

Kenny grew eerily quiet. He seemed on automatic pilot until they got to the hospital and he saw Dori. She was smiling.

When Kenny and Dori melted into one another, holding on tight, Cam felt a tug in her chest. She hadn't realized how much she'd grown to like this guy who'd picked on her all those months.

Jack swooped down, grabbed Jeremiah, and held him tight to his chest. Then he took his son in to see Macy. After a few minutes, Jack came out and pointed at Cam. When Jack motioned to Macy's door and said, "Go on in," Cam's chest threatened to burst with pride.

Cam stuck her hands in her pockets, and something pricked her right thumb. She remembered the shark's tooth. She fingered it. *Yeah, landscapes do change.* She slowed her breathing and went in.

Macy had Jeremiah on the bed with her, holding him. *Keep it together*, Cam chanted in her head. *Keep it together.*

And she did, for about five seconds.

Chapter Twenty-Four

Happy Tears

The air at the shop tasted like gritty-sweet maple dust. Kenny took deep breaths and got ready to get to work. He wasn't gonna stop until he was finished with both cradles.

When Kenny was leaving the mine with Cam and Jeremiah, it flashed through his head that the second cradle wasn't finished. He asked himself, what if he'd jinxed his babies by not getting the furniture done? What if they'd go away half-made because he'd only half done their cradles?

Then at the hospital, when the doctor said the babies seemed fine, Kenny promised himself that he'd finish the second cradle as soon as he could. He wouldn't rush it, because it still had to be perfect, but he wouldn't slack off on it anymore either.

Kenny sanded the glue at the seam between two pieces of maple. The back-and-forth motion calmed him, until a thought inserted itself into the rhythm of his work. Had he wanted Gary to fall? And if he did, why?

Thinking back on it, he grew angry. What made that bastard think he had the right to get into it with Kenny about whether or not he deserved kids? Kenny knew he owed Russ and Eileen a lot; he didn't need Gary telling him how far in debt he was. He didn't need to be reminded that if it didn't work this time, they couldn't afford to try again.

Kenny pried the lid off the can of stain with a screwdriver. He dipped the brush in and smoothed Autumn Maple onto the wood. His gaze went to the purple bruising around the knuckles of his right hand. When his fist slid off Gary and hit the ground, Jack had popped into his mind. For just a second, Kenny thought about how slugging Jack that day at Uncle Russ's had felt so good. But that feeling didn't last, didn't change the fact that when they were growing up, Jack was always better than him. Jack always outdid Kenny at everything, from football to making babies.

Did comparing Gary to Jack make Kenny want to kill Gary? It scared him to think that he could hate anyone that much. But did he? Maybe he didn't hate Jack so much after all. He was glad that Jack was finally stepping up, was gonna be a better father to Jeremiah. Kenny wasn't stupid; he knew that was best for the kid.

Maybe he was being too hard on himself. It was probably plain and simple fear for Jeremiah that made him act like he did with Gary. He couldn't blame himself for that. Even the cops said so.

Kenny decided none of it mattered. What was done was done. His family was the only important thing. Dori was relaxing some finally, and Macy and the babies were doing real good. Kenny wasn't going to worry anymore, because he knew Macy would stay on bed rest like the doctor said.

Cam was going to stay at Macy's to help her with Jeremiah. Kenny laughed out loud when he thought about catching Cam reading a book one day before Jeremiah went missing—*What to Expect When You're Expecting*. Kenny still found himself thinking of Cam as one of the guys, so it seemed dorky to him that she was reading that book. But then Kenny thought about seeing Cam at the mine—dirty and bleeding and wrapped in duct tape, of all things. He guessed he should cut her some slack.

Before Kenny knew it, he was done staining the new cradle. He ran his hand along the invisible seam of maple on the first one. Once the second one dried, they'd both be finished. They were perfect, down to the last wood screw. Now maybe his babies would be perfect, down to the last fingernail.

†

The green hospital phone nestled against Macy's leg. She'd left it there after hanging up with Sharon.

Macy hadn't heard from her mother all day and didn't really expect to. She would come around, or she wouldn't. Macy would be okay either way. At least the woman had shown a hint of compassion while Jeremiah was missing.

J-man was leaning against Macy as he read out loud from a picture book about trains.

A nurse came in and asked him, "Would you like to go out into the hallway and wait with your big sister?"

"Big sister?" Macy asked.

J-man leaned closer and whispered, "I told them Cam was my sister. Is that okay?"

Macy chuckled. "Yes, baby, that's okay."

"They know you aren't Cam's mama. And I told them that even though you're my mama, you aren't pregnant with my brother and sister, but with my cousins."

Macy laughed.

The nurse kept a polite smile on her face as she waited for J-man to go.

Jeremiah glanced at the nurse and lowered his voice even further. "I don't think they understand."

"Do you understand?" Macy asked him.

"Yes."

Her little man was so smart. "That's all that matters."

"Why you crying, Mama?"

She hadn't realized she was. "Because I'm happy."

"Happy tears!" Then he ran off to go hang out with Cam.

The nurse checked Macy's temperature and blood pressure. "Would you like me to move this?" She gestured toward the phone.

Macy hesitated and then handed it to her. "Thanks."

"Any spotting?" The nurse reached for the thin blanket.

Macy tucked it around her belly. "I just checked. No spotting." She had checked. Many times.

"Okay. Call if you need anything." And she was gone.

The door had barely shut behind the nurse when Macy heard the tapping. "Dori," she called, and Dori tiptoed in.

"Hey, how you feeling?"

"Much better." Macy patted the bed next to her, and Dori sat. She took Dori's hand in hers. "It's been scary, huh?"

"Yeah," Dori admitted.

"Well, it's all fine now."

"I know." Dori traced a vein on the back of Macy's hand with her finger.

There was a shadow of mascara under Dori's eyes. She hadn't bothered putting on new makeup. It made her look sweet but weary.

"You look tired," Macy said.

"Yeah. We all are. Cam's taking Jeremiah home. Jack's meeting them there to take Jeremiah for the night."

"Good." Macy had to let J-man out of her sight again sooner or later. She was just thankful that the staff had let him stay in her room the night before.

Macy scooted over to give Dori more room. Dori kicked off her shoes, pulled her legs up onto the bed, and leaned back against the pillow. Macy found Dori's warmth comforting.

"Where's Kenny?" Macy asked.

"He's at the shop, finishing up the babies' furniture."

Macy stared up at the ceiling for several moments before speaking. "When we were fighting in high school, I knew that couldn't be the end of us. I knew we'd be important to one another again."

"I seriously doubted that." Dori paused. "Sorry."

"You don't doubt me now, and that's all that matters."

The force of Dori's sob startled Macy. As she shifted to look at Dori, Dori buried her face in her hands. "What?" Macy whispered.

"I'm sorry."

Macy tried to comfort her. "Hey, we were just kids."

"I'm sorry for not having faith in you yesterday." Her sobs shook the bed.

"Yesterday?"

"You were talking like Jeremiah was... I just knew you'd lost it, like you thought you were pregnant with him again."

The image of Jeremiah, Mason, and Mya swimming in liquid hematite returned. *How much did I actually say out loud?*

Dori's sobs grew louder. "I thought that if something happened to Jeremiah, you wouldn't be able to give me my babies."

"Oh God." *What did I put her through?* "I was just trying to keep J-man safe. I didn't mean to scare you." She sat up. "Please look at me."

Dori faced her. Inches from one another, they stayed very still for several moments. It surprised them both when Macy didn't look away but held Dori's gaze. "I just wanted to make it right."

"Make what right? You and me? Jeremiah?"

"All of it." She didn't know how else to say it. She didn't know how to tell Dori that for once she was trying to find answers in the strength and love inside of *her*. "Dori, I would never hurt you like that."

"My head and heart knew that all along, it was just this thing in my gut." Dori pressed her fist against her stomach and looked away. She grabbed a tissue from the bedside table and ran it across her face, leaving smudges of tears and mascara. "Sorry. I should have had more faith in you."

"I should have earned your faith."

"You have."

"Maybe now." Macy smiled. "Lie here with me?"

Dori snuggled up behind Macy, and Macy took Dori's hand and pressed it against her belly. She could feel the heat of Dori's tears on her back.

Chapter Twenty-Five

Nesting

"So, you're all packed?" Sharon called over from her front porch.

"Yep." Cam threw her duffle bag onto the bench seat of her truck. It was the same duffle she'd come to Georgia with, but it wasn't all she had anymore.

Sharon shielded her eyes as her gaze swept across Michael's yard. "I guess with you leaving, the weeds will be right back."

Fighting her nerves, Cam walked over to Sharon. "Maybe not. They might be under control for a while."

"Well, you've done a great job over there."

"It was the least I could do," Cam said. "I'm still shocked Michael let me stay after all that happened."

"Michael is a good man." Sharon smiled. "Will you come in for a few minutes?"

"Yes, of course." Cam was stunned by the invitation she'd waited so long for, but she followed Sharon inside.

"You're moving in with Macy."

A blush swept across Cam's cheeks.

"She told me you were moving in to help out with Jeremiah in the evenings."

"Yep, that's the plan," Cam said.

It occurred to her then that Sharon seemed a little uncomfortable. It was nice to have her be the uneasy one for once, but she decided to just put it out there. "I used to have a bit of a crush on Macy, but we're just friends."

"I know."

"Now I care for her in a way that means a lot more to me than just thinking she's pretty and sweet."

Sharon nodded. "Good."

Cam wasn't sure why, but she couldn't seem to stop blabbing once she'd started. "This probably sounds cheesy, but her and Jeremiah feel like family."

"I know that's important to you."

She did? Cam couldn't help wondering if Sharon and Macy had talked about her. Well, of course they had. Cam knew the universe didn't revolve around her, but she also knew that Macy had been her cheering section when it came to Sharon.

"What about Jack?" Sharon asked. "Has he said anything about you moving in with Macy?"

"Jack actually likes the idea." It appeared Jack wasn't at all threatened by her.

Sharon traced the pattern of jagged yellow lines on the rug with her toe. "Jess would like the grown-up you."

Cam smiled. Why not? She was even beginning to like the grown-up her.

"I've got a few things I'd like to give you," Sharon said.

Cam's heart skipped a beat.

"It's taken me a long time, but I've finally started going through Jess's stuff." She took a deep breath. "I've set aside some pictures and some other things I thought you might like to have."

Cam nodded and stared at the blue and yellow of the rug Aunt Jess must have walked across a million times. Sharon led Cam toward the bedroom and took a deep breath before opening the door.

The queen-sized bed was neatly made, the foot of it covered in perfect piles of clothing. There were stacks of T-shirts, pants, polo shirts.

"I can fit in most of her shirts. Her pants are too long for me, though." She placed her hand lightly on the stack of Levi's and Dockers. "These might fit Dori."

"Maybe."

"Or is that too weird?" Sharon massaged her temples.

"For you or for her?"

She shrugged. "I don't know how to do this."

Cam wasn't sure if Sharon was referring solely to the clothes or to the bigger picture. She scanned the bedroom and tried to take in the general energy of the room without seeing anything too intimate. She looked at the dresser and immediately recognized a photo of her and Jess at the Inner Harbor in Baltimore. Cam had a smaller, worn copy of the same picture.

Sharon held up a large, white T-shirt from St. Augustine. "Jess loved this city. She loved the beach, the history, the food." She laughed. "According to Jess, any city could be rated by its food."

Cam stared at the screen-printed collage of the beach.

"They only had this in large, but she had to have one. I'm not even sure if she ever wore it. You should take it. It'll be big on you, but still…"

She held out the shirt, and Cam took the heavy cotton in her hands. She let it rest on her palms, feeling the softness, and tried to imagine Aunt Jess standing in that very room. Then she blurted out, "Where is she?"

"Part of her is in the mountains. Up by Helen, Georgia."

"And the rest of her?"

"I'm waiting a little longer, then I'm going to take her to St. Augustine. I'm just not ready yet."

Cam glanced around the room.

"In the drawer." Sharon answered her unasked question. "She's in the drawer."

Cam thought she might be sick, so she took several steps toward where she thought the bathroom was, just in case.

"No, don't go in there." The look on Sharon's face suggested she was as surprised by the force of her voice as Cam was.

Cam placed her hand over her mouth to convey the urgency.

"Please use the other one."

Cam ran to the bathroom near the spare room where Jeremiah had played Cam's first day in Augusta. She splashed water on her face and leaned against the counter. That day seemed so long ago. Finding out about Aunt Jess dying had torn something loose inside her, something that had just started to heal.

The biggest step toward that mending had happened at the kaolin mine. Cam was sure that Aunt Jess had been there, holding on to Jeremiah with her. Standing in her house, touching her things, she was still sure of it.

When Cam went back to the bedroom, Sharon was standing in the doorway of the master bath. Her fingers dug into the wood of the doorjamb. Tendons along the backs of her hands strained as her body shook.

"Sharon," Cam whispered. She wanted to reach out to her but didn't know if she should.

"I didn't want anyone to mess up the rug. I know it's silly, but it helps me to know it's in there."

"The rug?"

"Yeah, the bathmat. She wanted to help me clean. I told her no, she should rest, but she really wanted to. We'd washed and dried the shower curtain and the bathmat."

When Sharon looked at Cam, Sharon's face was streaked and her eyes were a little wild. After a brief moment, she turned back toward the bathroom. "I put the shower curtain back up, and she put the rug down. When she did, she left behind a perfect handprint in the fibers. I didn't notice it until she was gone."

Sharon took a few steps into the bathroom and knelt on the tile beside the bathmat. Her hand hovered an inch above Jess's indentation.

Cam thought maybe she should leave, maybe this was too intimate a moment for her to be witnessing, but she couldn't make herself go. Instead, she stepped just inside the bathroom door.

A tear fell on the back of Sharon's hand, and she pulled away, as if scalded. Then she laughed, a sloppy, sobbing laugh. "I loved Jess's hands. I loved Jess more than I loved myself."

Cam believed her.

"You told Macy you felt like another pair of hands was helping you hold on to Jeremiah," she said.

The sting of Macy repeating that to someone was sharp, but it quickly dissolved. Cam nodded so Sharon could see it without actually looking away from the mat.

"Jess's hands?" Sharon asked.

"Yes." Cam took another step into the bathroom.

"I loved her hands," Sharon said again. When she lowered her hand, it fit perfectly into Jess's print.

Cam was certain Sharon already knew it would match.

Sharon pivoted toward Cam as she lifted her hand from the rug. "Come here."

Cam squatted beside her and let her take her hand into hers. She held her breath as Sharon guided her toward Jess's print, expecting at any minute she'd come to her senses and close her out. She used both her hands to spread Cam's fingers just slightly, then she placed her hand, overlapping in every direction, into Jess's print. Taking a deep breath, she splayed her hand across Cam's and pressed it into the indentation, now stretched and distorted, reflecting the perfect way a family reshapes itself.

✝

Macy lounged on the sofa and watched Sharon, who sat on the other end by her feet. She drew her knees up to give Sharon more room, but Sharon didn't move closer.

Cam and Jeremiah came in from the kitchen. They were going out for pizza. A smile passed between Cam and Sharon as J-man pressed his mouth against Macy's stomach and told his cousins goodbye.

The door shut behind them, and Macy inhaled sharply.

Sharon leaned into her legs and squeezed her knee. "Hey."

Macy wiped away a tear. "Sorry. I still get weepy thinking about what could have happened."

"But it didn't. And everything's fine."

Macy nodded.

"So," Sharon said and leaned back against the sofa, "what do you think about my and Eileen's plan?"

"I think it's very sweet for you two to alternate days staying with me, but don't think you have to. I don't need someone with me all the time."

"We think you do. I can bring over my laptop and work from here. It's no trouble."

Macy knew if she wasn't up front with Sharon at that moment, she never would be. She had to be sure Sharon understood. "Before you make that decision, there's something you need to know."

"What's that?" Sharon cocked her head.

"It has to do with what you said about us never being together again."

Sharon raised an eyebrow, just slightly.

"Understand that's not acceptable to me. When this is all over"—Macy gestured toward her belly—"I have every intention of changing your mind about that. Be forewarned."

Sharon hugged Macy's knees to her chest and rested her chin in the crook between them. "When I was ten, my family vacationed at caverns in West Virginia. I wandered off from the others and ended up alone in a very dark place. Then my flashlight went out." She closed her eyes. "At first I was terrified. I strained to see something in the pitch black. But then I stopped fighting it, and this incredible sense of peace came over me."

Macy held her breath as Sharon opened her eyes and looked at her.

"When I look into your eyes," Sharon continued, "I get that same sense of 'I could get lost in there'—and I really like it."

Sharon held their hands up, one against the other, and studied them. Macy was noticing that her own fingers were longer and thinner, not a perfect fit, when Sharon brought their hands to her mouth. Her lips felt dry against Macy's skin.

When Sharon's tears started, Macy drew her thumb along the line of moisture under one eye. Macy looked at her and knew she was ready to not look away. She knew she could hold Sharon's gaze for always, but at that moment she wanted to hold all of her.

Macy made room for Sharon to lie beside her, longwise on the sofa. "Come here," she whispered.

And Sharon did.

Epilogue

Macy and Sharon walked into Kenny and Dorianne's backyard holding hands. Now that she and Sharon were together, Macy didn't want to let go. She grew warm at the thought of their lovemaking the night before.

"You're blushing," Sharon whispered into Macy's ear.

"I wonder why," Macy said. She stopped a few feet into the yard and looked around. "Wow, Kenny's dad is here." She was so pleased to see the proud grandfather fussing over the twins.

"Macy, Sharon, come on over here," Russ called out from his spot at the grill.

Hugs were exchanged among Macy, Sharon, Russ, and Eileen. The elder Ken Brewer gave Macy an awkward hug and offered his hand to Sharon.

"You're the lawyer," Ken said to her.

"Yes, sir."

"Thank you for helping out my son."

"It was my pleasure."

Macy smiled and turned to hug Dorianne, who was holding Mya. "Hi!"

"I am so glad you could make it." Dori looked over Macy's shoulder. "Hi, Sharon. It's good to see you." She gave Macy an extra squeeze.

Macy broke free. "Let me see this little stinker." She took the two-month-old into her arms and held her closely. "How's my precious girl?" she cooed.

With Mya in her arms, Macy turned around and leaned in to kiss the top of Mason's head as his daddy held him. "Hey, fellas."

"Hey, girls," Kenny said in a teasing tone.

Smoke from the grill carried the scent of burgers and barbecued chicken across the yard. The stronger the smell became, the closer everyone got to the grill.

Macy kept one eye on the backyard gate, watching for Jeremiah. It had taken a lot of getting used to, but she'd grown a little more comfortable with Jack taking J-man for overnights.

"My goodness," Sharon said as Mason gripped her extended finger, "you've grown just since last week."

"See," Kenny said to Dori. "It isn't my imagination that they're growing super fast."

Macy looked toward movement by the gate.

Jack shut the door behind him as Jeremiah and Bella bolted across the yard. J-man threw himself into Macy's arms as Bella plopped onto the ground and offered up her belly for a rub. From her squatting position as she hugged her son, Macy could see Sharon petting Bella. J-man hugged Macy back, tightly. "Mama," he said in a breathless voice, "I had fun, but I sure did miss you."

Macy's love caught in her throat. "I missed you, too," she finally managed to say.

Jack stood over to the side for a few minutes before taking the last couple of steps over to his ex-wife and their son. "Hi."

"Hi, Jack."

He handed Jeremiah a remote-controlled car. "Here you go, buddy. Don't forget this."

"Thanks, Daddy." Jeremiah took the toy and spun back around to face Macy. "See what I got!"

"Very cool," she said.

"I can make this car race from clear across the yard!"

Macy smiled at Jack. "I'm glad you could come by for a few minutes."

"Wish I didn't have to work. This new job is tough, but it's really good."

"I'm glad." And she was.

"I'm gonna go say hi to my mom and dad before I head out," Jack said. He stood talking to them for about fifteen minutes and went back over to say goodbye to his son. "See you next week, buddy."

"Okay, Daddy." Jeremiah hugged him briefly and ran off to play with Bella.

Russ was painting sauce onto the chicken, as Eileen spread a tablecloth over a picnic table.

"I'm going to see if I can give Eileen a hand," Sharon told Macy.

"Okay. Just don't stay away too long." She winked and turned toward Kenny and Dori.

"Your mama couldn't make it, Macy?" Kenny asked.

"No. She couldn't get away from Burke County and Harold."

"And my mama couldn't get away from her spite and meanness," Kenny said. Dori elbowed him. "What?" he asked.

"Your dad might hear." Dori nodded toward Ken, Sr., standing about ten feet away, beside Russ at the grill.

"Girl, don't you think he's already figured that out about her?"

Macy chuckled. She leaned closer to Dori. "No Grace?"

"I didn't invite her." She looked down. "I don't need someone who doesn't want to be around me when I have all this great family that does."

Macy nodded.

Jeremiah ran to the gate, and all heads turned toward it. "Cam, Cam, look at what my daddy got me!" He shoved the remote-controlled car toward her.

"Wow, that is very cool." Cam mussed up his hair and shut the gate behind her and the short redhead who was with her.

Macy couldn't help smiling about how silly-happy and blushy Cam had been since she'd started dating Wendy.

"Why does Cam's date look so familiar?" Eileen asked.

"Because she was one of my nurses when I was in the hospital when—" She stopped, unwilling to reference the time she had feared for Jeremiah's safety.

Eileen and Russ nodded in unison, and Macy knew they understood.

"Hey, everyone," Cam said as she joined the group by the grill. "This is Wendy."

"Hey, Wendy!" they all chimed together.

Wendy laughed, and Macy liked her even more.

"Don't forget I want to see your pictures from Grandfather Mountain," Macy said to Cam.

"I haven't forgotten." She blushed a bright red. "I've been kind of busy."

Macy was so happy that Sharon had invited Cam up to the mountains in North Carolina to spread the rest of Jess's ashes. Cam had told Macy that the invitation to be at the spreading of the ashes had meant a lot, but that Sharon deciding to spread them on the mountain that held so many memories of Jess for Cam had meant even more.

Sharon rejoined Macy. "Hey, you. Having fun?"

"I am. This is great."

"I would like to propose a toast," Russ said. He waited a moment for everyone to turn to him. "To family."

"To family!" everyone repeated enthusiastically.

Dori stepped to Macy. "I've never felt so blessed in my life." She kissed her daughter and moved closer to Kenny to kiss her son. "I'd like to toast Macy, my true sister. Thank you for the most beautiful, most incredible gift anyone could give."

"To Macy!"

J-man was hugging Macy around the legs, and she touched the top of his head. She smiled when Sharon gave her shoulder a squeeze. "I love you guys," Macy said to Dorianne and Kenny. She looked around the yard at each and every one of the people who were her family, by blood or by choice. "I love you all."

About the Author

Renee MacKenzie

Originally, from Virginia, Renee MacKenzie currently lives in SW Florida with her partner and their poodle. She enjoys photography, hiking, and exploring the swamp. 23 Miles will be her fourth novel; she has previously published three novels – Confined Spaces, Flight, and Nesting. Her fifth novel will be set in the backwaters of the Ten Thousand Islands area and she looks forward to getting out on the water and mangrove islands for research.

Renee MacKenzie

Other Books from Affinity eBook Press

Reece's Faith—TJ Vertigo   In the return of the main characters from the bestselling novel Private Dancer, we see the blossoming of bar owner, Reece Corbett, and actress, Faith Ashford's relationship. The two women explore new, uncertain territory together, using sexual intimacy as a glue of comfort, helping them become strong and whole. A trusting Reece shares with Faith the sordid tale of how she became The Animal and Faith finds herself newly empowered by Reece's ongoing trust and support. Jealousy arises when Faith has to kiss a man on her TV show and two amorous women stalk Reece. With the help of their friends, they always come back to one another's arms. When Faith is outed on her television show, things get really crazy, especially when her parents arrive on the scene. She has to somehow justify her lifestyle to them and defend her love for Reece. Just as she is learning how to do this, she discovers that nothing about her parents is quite as she once believed. This not to be missed passionate and erotic romance will have you begging for more.

Starting Over—Jen Silver   Ellie Winters, a successful potter, is living on a remote hilltop farm inherited from her parents. Her well-ordered life is shaken apart when her past

260

meets her present. Robin Fanshawe, Ellie's philandering long-term lover, has a fragile truce with Ellie. The arrival of women from Robin's present threatens to break that tentative pact. Charming Dr. Kathryn Moss, an archaeologist and an old lover of Ellie's, arrives on the farm searching for a new site to dig. When she discovers a previously unknown Roman settlement and ancient burial site on Ellie's farm, Ellie allows her to start an archaeological dig of the area. Will Ellie also allow the rekindling of an old romance or will she stay with Robin? Can that long term relationship, albeit tentative, recover from this collision or will an old romance trump everything she knows? Will Robin, seeing the interaction between Ellie and Kathryn, leave her womanising ways behind? Will she take a chance on giving herself wholly to the woman she loves? These questions and the mystery of whose royal resting place is disturbed at Starling Hill are answered in this classic romance of simmering passions, anguished loss, and the wonder of love.

Twisted Lives—Ali Spooner A twist of fate leaves Bet and her daughter Kylie stranded at the entrance of the home of Alex Graves, as she flees the control of an abusive husband. When custom –homebuilder Alex arrives to find steam boiling from Bet's car and a beautiful child asleep in the passenger seat, her heart goes out to them. Alex offers shelter to the pair setting off a chain of events that bring both mother and daughter close to her heart and danger to her door. A heartwarming story of true love that will keep you smiling long after you've finished the book.

Malodorous—Del Robertson Sequel to **My Fair Maiden** Something in Fairhaven stinks. Other than the mutton stew, that is. Gwen thought life after being a virgin sacrifice would be a bed of roses. Bodhi was just looking for a wench to bed. Neither less-than-dashing hero nor not-quite-so-pure maiden imagined they would meet again, much less be trapped together in a city the likes of the ill-named Fairhaven. There's a killer on the loose. Fairhaven's on lockdown, its citizens fearful for their lives. The local guards are corrupt. And, Bodhi's been accused of murder…

Desert Blooms—**Dannie Marsden** Luce's story continues in DESERT BLOOMS… When we last met Luce Velazquez in Desert Heat, she went through hell and back to salvage her soul and reputation. Hoping to get her life back on track with lover Beth Ryan, a woman who understands her pain and can relate on every level. Instead, Luce is in the hospital, and Beth in protective custody. Jessica Sullivan, Luce's friend and ex, has big doubts about the sincerity of Beth's love, and is in no hurry to release her from custody. Can Luce's new found happiness last, or is Jessica correct in her doubts? A heart stopping romance that will fill you with the wonder of friendship, anger of betrayal, and the everlasting vision of love.

Finding Her Way—**Riley Jefferson** Is it love or just great sex? After ending an abusive marriage, Jerrica Kerrison is finally alive and she's apologizing for nothing! She has a job with a financial firm in Boston, a townhouse in Newburyport, and a sports car she drives way too fast. Jerrica has everything except that indefinable emotion called love. Madison Jeffrey is a lost soul. A PR job in the south has always protected Madison from the pressures of her family. But one day, fate brings her back to New England, forcing Madison to face her long buried demons, and a sister who despises her. When a chance meeting brings Jerrica and

Madison's separate worlds crashing together, the attraction is instantaneous. After one passionate night together, Jerrica retreats into the safety of her world, leaving Madison to figure out what happened. Will Jerrica open up her heart to the idea of love? Can Madison finally believe that she is worthy of unconditional love? Or will a devil hiding in the shadows tear them apart?

HER—Lisa Ron Fox has been looking for that one person who will make her feel complete-her perfect match. Together with her friends, Megan and Tree, Fox continues her quest while dodging exes and clingers, laughing a lot along the way. When she meets Madeline, she instantly knows that she finds HER. Madeline has her own problems-notably a domineering husband. Can Fox win her heart? Can they make a life together? This story will make you laugh, cry, and hold your breath as the story unfolds. With the right person love can conquer all.

Bayou Justice—Ali Spooner Hell hath no fury like a woman scorned. When Kara, Sasha's, new lover is taken hostage as a diversionary tactic to allow the drug dealing Bellfontaine brothers to escape justice, Sasha springs into action. Kara is released physically unharmed, however, her emotions, and budding career in the District Attorney's office are left in shambles when she is held blame for their release, Appalled, by the failure of the criminal justice system, Sasha exacts her own brand of justice for the acts committed against her lover. From the Bayou's of Louisiana to the jungles of South America, Sasha plots her revenge.

Out of Retirement—Erica Lawson Melanie Stokes was a doctor—a very good one, or so she hoped. She was calm and cool under pressure, and very little fazed her. Until…Caitlin Joseph ran a small retirement home for older women in need. The fact that everyone in the house was gay was a coincidence, although it did cut down the number of women agreeing to live there. Mel took up an offer to do some relief work for a local community center when their regular doctor was away on holidays. As soon as she arrived at the home she knew something was different about the place. Was it the little old lady chasing the paper boy down the street or the sign saying "Dykes Retirement Home"? But there was something about the place that also appealed to her. Sure, Caitlin was cute as a button, but it was more the fact that she took very good care of her charges, despite their rather bizarre behavior. The older women seized the opportunity to introduce a woman into Caitlin's lonely life, using any means possible to keep Mel coming back. Their plans were boosted by the introduction of another woman into the house, who set hearts a fluttering and blood pressure rising. Now if she was a lesbian it would have been perfect…

Letting Go—JM Dragon A failed relationship puts Stella Hawke's life on the brink of chaos.

When her grandmother falls gravely ill in Ashville, Stella ends her army career to take care of the woman during her last weeks. Little does she know that an old army comrade, socialite Reggie Stockton, whose family owns the local newspaper, also lives in Ashville. Will she allow herself to accept Reggie's help to turn her life around and let go of the past? This is a journey where both women re-evaluate what they want out of life. Will that path lead to happiness or to a parting of the ways?

Through the Darkness—Erin O'Reilly Becca Cameron is a loner—by choice. She lives in a hundred year old farmhouse built by her great grandfather. A tragic accident in her home a year earlier drove away her lover, and Becca tries to accept what she cannot change and hang on to the belief that love can conquer all. Chase Hunter, had a meteoric rise in the Eastman Corporation and was, at thirty-four, the youngest vice-president. To Chase, her work was all consuming leaving little time for friends or lovers. There was simply no place in her life for anything but her job. When Becca and Chase meet at their work place, the attraction is spontaneous. Life begins to look brighter for both women as work takes a second seat to romance. Unknown to either woman, someone is watching their every move… Will passion outweigh doubt? Can love conqueror fear?

Beginning of the End—Alane Hotchkin What happens when life doesn't go exactly as you planned and you must protect others from your own fate? Escaping a horrific childhood, Nikki longed to find happily ever after in adulthood. What she found was Hell. Or did it find her? Finding the courage to break the cycle of betrayal, she opens her heart one last time. Alex lived a childhood others dreamed of. Her father never once denied the young rebel a thing. All her life she dreamed of protecting others; to follow in her father's footsteps. Soon though she learned sex and fists made the most powerful of weapons. Alex controls the women in her life through fear and sex, will breaking the cycle be too much to overcome? Will loving Nikki be enough to change her, or is Alex beyond help? Alex would give Nikki the world, but at what price? When a person's tightly controlled reality snaps what then…? This is the Beginning of the End for one of them and the ultimate sacrifice for the other. But who is who in this game of life?

Galveston 1900: Swept Away—Linda Crist On September 7-8, 1900, the island of Galveston, Texas, was destroyed by a hurricane, or 'tropical cyclone', as it was called in those days. This story is a fictional account of Mattie and Rachel, two women who lived there, and their lives during the time of the 'great storm'. Forced to flee from her family at a young age, Rachel Travis finds a home and livelihood on the island of Galveston. Independent, friendly, and yet often lonely, only one other person knows the dark secret that haunts her. Madeline "Mattie" Crockett is trapped in a loveless marriage, convinced that her fate is sealed. She never dares to dream of true happiness, until Rachel Travis comes walking into her life. As emotions come to light, the storm of Mattie's marriage converges with the very real hurricane. Can they survive, and build the life they both dream of? This second edition of one of Linda Crist's best-loved novels maintains the original story, while incorporating some reader-pleasing passages that were cut from the first edition. As an added bonus, the short story "Something to Celebrate" is included at the end of the novel, detailing further adventures of Rachel and Mattie.

Rapture: Sins of the Sinners—A. C. Henley & Fran Heckrotte A serial killer is targeting young lesbians throughout the state of Texas. Texas Ranger Cochetta Lovejoy is assigned to the case. Convinced she knows who is committing the murders, Ranger Lovejoy is willing to do whatever it takes to put the perpetrator behind bars--even if it means stretching the limits of the law by manipulating the judicial system. Detective Agnes Kelly-Elliott is one of Ft.

Worth Police Department's finest investigators. When Ranger Lovejoy appears on the crime scene of a recent murder, Agnes fears a dark secret that, if revealed, could destroy her family ties, and end her career. This is a dark, gritty, graphic tale of desire gone awry, and flawed characters looking for redemption in all the wrong places.

Absolution—S. Anne Gardner Games of the rich and famous, love, lust, and forbidden passions weave this tale that play out through decades and the world. The close ties the Alcalas have to the royal house of Spain provide them with an unspoken untouchable policy. Their passions and their secrets are about to come to light with a force that cannot be stopped. In this whirlwind is Cristina Uraca Alacala who is searching for a truth that has been denied to her most of her life and she must find. She is not unlike her family; Cristina does not stop until she gets what she wants. In the fog lies the truth that she must travel through to find. In this tale wealthy socialite Annais Francesca D'Autremond is a pivotal person of interest in Cristina's search for the truth. When these two women meet they find themselves drawn together by something greater than themselves. As the truth of a hidden past becomes clearer their passions grow beyond the realm of the no return instead of a status quo. Both tied together by destiny; will both survive the onslaught of past and present passions?

Denial—Jackie Kennedy Time spent in Somalia has Doctor Celeste Cameron accustomed to living and working in a war zone. Coming back home to America, Celeste is glad to see the end of the peril she has been in—or so she thinks. Danger seems to follow Celeste and she finds it in the shape of Amy. What Celeste feels for Amy scares her more than anything she has faced in war zones. Amy has the same feelings, but is in denial and vows to marry Josh, Celeste's twin brother, no matter what. When fate brings them together again, will they give in to their mutual attraction or will they once again deny what they feel.

Taming the Wolff—Del Robertson ONLY ONE WOMAN... As devastatingly beautiful as she is headstrong, noble-born Alexis DeVale abruptly finds her preordained life in upheaval. Abducted at sword-point, held for ransom, thrust into a maelstrom of lawlessness and piracy... HAS THE POWER... The strength of her passion, the depth of her love... TO TAME THE WOLFF... Mayhem. Brutality. Murder. These are the tools of the trade - and Kris Wolff is the master of her profession. Captain of the high seas, a roguish pirate, her heart hardened by life, her passion tightly controlled by the secret she's forced to keep. Faced with a new danger, The Wolff finds herself unable to guard her heart from the tumultuous desires that Alexis DeVale has awakened.

Private Dancer—TJ Vertigo Reece Corbett grew up on the mean streets on New York City, abused, used and in trouble with the law. Faith Ashford grew up wealthy, with all the creature comforts that money provides. When they meet fireworks begin.

Miriam and Esther—Sherry Barker Miriam thought her life would play out in the bustling metropolis of Dallas, but after a life-changing accident, she moves to the small town of Cool Lake, Texas to get her head on straight and regain her senses.

E-Books, Print, Free e-books

Visit our website for more publications available online.

www.affinityebooks.com

Published by Affinity E-Book Press NZ LTD
Canterbury, New Zealand

Registered Company 2517228

www.ingramcontent.com/pod-product-compliance
Lightning Source LLC
Chambersburg PA
CBHW051249260626
47162CB00002B/679